THE DECEPTION *of*
LIVVY HIGGS

ALSO BY DONNA MORRISSEY

novels

Kit's Law

Downhill Chance

Sylvanus Now

What They Wanted

children's

Cross Katie Kross

DONNA
MORRISSEY

THE DECEPTION of
LIVVY HIGGS

VIKING

VIKING
an imprint of Penguin Canada

Published by the Penguin Group
Penguin Group (Canada), 90 Eglinton Avenue East, Suite 700, Toronto, Ontario, Canada M4P 2Y3
(a division of Pearson Canada Inc.)

Penguin Group (USA) Inc., 375 Hudson Street, New York, New York 10014, U.S.A.
Penguin Books Ltd, 80 Strand, London WC2R 0RL, England
Penguin Ireland, 25 St Stephen's Green, Dublin 2, Ireland (a division of Penguin Books Ltd)
Penguin Group (Australia), 250 Camberwell Road, Camberwell, Victoria 3124, Australia
(a division of Pearson Australia Group Pty Ltd)
Penguin Books India Pvt Ltd, 11 Community Centre, Panchsheel Park, New Delhi – 110 017, India
Penguin Group (NZ), 67 Apollo Drive, Rosedale, Auckland 0632, New Zealand
(a division of Pearson New Zealand Ltd)
Penguin Books (South Africa) (Pty) Ltd, 24 Sturdee Avenue, Rosebank, Johannesburg 2196, South Africa

Penguin Books Ltd, Registered Offices: 80 Strand, London WC2R 0RL, England

First published 2012

1 2 3 4 5 6 7 8 9 10   (RRD)

LIBRARY AND ARCHIVES CANADA CATALOGUING IN PUBLICATION

Morrissey, Donna, 1956–
The deception of Livvy Higgs / Donna Morrissey.

ISBN 978-0-670-06605-6

I. Title.

PS8576.O74164D42 2012   C813'.54   C2012-903189-5

Visit the Penguin Canada website at **www.penguin.ca**

Special and corporate bulk purchase rates available; please see
www.penguin.ca/corporatesales or call 1-800-810-3104, ext. 2477.

ALWAYS LEARNING   PEARSON

FOR AMY

... ONE SWEET DAY ...

But the child's sob curses deeper in the silence than the strong man in his wrath!

—Elizabeth Barrett Browning

THE DECEPTION *of*
LIVVY HIGGS

ONE

I step carefully onto the iced side steps, knees creaking like an old stair, and fling feed to the grey hubble of pigeons *coo-cooing* about the doorplace. The air is stiff with morning, dawn yawning tepidly up the eastern skyline over Halifax Harbour. The houses on the street still sleep, their drawn drapes darker than mine. Something about my backyard twigs my attention—footprints. One pair. Leading across the fresh-fallen snow and out of sight behind the house. They weren't there ten minutes ago; the snow had been smooth as fresh-poured cream. I know, for when the hands of the clock touched seven I was already sitting up in bed, looking out the window as I always do and saying good morning to the souls resting in the cemetery that borders my backyard— most especially that dear wooden cross facing my window, its arms seeking to embrace me while lending shadow to that smaller cross that lies behind it. I hear a sound: someone—or something—is rustling through the cedar shrubs near the basement door towards the back of the house.

Laying down the feed bowl, I button my wool coat, go down the steps and trudge through the snow. It topples inside

the mouth of my rubber boots and presses cold against my legs.
"Who's there?" I call, and am more surprised than startled when
Gen, the young single mother living next door, quickly rises from
the shrubs. She's wearing her puffy red parka and striped-legged
pyjamas tucked into a pair of unlaced Ski-Doo boots.

"What're you doing outside so early," she scolds. "I can hear
you wheezing."

"What're *you* doing?"

"I'm looking for Ronny's hockey puck, he lost it here somewhere." She won't look at me, she's shoving something into her
pocket. "Brr, it's cold, you shouldn't be out, it's bad for your
asthma," she says. "Wrap a scarf around your mouth. Ronny's
asthma is acting up again, I told him he's catching it from you.
Did you see his puck? It's his lucky puck, swears he can't score a
goal without it."

She's clumping back through the snow towards her yard.
She's tall and big boned, with messy dark hair pinned above a
long narrow face that's usually brightened by big brown eyes and
showy white teeth. She's not smiling right now, though, and keeps
her eyes from mine as she straddles the railing separating our
backyards, still talking about Ronny's puck. "It must be buried in
the snow," she's saying. "He shot it from the back steps and said it
landed in your bushes."

I keep watching her. If there's one thing life has taught me, it's
how to spot lies, and they're hopping from her mouth like little
green frogs feigning to be words.

"Why're you looking at me like that?" she asks. "You think
I'm snooping or something? Well, I am, you've dead bodies in
your basement, I saw through your window. You push old ladies
down the stairs and feed them to the cats. Oh!" She stares at me
with stricken eyes. I turn from her, retracing my steps through the

snow, and she comes after me. "I'm sorry. I— Oh my God, I'm sorry, I don't gossip, I never listen to gossip. Livvy!" She tramples up behind me, her hand touching my shoulder. "Livvy, I've secrets big enough to eat us both, swear to God I do. Not that I think you've secrets—oh, frig, why don't I just choke myself!"

I turn back to face her. I look deep into those young eyes filled with morning light, yet still holding that ray of dark I'd seen upon first meeting her a year ago. The ray has darkened considerably this morning, and her smile looks strained. "Be careful of secrets," I say. "They've ways of shaping your path."

A flicker of guilt swipes her face and my eyes are drawn to the bulge in her pocket. She tries to cover it with her hand and looks with relief towards her eight-year-old boy, Ronny, who's busting through the front door, yelling, "Livvy, Livvy!"

I smile to see the round, sweet face running towards me, dark hair curling across his brow, his unzipped parka flapping open. He's holding a brown paper bag in his hands.

"Wait, Ronny, wait," Gen calls, clumping though the snow towards him. "It's not wrapped, Ronny, it's not wrapped." But he's already coming through my gate.

"Careful you don't break it," he says breathlessly, passing me the bag. "And we forgot to buy wrapping paper."

"*Wrapping* paper—what's this now?"

"We didn't forget, you've not given me time," says Gen. She looks at me apologetically. "It's just a little thing. Take it inside and open it. Just a little thing from Ronny—There's that cough again, Livvy. Why aren't you wearing a scarf? You too, Ronny, I can hear the both of you wheezing."

The boy's not listening. He's staring at me, his eyes intent, his mouth curled into an eager grin. A heavy silver frame slips out of the bag, and I clasp it with both hands. It's a photograph of a wispy old woman standing on the sidewalk—a wispy, wrinkly old woman with greyish white hair and purplish sacs beneath shrivelled eyes that glitter like fish scales.

"What's this, what's this now?" I look impatiently at the boy and his mother. Even through the ashy dawn I can see the blush in their cheeks, their eyes glistening. I look back at the picture of the sickly old woman. And then I see it. I see the collar of my old, worn-out blouse sagging around the clawed front of my throat.

I clutch onto the fence post.

"Isn't it gorgeous the way the sun lights your hair?" says Gen. "I took it when you weren't looking. A few weeks ago. Ronny's been saving it for your birthday. Remember last year you gave him cake for his birthday? Well, now he wanted to give you something." She and her boy are smiling, staring at me with a growing expectancy, wanting some notion that I like their gift, that I like this reflection of myself, the first I've seen in God knows how many years. I must've stopped looking in mirrors. When did I stop looking in mirrors?

Eighty. I speak the word slowly. I speak it deep. I need to hear it spoken to mark it in time, to keep it from slipping from my memory like tap water through cupped fingers. Eighty. The figure startles me as it might a weatherman recording an absurdly hot day in late fall. Gen eyes me critically, not surprised at all. I squint at the picture. I hold it closer. I see what she sees: a corroded face, bald eyes and a wrinkled throat.

Gen shifts impatiently. "Why're you staring like that? Lord, you're acting strange this morning. I'll be your social worker when I graduate in the spring. I'll put you in a home if you keep acting weird. Stick the damn thing in a drawer if you don't like it. I burn every picture that's taken of me."

I sniff. "Young thing like you, supple as a baby."

"I'm thirty-two, oldest in my class."

"How did that happen?" I ask with vague interest, still looking at the picture, still grasping at the image of the old woman.

"I'll stop in for coffee and tell you sometime."

I look at her. It occurs to me that I know nothing about Gen, except for her love for her boy and her seeming compassion for this cranky old woman. The frost cuts deep into my lungs, making me cough. "I—I must go in."

"What about groceries?" she asks. "I haven't shopped yet this week, I'm writing term papers. I'll go this evening—you have your list?"

"I went yesterday," I lied, not knowing why, wanting only to go inside now. "Wait, Ronny, wait there," I call to the boy who's stomping down the untrodden snow by the fencing.

"Sure there's nothing you need?" asks Gen as I start back up the steps. "What about your meds? Hey!" She comes up the steps behind me. "Livvy, I'm sorry—those old stories, they must make them up to scare children, to keep them home."

"Your morning's wasting, get yourself to school," I say more gruffly than I intend.

"It's Saturday, and here, this is from me." She wraps her arms around me from behind and hugs me tight. "Happy birthday, Livvy."

She lets go and bolts down the steps with the mischievous grin of a naughty youngster and I shuffle into the porch, my face flushing like a foolish maiden's. Fumbling through a grocery bag of perishables I sometimes keep there, I take out a fully red apple, step back out and offer it to Ronny. "So you'll never grow old," I say.

He shuffles through the snow towards me, grasps the apple and runs through the gate after his mother, looking back with a furtive grin. We too have a secret, the boy and I. But I've been out too long, I'm starting to shiver.

"I ran into your minister from the hospital," Gen calls from her doorstep. "He said you haven't shown up the past couple of weeks. The nursery's full of squalling babies."

"Eighty years old, it's me needing rocking," I mutter, going inside again and kicking off my rubbers. Opening the inner porch door, I trail inside the living room, placing the framed picture face down on the side table. Willaby hops from the rocker and Tuff stretches from beneath the sofa, the two of them swerving through the darkish room and circling my legs like trout through brackish brook water. Breakfast. I must give them breakfast but I've been outside too long, I feel a weariness. Gen's words about the neighbours talking, they disturb me. It's been so long and they still talk. At least, those old enough to remember.

I go to the rocker and sit for a moment. The photo, it disturbs me too. While sitting and gazing about this darkened room, mollified by gentle purrs and the distant whirr of life outside my picture window, Time has crept up on me. It has stealthily greyed my hair. It has shed my brows and lashes and shrivelled my eyes. I lower my chin beneath my collar and sniff: I smell like the dust that has long since settled on old things.

Ahh, what's this, what's this now, I've suddenly become old? Brushing away the irksome thoughts, I lean back into the rocker and pull a woolly blanket over my legs. Tuff curls against my side, Willaby against my chest, his ears twitching against my chin. I rock, murmuring to the cats as might a mother to her babies, and soon I'm drifting into sleep, a discomfited sleep. I dream of bones, a little sack of bones taking the shape of a girl sleeping by an unlit lamp. Her breath is white with cold in the moonlight. I hear the sea hissing over the rocks nearby, can smell its brine, can taste the salt stinging my chapped lips, and I know I'm back on the western shores of Newfoundland again, where I grew up. A light emanates from the lamp. It grows brighter, draping its glow over shorn grass and the girl sleeping upon it. I stretch out my hands, I want to touch her, I want to see her face, to look into her eyes. A great urgency pulls me towards those sleeping eyes and I'm almost touching her brow, but something tugs at me from behind and pulls me back. "No," I plead, and I grasp for the girl but I'm being pulled, pulled from the underwater of sleep.

I open my eyes, my body quivering, my hands pawing the air for the girl. What's this, what's this now? I sit back, feeling faint. Willaby is purring, kneading his claws into my chest, and Tuff prowls; they're hungry.

"A minute, just a minute." I breathe slowly, my hands quivering. It has been sixty or seventy years since my father ousted me from his house in Sables d'Or, the French outport on that French shore of Newfoundland, and this is the first time I've dreamt of it.

Willaby kneads his claws deeper. "All right then, all right." I scratch his neck, set him aside and make my way to the kitchen and the bag of dry cat food. As though summoned, I hear the girl call out through her dreams—"*Mommyyy, Mommyyy!!*" She's calling from the deep dark of my past that I've buried— "*Mommyyy, Mommyyy, let's go to the dunes, let's go to the dunes, Mommyyy, Mommyyy, let's go to the dunes.*"

I close my ears. I'm too tired for company and too old for ghosts. If there's one good thing age has taken from me, it's the burden of memories. In the past eighty years they've burned themselves out, leaving little more than a spattering of images that dim and glow like embers in the receding path of the fire they once were. It's Gen's words about gossiping neighbours, and the photo—they've stirred things up. And Gen herself. I know little of her beyond backyard banter and her kindness in doing most of my shopping. But I know when something's up, and there's been a strain on her face these past few weeks. I've seen her standing outside her door and staring down the road, brooding. And she hid something in her pocket—and she lied.

There's a knock on the door. Ronny. I knew he'd be back. "You'll be late for school," I scold, opening the door to his eager face.

"It's *Saturday.*" He waves goodbye to a skinny young man who's just now leaving through Gen's front door. I stare at the fellow, at the huge yawn overtaking his face and the bulging knapsack dragging off one shoulder. I stare at his black spiked hair and what looks to be a silver-studded dog collar buckled around his neck. He returns my look of apprehension with a grin and dawdles to the curb, red underwear poking through rips in his too-tight jeans.

"Who's *that?*" I whisper in alarm to Ronny.

"Uncle Stu. His car's in the garage, his friend's picking him up."

"Your uncle?"

"He's going to university too, he's going to be a doctor."

"He'll need one to fix that hair." A rusty red truck rattles to a stop in front of the house and the young fellow carefully lowers his head as he climbs inside. A brother. I don't remember Gen mentioning she had a brother. She talks as little about her family as I do mine. I wonder now if he's the reason for her moodiness of late. The truck roars off and I quickly turn to Ronny, who's scraping back the heavy side bolt holding the basement door shut. He drops onto his bottom and my stomach sickens as he *thud thud thuds* down the steep wooden steps into the dark mouth of the basement.

"You need to be careful," I say, creeping down behind him, taking care never to touch that bottom step, stained with a blood my mind can never wipe clean. I sit on an upturned bucket, watching through the dusky light as three black kittens with white paws scamper and topple over Ronny's chest and face, nipping at his chin, tickling his throat and making him giggle.

A low hiss sounds from the mother beneath the steps, her amber eyes glowing with warning. She hisses again, but more from fear than hostility. For she remembers. It is this boy who rescued her and her kittens from the gutter near his school, half starved and nearly frozen. She remembers, too, a friendlier home than the alleyways, else she never would've allowed Ronny to touch her and bring her here. Abandoned, most likely, and fears being tossed out again.

"You've to ask your mother this evening," I say to Ronny. "I have to call the shelter soon. They're six weeks old now."

"No, no, don't call yet."

"Where did he come from—your uncle?"

"He trans-*ferred* from another university. Will you keep one, too?"

"No, I've enough. Will he live with you?"

"Nooo, he lives by my school. Think she'll let me keep two?"

"You'll have to ask her. Does anybody else want one?"

"Geddy does."

"Has he asked his mother? Tell him to ask his mother. Watch now, the queen's getting nervous," I say as the mother hisses again.

"Did you feed them yet?"

"I'll soak some food."

"Can I help?"

"No, you'll be late for school."

"I told you, it's *Saturday.*"

"Come back after you've asked your mother. Is he really studying to be a doctor?"

The boy's not listening. He's giggling into the furry belly of a kitten stretching across his face. "You best leave now, I have to feed them."

He puts the kittens back into their nest and then bounds up the steps on all fours. As I follow slowly up after him he carefully jars open the porch door, peeking out. "All clear. I'll ask her after supper, I'll ask if I can keep two."

"Tell Geddy to ask his mother too. Tomorrow I call the shelter. Here." I dig a block of chocolate from the bag of perishables and pass it to him. He takes it with a great grin and dashes out the door and out of the yard. I watch for a moment as his step slows and he sucks the chocolate into his mouth. He'll hold it on his tongue and swarm it with spit until it becomes soft and gooey. He'll swirl it deep onto the back of his tongue and then hold it because that's where sweet tastes strongest. He knows that because it's what I taught him, it's one of the few things I've learned within the shrunken corner of my world: how to salvage the most from the sweetest.

Willaby meows loudly, Tuff joins in and I make my way to the kitchen, divvying up the last of the dried cat food and putting some to soak for the kittens. It comes to me that I told Gen I'd already done the shopping. The thought of readying myself and walking to the store tires me. And I'm winded from my useless lungs. And I feel like napping again—ahh, the complaints of the old!

I feed and put out fresh water for the two cats, noting the cat hair and dust starting to mount in the corners of the hardwood floors and around the legs of the settee and cabinet. Needs to be swept. The whole place needs to be swept. Lifting the broom from its hook in the closet, I go down the hallway to my room, straightening my shoulders to shake off this growing feeling of lethargy. I pause at the foot of my bed, suddenly overwhelmed by a sense of dread, and put my hand to my heart, feeling faint. I hear the girl again, her voice a distant cry, yet filtering more clearly through the house than early morning birdsong: *Mommyyyyy, Mommyyy!* The air swirls around my face and I clutch onto the bedding—what's this, what's this now? It feels as though I'm taking my last breath. It feels as though I'm at the crossroads of a great wind. It pummels me backwards, fanning the most distant of memories. I chase after Mother down the yellow sand beach of Sables d'Or. She is big, the wind tenting her dress around her chunky legs and flailing her reddish hair about her rounded face that stays pretty even when she scowls and is uttering angry words to the sea and to herself and to me: "Paltry white bastard, your father's a paltry white bastard, he don't care about *nothing,* and oh, I'm a stupid *cow* I suppose, I don't iron his collars good enough, don't clean the house good enough, can't even pick up the mail. Imagine that, not allowed to pick up the mail—might *lose* it. Ahh, bastard, he's like my mother, he's like your Grandmother Creed. They think I'm stupid, they think I'm a fat, clumsy cow." She walks and walks. She walks till she's tired. Then she stands tippytoe atop a rock and holds out her arms like wings, her hair trailing a burnished windstream behind her, her eyes filled with sky. I try to do the same and teeter onto my butt with a shriek and she laughs and swoops over me, gathering me against her bosom soft as down, her hair folding warm about my face.

Mother breaks through the thatch of trees that blocks our house from the wind and comes onto the yellow sand beach. Her hair plays with the breeze. She looks up the shore to Sables d'Or, its stores, stages and slipways spilling onto a shoreline that's already littered with boats and nets and huddles of fishermen tending to their fish, split and salted and laid on flakes to dry in the sun. The Anglican church with its bell tower sits amidst a freckling of brown, red and yellow houses, blocking from view Father's store that sits just behind it.

"Hypocrite," mutters Mother. She walks the opposite way down the shore where the beach is bare of all things but sand, sea and dune grass, muttering as she walks, "… don't starch his collars good enough, don't clean the house good enough and oh, I'm a sow, I suppose, because I don't dress fancy enough. Don't wear them silly flapper dresses, don't go to church. Ah, what's the sense of going anywhere around here, everyone's *French*! He brings me to a *French* outport. He never told me they were all French that lived here, and I'm stupid now, because I can't learn French. Fine then, starch your own collars. You're like my mother. Your father's like my mother, did you know that, Livvy? Your father's like your Grandmother Creed. They thinks themselves better than every-body else, got chafed necks from their too-high collars. Imagine now, your father, building his house in the woods. Too *proud* to live amongst other people, just wants their money is all, paltry white bastard."

She keeps walking. She walks till she's winded, till her body droops like a windless sail, and she sits on a rock and lights a cigarette and smokes and smokes, watching the sea crumple at her feet. I want her to look at me. I jump up and down and twirl around with the wind. I scoot like a crab over the sand, digging out the tiny silvery fish called lances and dropping them cold and wriggling at her ankles. She shrieks, brushes off her ankles and starts wandering again along the shore.

The sun is hot and high and I chase after Mother down the yellow sand beach. She wanders till she's tired and then settles heavily in the lee of a sand dune. I burrow like a bunny beside her as she strikes a match to a cigarette and then she lies back, pillowing her arm beneath my head. We look through her smoke clouds at the real ones floating overhead and her eyes are squinty, half moons of blue, her heart thudding against mine, thudding her words through my bones, they are the same, they are always the same: "... paltry white bastard, *disappointment,* I'm a *disappointment* because I don't *dress* fancy enough, can't learn *French,* don't *iron* good enough. Serves him right. He's a hypocrite like your Grandmother Creed."

Heat quivers from the woodstove. With the trapped heat from the sun, the house is doubly hot. I trail from my room, whining, "Mommy, Mommy, let's go to the dunes, let's go to the dunes." She points me towards the washstand: "Wash up, suppertime. I hear your *faaather* coming," she adds, mocking the word. Butting out her cigarette, she hurries to the washstand behind me and brushes her teeth and rinses her mouth. She carefully puts on pink lipstick, brushes her hair till it fluffs around her shoulders and then stands back, smiling prettily at herself. She takes off her apron, smooths down her nice frilly dress and shoos my cat, Tabs, from the room. I wash my face and comb my hair, watching as she brushes the tablecloth clean of wrinkles and places a plate of chicken in the centre. She scowls at a burnt piece, puts it on her own plate and goes back to the stove for a bowl of creamed potatoes and green beans.

"Mommy, I'm ho-ot."

"It's scarcely June, enjoy the warm spell, it'll probably snow tomorrow. Here, let me see your face." She searches it for dirt, smiles into my eyes and swats my butt towards the table. Perching on her chair, she watches the door. I see through the window that Father is walking up the path the way he always walks—his step long and sure and hurried, like he's going somewhere important. He is big, but not like Mother; his body is hard. Once, when I was small and wanted to climb a tree, he sat me astride his shoulders to reach the branches and it was like sitting on rock. Frightened of falling, I grasped at his neck but found nothing to grip, his flesh too taut to pucker beneath my fingers, and so I clung to his ears. He laughed and said pity I was a girl, I would've made a good sailor, climbing the riggings on his ship.

"You always talk as though you owned a ship, why do you talk like that?" Mother asked from the doorstep.

"Goddammit, a man can't talk to his own youngster?" he snapped. He put me down and headed for his shed where he cleans and sorts tools and things, and has a little office to the side where he works on his books.

He opens the door now, slipping off his shoes and standing with the sun slanting over his shoulders onto the pretty patterned rug he recently brought from his store. His eyes shine like new nickels and I'm glad Mother took extra care with sweeping and dusting today, and I'm glad she's wearing a nice dress and her hair is fluffy and tucked neatly behind her ears.

Father takes off his fedora, his head shiny without hair, a pleased smile softening his big-jawed face that sits square on thick shoulders. He slips his tweed jacket onto a hanger and comes to the table, loosening his starched collar and cuffs as he sits, and he pats my head with the same pleased look that he patted the mustard-coloured sofa on his way to the table.

I stare at his eyes, wondering what pleases him, but unless he tells I shall never know, for unlike with Mother it is my eyes that know him, not my heart. He looks at my hands and too late I see my fingernails are dirt-grimed from digging sand at the dunes. Quickly, I hide them beneath the table, squirming beneath his pitying look.

"God, Cecile, can't you clean her? Enough dirt to plant spuds."

"I've cleaned her five times since morning." They look contrarily at each other. Mostly they never look at each other. Mostly they trade silence throughout our meals, the silence of storm clouds building overhead. Today Mother quickly turns her sour mouth into a smile.

"Livvy will be six this coming February. We can start her in school in September, if we want. Lots of children start school when they're five. She'll be real good at washing and keeping her hands clean, won't you, baby?" Mother adds as Father mashes mustard into his potato with his fork. "It's time I started working in the store. Like we said."

Father doesn't look up; he fills his mouth with potato as though he doesn't hear. His face is smooth, clean and pinkish. He has tiny red hairs that peek from his nostrils and ears. There are reddish shoots around the back of his head that, caught by the sun, sparkle like flankers as he shakes his head at a piece of chicken. "It's burnt."

Mother quietly cuts the burnt part from the other piece on the plate and places it on his. "It's another three months yet before school opens. Lots of time for you to plan what I can do."

"For gawd's sakes, Cecile." He glances at the cluttered sink, at the rumpled blanket and pillow on the sofa, the Eaton's catalogue splayed open on the end table, a basket of wash waiting to be ironed. I want to run and fold the blanket and push the catalogue under the pillow, hide the wash and kick our muddied shoes and wet socks outside on the stoop.

"You always sees what's not done," Mother protests. "What about everything that is? Frig, I *told* you I'm not the great housekeeper, you *know* that, you said I'd be working in the store, that's what you said." She falls silent as Father's eyes drop onto her plump shoulders and tenty dress. She stares at his soured mouth and stiff shirt collar and I stare at the chicken and strain to breathe.

"Eat your dinner," Father says to me. I nibble a bite of chicken and he picks around the burn on his and Mother's voice becomes more insistent.

"You said I'd work in the store after Livvy was born. Then it was after she started walking. Well, now she's soon starting school. It's time."

"You can't speak French," says Father. "Most of my customers are French."

"You knew that when you brought me here. You still said I'd work in the store."

"Learn the language," he says impatiently. "And Indian. Get a feel for the words. When I opens a new store down the peninsula, perhaps you can help with stacking the shelves."

"You always talk of a new store. It's been five years and you haven't opened a new store yet. Wait, listen to me," she pleads as Father shoves away from the table. Her voice goes hard as he starts towards the door: "You paltry white bastard! Who else have you tricked with your lies?"

Father stills as though struck. And Mother stills. The stringy chewed chicken stays in my mouth and my heart holds back a beat. It waits for something to happen. Nothing does, just the horrid stillness of a moment broken from time. I swallow the chicken and it lodges in my throat and I choke. Father leans over and thumps my back. Mother holds a glass of water to my lips and Tabs leaps onto the windowsill with a loud meow and things are moving again. Father walks out the door towards his shed as Mother starts pushing things around on the sink, neither of them moving too quickly as though they, too, felt the stillness in that broken moment, felt the fear of time stopping and having to restart, throwing things off with its tremor and nothing ever matching onto itself again.

Swinging a large cloth bag over her shoulder, Mother sets off for the outport. We take the path leading through the tall grasses of the marsh that swish and sway with the breeze and smell like ground rot. Soon we break through a batch of alders, and to the right, on top of a knoll, is where the old Irish teacher, Missus Louis, lives with her French husband, Mister Louis. They're one of the few families that speak English, and theirs is the only house Mother visits. Today she walks right past it, and keeps her head down as she walks through Sables d'Or for fear of encountering any outporters and having to struggle her way through their broken English. I gape at the youngsters hollering and darting about, but like Mother I am shy of their talk, and when they gape back I turn my head.

Hurrying to Father's store, Mother pauses, brushes down her pretty new dress and pats her hair coiled neatly at her nape. Then she brushes down my dress and pats my hair that's pinned at my nape like hers, and, tweaking my nose, she opens the store door. A bell tinkles overhead as we enter. It is deep and shadowy inside from the light entering through long windows at either end. I stare at a row of wooden barrels, each with its own whiff of apples or prunes or dried apricots.

Father looks down from a stepladder, his jaws swelling over his tight collar, his sleeves rolled above massive forearms. He looks cross to see Mother and her smile fades, her hand tightening around mine. Stepping down from the ladder, Father smooths back his scalp as though it still has hair and smiles at me. "Can I help you, young miss?" He passes me a peppermint knob and I pluck it from his fingers, pop it in my mouth and lick the pink flecks of sugar from my fingertips.

"Don't put your fingers in your mouth," he says with an impatient click of his tongue. I dart behind a pickle barrel, licking my fingers, and Mother, laying her bag on top of a barrel, goes behind the counter with a tilted chin.

"Yes, can I help you?" she asks an imaginary customer. "What, a pound of cheese, will that be marked in your book? Oh, you've money, you'll pay today?" She looks at Father with a pleased smile and his shoulders tense near to his ears. "See, they pay me money. With you they charge it. I will make an excellent merchant." She reaches for a credit book and Father impatiently slides it out of reach. She bends to sniff the opened face of a round of cheese and he juts forward an arm, drawing the cheesecloth over it. She touches the red-painted tray of his cast-iron measuring scales and he pushes her hand aside.

"Teach me to use them," says Mother.

"I've not time, for God's sakes, Cecile."

"There's lots I can do here. I can weigh out flour and potatoes.

And I can measure fabric, organize things." She stands back as the bell tinkles and two women come in, speaking rapidly in French.

"Bonjour, Mesdames," Father greets them. Mother smiles uncertainly as the women nod pleasantly towards her. They nod pleasantly at me too, then turn to Father who's speaking to them in French, commandeering their attention to something out the window—the weather perhaps, for they're all speaking and nodding agreeably towards the sun sparkling off the sea.

Mother steps quietly out from behind the counter, takes a molasses jug from her bag and goes to the back of the store. Placing the jug beneath the spout of the molasses barrel, she twists a knob and stares sullenly at Father. Thick, black molasses pours from the spout. I whip my fingers through the gooey stream and suck them into my mouth. Father coughs loudly and the women raise their brows towards the thick brown drools dripping from my chin onto the front of my dress.

Mother turns to me and gasps. Snatching my hand from my mouth, she smiles apologetically at the women. "She's a bugger for sweets," she says, her face flushing. Knowing the treat is nearing its end, I swipe another four fingers through the stream of molasses and duck behind a row of fabric, licking them. The women smile. Father laughs too loudly, his big forearms gesturing expressively, drawing the women's attention back to himself as he shares some joke that makes them laugh too. Mother keeps smiling towards the women. She tries to say something but her voice is overridden by Father's as he continues talking. Her face turning pink, Mother grasps my hand and we slip outside, scarcely noticed.

"Bastard!" Mother utters as the door shuts behind us. She takes to the beach instead of the road through the outport and nods politely to a knot of dark-skinned Frenchmen heaving coils of rope and fishing gear out of a boat hauled up on a slipway.

Further down the shore, she throws an angry look back at the store. "Bastard, he don't care, he's never cared." Her voice is choked. I look up in alarm and see tears in her eyes. I've never seen her cry, and a chill creeps through me as she keeps uttering words I've not heard before. "… I'd leave if I had somewhere to go, I'd pack my bags and leave, perhaps I *will* leave. Perhaps I'll go back to the mainland somewhere."

I trot tight to her legs as her new words keep landing like cold rain on my face. "I should've left when he first brought me here, when I knew he didn't care. I've always known. Big-time merchant." She sniffs, looking back over her shoulder. "Thinks I'm stupid. Can't even pick up the mail. Oh no, I might *lose* it, I can't do anything right, don't dress fancy enough, don't clean the house good enough …" And she's uttering her old words again, strings of syllables entwined like a lyrical lullaby, but I've been awakened by her tears, her new words. They force me to listen anew to the old ones, to break them into the meanings they first held before familiarity stole it from them. "… he's like my mother, got chafed throats from their too-high collars and I'm a *disappointment,* don't wear them *silly flapper dresses*— Ahh!" She throttles a laugh. "They're just alike, Livvy, your father and your Grandmother Creed. They think themselves better than me, they think I'm no good at nothing …" Her voice grows deeper and throatier with each word spoken and I struggle to hear if it's Father or Grandmother Creed she's fighting with.

I crouch in the shade of Mother's chair on the veranda and catch fluffs of wool floating from her lap as she sits carding wool and complaining about Father to Missus Louis. Missus Louis nods, tucking coarse white hair behind her ears with fingers that are scaly and red from work. She watches through eyes dark as pitch as Mother clumsily rolls a fluff of carded wool into a cone and sets it on a mat at her feet. "… thinks I'm not good enough, I'm too stupid," she repeats, tiresomely.

"You sure now, luv, you sure it's not yourself thinking those things. I see that in you, Cecile. You sure it's not you wanting one of those flapper dresses."

"Sure, I can wear them while I'm making suppers for his lordship. Ahh, they named it right, the last supper. Two thousand years later and we're still stirring their tea and kissing their feet as if they're Christ."

Missus Louis laughs. "The *everlasting* supper is what we ought to call it. You're right, Cecile, you're right on that one. But a little kissing don't hurt sometimes, luv. My man in there, Louis," she says, calling Mister Louis by his last name as she always does, "well, girl, he's old and cranky but he likes a squeeze sometimes."

"Providing you looks good doing it, else there's more blasphemies for the saints to pray over," says Mother.

Missus Louis shakes her head. "I worries for you, luv. I'll pray for you at Mass. I'll pray you start thinking yourself queenly— perhaps that might start adding a different flavour in the pot. Do you care anything for him, Cecile? My soul, it's not a thing to feel bad over, loving your husband," Missus Louis exclaims as Mother raises her eyes like a youngster caught doing something bad.

"When he don't care it is," cries Mother. "He cares about nothing. He truly cares about nothing. When I think of it now— how showy he used to be when I first met him, how he was always hugging me. He couldn't keep it going, though, could he. It's not in him, I swear, it's not in him to love. Truly, he's so deep into himself he sees nothing of anybody else."

"But he must have cared," says Missus Louis. "Why would he have brought you here, to a French outport in Newfoundland, if he didn't care? He would've known the hardship. Tell me again how you met."

"Ohh, I've no heart for that right now. You've such a curiosity about him—and my mother. I sometimes think you're more interested in them than you are in me."

"There. There it is," says Missus Louis. "Always putting yourself on the bottom rung. That's why I like hearing you repeat things, so to be sure I'm hearing what's real and not what you imagines. How's he doing with Livvy? Such a sweet child, he must care for her."

"The part of her that's his, he cares for."

Missus Louis suddenly notices my sitting there and touches Mother's hand in warning.

"My, I thought you'd gone with the others," says Mother, pulling me to my feet, the wool fluffs falling from my lap.

"*Macushlah,*" Missus Louis croons, patting my cheek, "why didn't you go with the grandchildren, I thought you'd gone swimming with them."

"Go on then, go find the girls." Mother pats my behind and I wander off the veranda, hearing her say to Missus Louis, "I says too much in front of her. I should make Durwin take her to the store with him so she can play with other children. Learn to speak French. But he's got no interest in her, and I need her for company. I'd go mad without her chattering and running about."

Esmée, Missus Louis's daughter, calls to me. She's older than Mother and is standing near the doorway of her squatty yellow house, a spit away. She looks like one of her boys in her trousers and buttoned-down shirt, and gives me a dimpled smile that softens her longish face as she saunters towards the pig pen with a bucket of feed. "The children are at the *rivière,* Livvy. Go swim with the children in the *rivière.*"

Throwing a last look back at Mother, I run to the riverbank where Suzie and Colette, the two eldest girls, call up to me. Dropping onto my bum, I slide down through the soft-stemmed bushes and thick grass to where the girls are now swimming with the rest of their brothers and sisters—two of them dark like the French, three fair like the Irish and two with the ruddy, freckled face of their rogue English father who is never home from the seas. They all shout at me in a mixture of English and French with an Irish lilt: "Jump, jump into the *rivière,* the *rivière,* jump!"

I skim down naked and jump into the cold water. The girls poke at the boys' dickies and the boys point at the girls' thingies and titties and I forget about Mother as we flounder neck deep into the river to hide ourselves, splashing and ducking to see through water that burns our eyes.

Soon, Esmée's eldest son, Henri, appears on the riverbank. He's dark and marches along wearing wrappings around his legs like his grandfather, Mister Louis, who used to be a French soldier. He carries a stick gun across his shoulder and points it at us, shouting in a lazy, rough voice, "Get home, you little *bâtards,* Mam's got supper ready!"

I scrabble into my clothes and run to Mother, who is squishing out a cigarette by Missus Louis's back door. "Come back tomorrow, *macushlah,*" says Missus Louis, cupping my face, then Mother takes my hand and we run to the front of the house into a stiff breeze blowing off the sea. "Not a word to your father," cautions Mother, "not a word to your father where we were; he'll have a fit. Give me a kiss, here, give me a kiss."

It is another day and it is many days that pass and embers of memory ignite into a flaming wall of fire as I race each day with Mother through the marsh to sit and talk with Missus Louis, sipping tea and baking bread, me always being sent off, soon enough, to swim in the river with her grandchildren, to race with them along the riverbank and over woodpiles and through grass higher than our heads. Mother starts learning to shear the sheep alongside Missus Louis, and when Esmée calls to her eldest girls to go inside and do chores, I stay outside with my mother, helping her carry armloads of wool to the river to wash it.

Missus Louis rises, hefty and shapeless in her long dress and petticoats, from amongst a flock of sheep. "Did you scrub it with lye?"

"Yes, yes, I scrubbed it with lye," says Mother, hanging the dripping wet wool over the fence to dry.

"That's good, that's good, my girl." Missus Louis lumbers towards us and helps with the hanging. "Look at ye, more soaked than the wool. That's good, neither of you are squeamish of work. Soon we'll be spinning. Now there's the never-ending job: I spin in the kitchen, I spin between sweeping and mopping, spin while singing lullabies—day after day, week after week. I've got grooves trod in the kitchen floor from walking to and fro the spinning wheel."

Mother laughs, her hair flamed by the sun, her face bright and pretty. "Least it's good, honest work, not standing at a table for hours and hours ironing wrinkles from a bloody shirt sleeve." She calls me to her, "It's time to go, Livvy," and Missus Louis comes with us to her door, handing Mother a pan with dumplings and a jar of gravy.

"For your man's supper," she says with a wink. "Tell him you made them yourself—he'll think you're that fine maiden, Magdalene."

At home Father fights with Mother over the messy house and the soggy dumplings and Mother runs off into my room where she always goes after fighting with Father. "Too bad, too bad you don't like *dumplings*! Make your own damn supper," she yells through the door.

Father gives me a disgruntled look, lifts his work jacket off the hook and leaves the house for his shed, where he always goes after fighting with Mother.

"I'll bring the catalogue and your cigarettes!" I call out to Mother, and finding her smokes hidden in her coat pocket and the catalogue on the side table, I run to my room and tuck into bed beside her. She lights a cigarette and opens a window for the smoke so Father won't smell it and we play our game of my picking out the prettiest dress on each page and she picking out hers, and me reverently promising to buy them for her when I'm bigger and get lots of money.

"You like black shoes best, right?" I ask.

"I like all the shoes, I like all the pretty dresses and shoes. Shh, don't tell your father, it's our secret." She smiles at me as though I've already bought them for her, and with my heart bursting with importance, I hurriedly look for more pretty things to keep her smiling.

Evening shadows the path leading away from Missus Louis's door as Mother tugs my hand and bends to straighten my skirt and tuck in my blouse. She smells like smoke and wet grass. "Not a word to your father where we were." Kissing my face, she takes my hand and we run down the knoll to the marsh path. Mother stops, pulling me beside her. It is Father. He is hurrying past the last house in the outport and towards us. He's wearing his tweed jacket and wide-legged trousers, and his eyes widen with surprise beneath his fedora as he sees us.

"What're you doing? Why were you up there?" he asks, glancing at Missus Louis's house, his voice thin with astonishment. "Goddammit, Cecile, *you were in there?*"

"What, I can't have friends now?" asks Mother. "Is that why you built your house in the woods, you don't like my having friends?"

"You took my daughter into that *murderer's* house?"

"Oh, and I don't know enough to be a good mother, do I? I don't know murderers from good folk like you?" She makes to run along the path, but Father stands before her, squaring his massive shoulders.

"They drowned my father," he says in a low, grim voice, and Mother's eyes fill with scorn.

"*Drowned* your father, hah! You know only talk! Dead man's talk. You crap out the past like yesterday's breakfast."

"I was there, you fool! You dare snoop behind my back with those *murdering thieves?*"

"I'm a snoop too now? My, that's some high opinion you got of me. Perhaps you should check my pockets, perhaps I got your silver in there, perhaps I'm a robber too." She steps back as Father's face flushes. He raises a thick, knuckled fist as though to strike her.

She laughs. "Go ahead, and let's see what good can be said about that." She spits at his feet. "I'd leave quick as that. Perhaps I will anyway, perhaps I'll just leave." She looks meaningfully at Missus Louis's house and darts off the path onto the beach, holding out her hand for me to follow.

Father seizes my arm as I'm about to run past him. "You'll go alone," he says hotly to Mother. "You remember that."

"Oh, going to try your hand at fathering?" Mother gives him a pitying look as he tries to pull me along the marsh path and I dig in my heels.

"Come along now, you won't get sand in your shoes if you walk on the path," says Father, softening his voice. I wrench free from his hand and run to Mother, who's looking sadly at Father. I look back too, and see the injured look on his face as he stares after me, the same look I saw on Tabs's face once after he sprang after a fat red robin and missed, his paws sinking into the sharp prickles of a blackberry bush instead.

A fierce wind blows off the sea and tastes salty on my lips. Rocks rattle beneath my feet as Father grips my hand, near lifting me sometimes, as we walk up the shore to the far side of the outport. Holding onto the brim of his flat leather cap, he turns back to a shout from Mother. She's chasing after us. She clings to her wrap, shouting for Father to bring me back. He keeps going, pulling me along. The wind stings my cheeks and I cling to his hand as seagulls scream and the rocks grow into ledges jutting into the sea, their ragged edges protruding through foaming white water. Father lifts me to his shoulder and walks straight into the gale and I wonder if there is a wind that can bend him. He comes to a ridge of rock twice taller than me and rounded at the top and he sits me there, pointing to the small rocky cove on the other side, inaccessible except by boat. Scattered high on the rocks are the bones of a ship whose rotted hull sits high up from the water, wedged into a cliff and splattered with gull's shit. Father kneels, looking down into the cove. His shoulders fall forward, his coat and V-neck sweater open onto a neck as thick and wide as his face. Lifting off his cap, he bows his shiny bald head before the broken bones of the ship.

"You're my daughter. There are things I want you to know," he yells over the wind and the sea rushing at the rocks. He leans closer to me. "That boat was going to be mine. My father—your grandfather—was tricked. He was the captain and he was tricked onto the rocks. The old Frenchman, Louis, and his father did it. *They drowned my father.*" Those last words he flings at Mother, who's caught up with us now and stands trying to catch her breath, her face whipped red by the wind.

"What do you mean," she asks, *"going to be yours?"*

He pulls me tighter, speaking steadily and intently into my ear. "They put out the false light. They shone a light—like a light-house light—and lured him onto the rocks in the fog and the stormy water."

"Tell me, why was the ship to be yours?" Mother yells. "It was my mother's. You worked for her!"

"They were after our cargo. They're greedy bastards, no more than pirates."

"*Our* cargo? When did it become *your* cargo?" Mother is hauling on his shoulder. "It was my *mother's* cargo. Stop telling her lies, why are you telling her lies?"

"They stole it and blamed it on the storm. I would've drowned too if the sea hadn't hove me ashore." His face almost touches mine and I smell the musk of his skin as he points to a craggy rock ledge being beaten by surf. "I clung to that ledge—see that rocky ledge, Livvy? They were shamed out of hiding, the greedy French rogues, and they dragged me ashore with five more from our crew. Two others drowned with Father," he says more loudly towards Mother. "Three men they drowned with their greed."

"That's how you *want* it to be," Mother shouts. "Mister Louis and his father, they just happened to be there. They saved you."

"You *fool,* they near *drowned* me. You betray me, and you teach my own daughter to betray me."

"Oh, it's *me* who betrays? You bastard, you've never cared for me, why did you marry me?" she asks, and Father's eyes harden with contempt, yet their centres are soft and pulsating like little dark hearts. He shifts me aside on the ledge and climbs on top as though readying himself to make his way down into the cove, but a knuckle of wind fists his face and I cry out with fright as he sways towards the sea rushing at the rocks. Just as quickly he lowers himself down, grasping at the ledge with gloved hands, his face blanching as he stares at the sea licking at his feet. Mother has taken hold of me, and she too had cried out with fright, her hand still reaching out for Father's. He stares at it derisively and she pulls it back.

"I'd be scared of dying too, if I were you," she says, and wrapping her arms around me, she lifts me off the ledge and we start walking down the beach, the wind tearing at our clothes and cutting tears from our eyes that run cold down my face. A sharp pain hammers my heart and all goes dark and I am assuaged with a weariness that scarcely allows me to lift my foot. I open my eyes to light and the white of my bedroom ceiling.

What's this, what's this, now? I am lying across my bed, clutching onto a broom. Did I faint? I was about to sweep the floors, I must have fainted. I close my eyes, breathing fast, then open them again to a siren wailing from way off. My chest hurts and my heart thumps hard. I look at the phone beside my bed in alarm. Did I call an ambulance? But no, I would remember such a thing. Grasping the bedpost, I pull myself up, the pain slowly easing from my chest. Asthma. I must have had an attack, a bad one.

TWO

The siren wails to a stop outside my house. I carefully lift myself off the bed and shuffle down the hallway, the wind, the ocean still thundering through my ears. Pulling aside the drapes, I gasp to see Gen running to the ambulance, her dark hair tumbling about her shoulders. Ronny lies limp in her arms, his head hove back. Goodness, my goodness, what's this? I hurry into the porch and out onto the side steps, coughing as the winter cold cuts across my throat. I call out to Gen but she's swallowed by the ambulance, its white doors closing like teeth behind her, its siren screaming and flashing towards the hospital.

I cling to the door handle. What's happened to the boy? An asthma attack. Yes, yes, it must be an asthma attack. I knead my hands, staring after the ambulance. There's no one about, no one who's seen. There's a car parked on the corner. It seems odd for a car to be parked there. It's partly hidden behind the thick trunk of a blue spruce with its door open and a man standing beside it, watching after the ambulance. The man looks back to Gen's house and keeps staring at it. There's something about him, something familiar. He notes me watching and ducks inside the car as though not wanting to be seen. I watch him for a moment, but my thoughts are too taken up with Ronny. He looked so limp. And he was white, ghastly white.

I go inside and sit in the rocker. No, I mustn't sit, the cats have to be fed, they're hungry. I'll open the inside porch door to hear Gen when she returns.

A whiff of souring cabbage comes from the garbage bag in the corner: I must change the bag. Willaby and Tuff leap onto the settee, watching me. Calm yourselves, I say, trying to soften my voice. Mostly they sleep during the day, but they sense my distress; it has become theirs, although it is I who needs calming. I root through the cupboard for cat food, then remember I'm out. "Anyway, you've already fed them," I tell myself loudly. There, there it is, the mind going.

Wearily I return to the living room and sit in the rocker, pushing the dream away, pushing Ronny away, my stomach nause-ated. I try to think whether I've eaten today. Is it noon yet, or still morning? I feel a sense of dizziness without the grip of time. Grasping the arms of the rocker, I strain to see the black hands of the wall clock behind me. It's only ten past nine. A thousand childhood hours have passed and it's only morning. I think about the girl. I think about Mother and that moment outside of Missus Louis's when she threatened Father that she'd leave him. How different would things have turned out if she had.

But there it is. Sometimes a moment holds too many things in its brokenness. Perhaps the bulk of what she said caught up with her later, frightening her with its threat of things changing and nothing ever matching onto itself again. Perhaps, by the time she'd paced through the house later that evening, her fear of different rooms, of different roads and wants, held her back, kept her clinging to those she already knew.

The phone rings and I push aside the memories. Yesterday I was bereft of them: of what use are they when death has silenced those I shared them with? "Hello," I say into the receiver. It's Reverend Wright from the hospital. When are you coming back, he's asking, there's seven newborns squalling to be rocked, the nurses are missing you.

"I've a cold," I tell him. "Can't be rocking babies with a cold. I'll be in tomorrow." It's only been a few days since I've been to the nursery, but he's called thrice now, and is always relieved when I answer the phone. "I'll let you know if I pop off," I say and replace the phone, going again to the window, wringing my hands with worries of Ronny. I sit in the rocker, wishing I was at the hospital right now, nestling a bundled baby to my chest, smelling its sweet-born breath and resting my cheek against that downy soft crown as its little red fist clenches my finger and it nuzzles towards me as though I'm its source of life. Too late I think to ask Reverend Wright to go find Gen and Ronny. His number, I've his number written somewhere, I think, or I'll just call the hospital and ask for admissions.

I pull the phonebook from its shelf beneath the side table and am about to start dialing when a car pulls up outside. It's Gen, she's in a cab.

Rushing into the porch, I push open the outer door and hold my hand over my mouth as the cold air cuts a cough from my throat. "The boy," I call as she gets out of the cab and it drives away from the busy curbside. "What's happened?"

Gen's hurrying to her gate, her hair flicked back in a ponytail, her eyes stark on a pale face. "Oh my God, he had a seizure. It ended before we got to the hospital. Go inside, get your coat on and I'll tell you in a minute—the cab's coming back for me." She rushes inside her house, and I pull on my coat and am standing on my steps again when she rushes back out with a duffle bag, hugging a tattered teddy bear beneath her arm.

"A seizure, a freaking seizure, can you imagine—a grand mal," she blabbers, coming through her gate towards mine. "Did you see him—oh my God, did you see him? I thought he was *dead!*" She clasps her hands to her face.

"But he's all right now?"

"Yes, yes, he's fine, but did you see him?"

"Yes, yes, I saw."

"He'll be in the hospital for three days' observation. They'll put him on a drug if he has another. He'll be fine—I'll *make* him fine." Conviction ripples like a muscle through her words. She smiles, a crazed light brightening her eyes as she runs to the cab that's pulling back up to the curb. "Oh, Livvy! Just a minute." She motions for the driver to wait, and comes to my gate. "A favour, can I ask a favour? I have an exam on Monday. Can you cab it to the hospital and sit with Ronny?"

I open my mouth to speak, but I'm suddenly overwhelmed by a terrible feeling of foreboding. I grip the doorknob, that earlier feeling of fatigue descending like lead upon my bones. I start trembling. I try to speak but my tongue thickens as Gen stares at me with disbelief.

"Don't worry about it," she says abruptly. "I'll skip the exam. Go inside, you're wheezing."

Wait, I don't feel well, I try to say, but my voice is little more than a whisper, the last gasp of a dying wind, and she's already inside the cab, driving off. I clutch the door jamb, holding myself up. What's this, what's this now? My heart's racing and I'm trembling from fear and utter weariness. I glance over at Gen's house, and it looks so silent with her windows draped and without her hanging off her front step, ordering me inside to put on a coat, to wrap a scarf around my throat, or hollering at Ronny who's eternally howling with glee or pain and stomping through snow in the backyard with other boys, throwing snowballs that splat like heavy cream on each other's faces. They are sounds I hadn't really listened to till now, in the silence of this moment. I keep gripping the door jamb, trying to deepen my breathing, but it's the fear that deepens inside of me. It circles my heart. The girl, she is here again, I feel her. I feel the silence. She was frightened of silence. She knew. Somehow she knew of that great silence about to descend upon her.

"Can I lend you a hand?"

It takes a second for the voice to penetrate. It is smug with virtue. It's the neighbour, Sunderland, hunched over his cane, his wet, puffy eyes staring at me and at my house.

Why do you look at me like that? I want to ask, but he jabs at the sidewalk with his cane, hobbles across the street and enters his yard, pristine with untouched snow. Juncos charm the air around the feeders decorating his walkway. I look down the street at the Pilgrims' house, and the Pillars', and the Hatchers', their walkways neatly shovelled and their windows twinkling with ornaments of glass. I look to my flaking brown house, its windows rheumy with street slosh, its doorplace splattered with pigeon tracks and droppings. Like me, it has been encroached by age and neglect.

Sunderland opens his front door and stands staring back at me. I feel the pitying look in his eyes and it stirs me with an almost forgotten anger. He's old enough to remember my past, leastways the past he believes he knows. Perhaps it is his tongue that wags still, that fills the ears of Gen and others curious enough to ask.

Enough, I say to myself, and go inside. Pushing Willaby off the rocker, I sit, wrapping myself against this silence that presses cold against me. It is the memories, those silly memories that continue to haunt me this morning. They bloat like undigested food in my stomach. I sit forward, the pain from earlier coming back in my chest. Curse the silence, I'm paying too much attention to a little ache. There, that's the mind for you—if you think about your little toe enough, it becomes bigger than the foot.

I shift for comfort. My stomach feels nauseated again. What's this, what's this now, I feel like crying, I feel tears burning my eyes. Willaby brushes past my legs. He sits and stares up at me. He knows something's not right. I lean forward as the pain grows, squeezing my chest. I feel faint, darkness crowding in. A crevice of light splits through the dark and I'm squinting through a crack in Missus Louis's door. I see Mother, her words dripping like tears onto Missus Louis's table as she cries out the story Father told her of Mister Louis waving a false light that brought the ship upon the rocks and caused his father's drowning. Missus Louis receives them in silence, any words she might've offered in return overthrown by a series of mutters and grunts sounding from Mister Louis as he barges out of his bedroom from his afternoon nap, a bluish war cap circling the top of his shaggy white head.

"*Bâtard! Bâtard Anglais!*" he shouts.

"My soul, he's awake," says Missus Louis.

"I hear, not for the first time, I hear the *bâtard's* lies. What, you think it good for me to be blamed?" he roars towards Mother. "I dredged his arse from the sea. Blame his big *capitaine* father— *capitaine!* Ah, what *capitaine* runs his boat on the rocks, hey? What *capitaine* drowns hisself and half his crew—and his own son too, but for *moi! Moi!*"

He thumps his chest, tossing a surly look through sunken black eyes at Missus Louis as she scoffs, "Shout louder, man, shout louder, we're only half convinced."

"I tell you, I near drowned," he says, thumping his chest harder. Lowering his voice, he turns to my mother. "Why he don't tell you that, hey? I hold his collar in my teeth like a dog and I dragged him ashore. I swim that sea—ah! He cling to my neck, weeping *prières,* and I swim that sea like a duck."

"Pumping yourself with pride! Shame for pumping yourself with pride," chides Missus Louis.

"Shame! Ahh, shame, is it?" Scraping back a chair, Mister Louis sits, rapping his fist on the table. "I tell you what shame is," he says to Mother, his anger turning to scorn. "They starved us. Yes, I tell you, the Limey merchant *capitaine* and his father, they starved us. No credit, they gave no credit. My *grand-père,* he lived on bark a full winter, yes. He lived on bark and his bones there, his bones poked holes through his skin. *Traîtres!* The Limey *bâtards* call us *traîtres.* Long before my *père,* they starve the *Français.* They don't want us here—the *Anglais,* they want the sea with the fish for themselves. That make them feel good to call us *traîtres.* They have reason now to starve us more. We won't swear to their flag so they give us no credit, the merchant *capitaine* and his father—and all the rest of the merchants, hey—all up and down this shore. They say we will keep our furs come spring, that we won't pay our bill, so they won't give us credit. They think we cheat and lie because we don't bow to their flag. I cheat no man! I cheat no man and the *capitaine marchand bâtard* starved us."

"He talks like it's yesterday," Missus Louis sighs. "Let it go, man, it's old strife."

"My *père,*" says Mister Louis to Mother, "his bones popped through his skin. Your *capitaine marchand*—he and his *père* starved us. Does your man tell you that? Ah! He is a Limey *bâtard,* your man. He knows what his *capitaine* did—all *Anglais* are *bâtards.*" He laughs. "A *Français,* we find you a good *Français,* yes."

Mother's tears have stopped. "You tell the truth? Durwin's father starved you and your grandfather?"

"*Oui, oui,* I tell you no lie, his father starved us."

"A good Irishman, luv, you need a good Irishman with a song in his heart," says Missus Louis, "not strife. Hey Cecile, what do you say?"

Mother gives a shaky laugh, wiping her eyes. "The good Lord gave me a merchant, a merchant who wants a boat to master."

"He got you to master, you're his boat. Listen, listen to his self," Missus Louis says as Mister Louis starts up again about the Limey captain. "You be as well off whistling jigs to a wall as getting a word in with him. Go milk the goats, old man. Go lay an egg—and stay out of the woodhouse," she calls as Mister Louis shuffles, grumbling, out the door. "He can build a house but he can't stack a tier of wood without it foundering," she complains to Mother. "He'll maim a youngster yet, watch if he don't. Now tell me, Cecile, what is it that you're thinking, tell me, luv."

"They've done something. Durwin and my mother, they've done something."

"Are you sure? You've a hard view of your mother. I wonder at your hard view of her."

"She lies, she always lies. She's clever like the fox, always setting her little traps, twisting things, making lies out of truth—or truth out of lies, who can tell? Even now I can't figure what was real or a lie with her. I can't explain her, Missus Louis. She was forever talking down anything I liked. Even dancing—not because she didn't like dancing, but just to turn me from something I liked. Ohh, I can't explain her, I can't." Mother near weeps as she goes on to talk of her father, her poor, poor papa, nearly pecked to death for being a dentist and not a surgeon.

I strain to listen as she describes her papa as a big soft thing slouching on the sofa in their home in Halifax. He gave her new toothbrushes in pretty packages and told her they were made from hog's hair and that tooth fairies lived in her mouth. *Teach her something useful, Orrick,* her mother was forever whining at him, *you must've learned something besides tooth rot and fairies.* "Then, when Papa dropped dead, she becomes all weepy with the neighbours: *A saint, a learned man he was, his heart too big for the pain of medicine so he healed mouths instead and was forever reading the great works of all the saints. God help us, he's gone.* Ohh," says Mother nastily, "for sure his fat bank account and merchant ship helped."

"I've never understood how your father, a dentist, came by a merchant ship," says Missus Louis.

"It was left to him by *his* father, my grandpapa, who was a merchant. Papa had no mind for it and would've sold it. But my mother wouldn't allow him. *It's making us money, why sell something that's making us money. I've been studying the books, I'll take care of it.* That was her argument, always the same. She persuaded him to keep on Captain Higgs, who'd been sailing the ship for ten years and knew its business far better than Papa. Ohh, I can see her now, looking so fake."

"Tell me, why do you think her fake, Cecile?"

"The way she would sit at the dining room table in her fancy dresses and fancy hairstyles, the logbooks opened on the table as though she were studying them whenever Captain Higgs came to visit—"

"You think she was keen on him?" Missus Louis cuts in.

"She was keen on herself. She loved sitting there with the accounting books, acting like the big businesswoman and her hair so perfect."

"Perhaps she did study them, perhaps she was smart."

"She is smart—that just makes her more sly."

"You scorn her. You scorn your mother as much as you do Durwin."

"I *despise* her. She never felt nothing when Papa died. She sold his dentistry tools within a day of his funeral. And of course she kept the ship and Captain Higgs. Ohh, it's obvious to me now that they cooked up some scheme—she and Captain Higgs and Durwin."

"Tell me again about when you met Durwin."

Rubbing tiredly at her neck, Mother tells of how Durwin came to Grandmother Creed's house with his father. Captain Higgs was brutishly big, his fists strong enough to hammer nails, his voice booming through the house as he sat in the dining room, talking numbers and cargo with Grandmother Creed. One day, just a week before Captain Higgs was to set sail to England, he brought his son with him. Grandmother Creed was all jittery, nervous, as though she already didn't like the son. Still, she kept smiling that fake smile. *Come, Cecile,* she called, *and meet the captain's son, Durwin.* He stood stocky, big jawed and well dressed beside his father. Mother was sixteen and hadn't had a boyfriend yet. She liked Durwin's nice clothes. When he said no to Grandmother Creed's offer of tea and invited Mother for a walk instead, she liked him more.

But I've made a pot of tea, Grandmother Creed had protested. *I prefer if you sat with us. Cecile, come sit, dear.* But Mother didn't, she was smitten by the shiny grey eyes of the captain's son and followed him like a puppy from her mother's door.

Every day after that, for the whole week before Durwin set sail on the boat with his father, she walked the streets with him. She listened as he painted pictures of intrigue about the merchant store he owned with his father on the old French shore of Newfoundland. He told her of the other stores they were to build soon, and the merchant ship he would soon own. She said nothing to Grandmother Creed, sensing her intense dislike of Durwin, but that's only what Mother expected. Anything or anyone she liked, Grandmother Creed was sure to take apart somehow. "She once told me this girl was mentally ill and on drugs for trying to kill her baby sister. All because I liked her and was becoming close friends with her."

"No, dear, did she? Did she go that far?" asks Missus Louis.

"Yes, yes, that's what she was like. And they were so big, her lies were so big, you'd never think not to believe them. She took apart everything I liked. She liked me being home and her and I wearing the same dresses. Oh, she was so vain, she loved that, the two of us wearing the same dresses, it made her look and feel young to be dressed like her little girl. *We're so tiny, we've the bones of birds,* she'd say. And then I started getting fat, just to spite her. Ohh, you don't know, you'll never know the things she did. Nor me either, how can I? How can I go back, taking apart everything she ever told me from the cradle up? Ohh ..." Mother holds her hands to her head as though to keep it from spinning. "And she followed me around the house like the plague after I met Durwin. *Are you seeing him, Cecile? You must tell me. He's not to be trusted, dear, him and his father, they're not to be trusted.*

"But you said she liked Captain Higgs. Why did she stop liking him?"

"And that's the mystery," exclaims Mother. "First everything was Captain Higgs. And then suddenly he's not to be trusted, him or his son. There was something come up between them, something more than her not liking his son. But I was only thinking about Durwin back then. Figuring my mother didn't like him because he didn't give her any attention, but was giving it to me instead. She was always so vain. And that's what made me like Durwin even more, that he didn't pay heed to *her.* God, I so despised her trickery, her *evil,* I would've run off with anybody back then.

"Ooh. If you only knew what it was like," moans Mother, and continues talking to Missus Louis about those days before Durwin set sail with his father, how she kept meeting him by the back of the graveyard behind Grandmother Creed's house. He never noticed her weight, her fat legs and arms and biggish dresses and clumsy footing, he saw only her eyes as he painted pretty pictures for her of his house, off to itself behind a marsh and with tall, straight evergreens growing around it, and yet only a ten-minute walk down a yellow sand beach to his store. Mother listened. She dreamed. She painted herself into his picture, she put herself behind the counter of his store, and he led her along with promises of more colour to come.

Then he was gone. Sailing for England with his captain father aboard her papa's ship with a load of cargo. *It's good he's gone, dear. He's cold. He's cold as his father. Stay away from him, Cecile.*

"Ah! *Cold*—imagine, Missus Louis, she calling Durwin cold, she with her ice heart."

"Was she really cold, luv? She must've cared, she probably didn't know how to show it."

"She's a different kind of cold, she takes *everything* and gives nothing. Durwin takes nothing and gives nothing." Mother falters. She rubs her brow, she rubs and rubs her brow.

"It's hard on you," says Missus Louis softly. "I can see it. Why did he woo you if he didn't care?"

"I told you," says Mother, tiredly. "They did something, Durwin and my mother. It's easy to see, looking back. When word came a few days later that the ship had foundered and Captain Higgs had drowned, my mother tried to look upset. I can see her now, trying to dig tears out of her eyes. *So sorry, dear, such a horrible thing, Durwin drowned with his father. You'll get over it, dear. Time will help you, I promise.* But it was the ship she was worried about: that first day she heard about it going down she was off to the insurance people, adding and counting her losses."

But Mother was heartbroken. She wept for days. She wept for her lost love and her lost canvas of a new story, a new life that had grown deeper and deeper in fantasy since Durwin had left on the ship with his father. She dreamt of him at night, her heart burgeoning with love and grief.

Then, as if in a dream, she heard him calling her name. Three weeks after the ship went down, she was strolling through the graveyard with a weeping heart when she heard him call. He was sitting against a time-bitten headstone, waiting for her, with his eyes wild with anger, his ears echoing with the cries of drowning men and the sea smashing his face. To think, she exclaims now to Missus Louis, she was overjoyed to see him! Overjoyed and too simple-minded to ask why he hid from Grandmother Creed, why he was so urgent in his courting her. He took her one night, and another, and again in Point Pleasant Park, beneath the swooping, moth-winged branches of an old spruce. Moonlight dappled his face, brightening his eyes with a promise that seeded in her belly and whitened Grandmother Creed's rouged face with fury as Mother hurriedly packed her things while Durwin waited outside by the gate. *You fool, you poor fool, you'll rue this day. I'll have him jailed. He thinks he can out-trick me, I'll have him jailed.*

Mother kept packing. She went into the hallway, hearing Durwin and Grandmother Creed arguing in strained whispers by the door. Closing her ears, she went back to packing. Her eyes were still bright with moonlight, her belly growing with promise, her heart with hope, and she wanted nothing of those wretched whispers tangling like vines around Grandmother Creed's and Durwin's throats. She feared they'd strangle around hers too, strangle the dream of escaping Grandmother Creed, of losing the story she had written of love and adventure waiting for her on a foreign shore where she'd be a wealthy businesswoman. For that's what Durwin had promised her for moving so far away, to an outport that had none of the shops and streets and movie houses and restaurants of the city of Halifax. He promised she would create a new life with him, that she would work in his stores and never, ever again would she have to live with Grandmother Creed who tried to command her every thought, her every move, who tried to slip her own aged bones inside of Mother's and wear the youthful flesh of her daughter as others wore a store-bought dress.

"It's my fault, I should've listened. I heard them arguing, I should've listened," Mother laments.

"Tell me about the ship. What do you remember of Durwin's father and the ship?" Missus Louis probes, as though looking for some little thing Mother might've forgotten, some new thing she hasn't thought to tell.

I get bored with listening to the repeated details of the story and wander outside to Missus Louis's porch. Her daughter, Esmée, is calling to one of her youngsters, the eldest, Henri. She's wearing the same trousers and buttoned-down shirt and is running towards Mister Louis, who's holding a squirming Henri by the scruff, calling him a little *bâtard*.

Henri bolts off. "You ol' fecker, *Grand-père!*" he shouts, and Esmée covers her shocked mouth with her hand, then points disapprovingly to Mister Louis.

"You're hard on him, Da. You're too hard on him."

"He sucked the eggs again. Next time he robs my eggs and sucks them dry I *battre* his ass."

"Next time I *battre* yours," says Esmée. She grins and swats her father's behind as he grumbles past her. Stepping around squawking, fluttering hens, she pats the rump of a bleating goat with bloated teats and shouts to her boys who then shout to each other as they scatter—some to the woodhouse, others to the porch for the water buckets. She shouts to her girls and as they skim the smaller ones off her legs she beckons me inside her yellow house, where Suzie is cutting meat for supper and Colette is scooping eyes out of spuds. I corral the toddler who's still in diapers and he falls backwards onto Teenie, the youngest girl, who screams *Tabernac! Tabernac!,* and Mother calls and takes my hand and we run through the tall, rustling grasses of the marsh and she's urgently whispering, "Don't tell your father, shh, shhh, don't tell your father ..."

I crawl through long shadows in the underbrush with Tabs. I peer through fern fans of green and see Father just home from work, his fedora low on his forehead despite the heat, his collar unbuttoned. He's standing square-jawed before a skinny woman who looks like she stepped from one of Mother's catalogues with her flapper dress frilling below her knees and a tight bell-shaped hat shading her eyes. They stand stiffly, staring at each other, armoured behind collars and wraps, agile in good manners as they whirr and slash each other with strange words: *manifest, lading, lloyds, cargo.*

They both quieten as Mother comes out of the house. The skinny woman reaches towards her, gold bracelets chiming around her wrists and her voice turning soft as moss. "My darling, I so hope you don't mind my coming. I wanted to see you. And I so wanted to see my granddaughter, I haven't seen her since she was a toddler."

Mother, her mouth opened with surprise, allows the woman to embrace her, and then stands back, looking from her to Father. "When—how did you get here?"

"I crossed last night on the ferry, dear. My suitcase is at the train station; I walked here through that marsh path. Do you mind that I've come without writing first? That ferry boat is so absolutely terrible, I was afraid I'd chicken out once I got to Sydney. That last time was such a horrible trip across, I swore I'd never do that crossing again. But"—she shrugs her thin shoulders—"if I don't come, how could I see you? You never visit."

I scrabble out of the underbrush and run to Mother, shouting, "Mommy, Mommy," and she kneels, gathering me before her like a shield.

"Such a mess you are." She makes a funny laugh and brushes sticks and stuff off my hair and clothes. "Livvy," she says quietly, "this is your Grandmother Creed. You were only two the last time she was here."

The skinny woman stands before us. I stare at her flapper dress and tight hat and shiny necklace. I look into her squinty eyes, half moons of blue like Mother's. I stare at her lips, pink like sunset, her cheekbones like powder-dusted hillocks. She leans towards me and a rush of scent wafts about my nose as she speaks in her funny way.

"Indeed, she's a bonny little thing. Hello, my dear, how are you? I sound too British," she says to Mother as I stare at her without answering, and she leans closer as though I'm hard of hearing. "I've come all the way from Halifax—a big city in Nova Scotia—just to see you and your mummy. You were such a cute little tot the last time I saw you. I think she's grown into a tomboy," she exclaims to Mother, touching my tousled hair.

"I don't have a dickie," I declare and am about to pull up my dress to show her when Mother grabs my hand and Father grunts irritably.

"She's only *five,*" says Mother, and I hold up five fingers to the grandmother. Mother makes a bleaty laugh and I remember her angry words about Grandmother Creed those times we walked the beach and so I stick out my tongue at the grandmother.

"That's it," Father shouts. Grabbing my wrist, he marches me inside the house, whacking my elbow on the door jamb, and I scream *Tabernac! Tabernac!*

Peering from my room where I've been banished by Father for saying some word the night before, I hastily comb my hair and do up the buttons on my good dress that Mother laid across my bed this morning. She's wearing a new flouncy dress too as she moves quickly about the kitchen, her hair bundled tidily into a ponytail. Her face flushes as she drops a knife. She leans over to pick it up and drops it again, flicking looks at the grandmother, who's taking a seat at the table. Father is bent over by the door, his collar pinching his throat as he buffs his shoes. He, too, keeps glancing at the grandmother who's now sitting twiglike on the edge of her chair, sipping tea. Her hair is buttercup yellow and is swept back from her forehead in deep-trenched finger curls. Her cheekbones are shiny smooth without powder, her eyes squinty bits of blue as they scrutinize Mother's fumblings.

Seeing me, Mother smiles as though I've granted her relief from a stubbed toe. She sits heavily at the table, beckoning me to her. "What a pretty frock," says the grandmother. She pats my cheek.

"She's a little shy," says Mother.

"Perhaps she'll come visit me sometime. What do you think, Livvy?"

"I'm five," I say.

"Yes. Yes you are, dear. Now let's see ..." She examines my face. "You have your father's eyes. Your mother's hair and the same skinny arms and legs. When she was a girl, dear," the grandmother quickly adds as I pat Mother's thighs that are plumped like pillows beneath her dress. Mother's face flushes and I look at the grandmother's curled hair.

"Are you going to church?"

She smiles, shaking her head. "Us old women dress to amuse ourselves. We're not busy like your mummy, dear. Besides, it's Saturday, not Sunday."

"Where are your titties?" I ask, staring at her silky dress that sits flat on her chest.

Mother puts her hand to her mouth and Father snaps a hand around mine, leading me back to my room as the grandmother exclaims, "What a *cheeky* little bugger."

It is past supper and Father sends me outside to play with Tabs. He seems angry, and I'm reluctant to leave Mother sitting at the table with him and the grandmother. But Mother nods for me to go, so I sit on the stoop, watching Tabs bat at flies, listening to their voices rising and falling inside. They use angry, indecipherable words that echo through the house like the distant squabbling of a murder of crows. Evening falls quickly through the trees and Father opens the door. "It's bedtime," he says, his voice hoarse, his words heavy, and I enter a house caught in silence. There's a ribbon of light beneath the grandmother's door, darkness beneath Mother's, and another ribbon of light beneath mine. I open it to Mother lying in a sullen hump on my bed, her nose red from wiping it with a crumpled tissue. She pulls me to her with clammy hands, stripping off my dress and socks, and I shimmy into my nightdress.

"Go get Mommy some matches," she says. "I don't care if he sees you."

I creep out of my room. Father is leaning against the counter, staring into a glass of whisky. Sensing me there, he looks up and takes a gulp of his drink. Quick like a minnow, I dart to the matches on the mantel and stow them behind my back.

"What're you doing?" he asks.

"Nothing." I dart back to my room, close the door and squeeze onto the bed beside Mother as she lights a cigarette and puffs the smoke out the window.

"She wore my clothes, your grandmother wore my clothes," she whispers harshly. "They were too tight, she used to wear my clothes and think herself young and pretty and prance before the neighbours, *How charrrrming, simply charrrrrrming to be sharing dresses with my little girl. How tiiiiny my waist must be, we have the bones of birds* ... Ah, I fixed her—did I tell you that, Livvy? I fixed her. *You've gotten fat like a sow, step lighter, step lighter! You got the bones of a shepherd girl, you clump through the rooms like a sow, you clump through the rooms like a sow on wooden legs."* Mother laughs. It sounds like the bleating of a startled sheep. *"Doctor, doctor, I don't know what to do with her, oh doctor doctor, she keeps getting fatter and fatter, my little girl's a sow and she's doing it on purpose, dear doctor, dear doctor ..."* Mother's laughs sound like cries now and I press into her breasts that jiggle like jelly. I nose deep into her armpit, into the deep, damp sweetness of her, and I want to go deeper to keep her awful sounds from thudding through me. "They'll burn in hell for what they've done, I pray they burn in hell," she whispers suddenly and with such force that her body jolts forwards. "Shh, it's okay," she soothes as I pull away from her and start to cry, "it's okay, it's okay."

Sunshine falls across Mother's face as she breaks through the woods, her dress flapping in the wind, her smile framed by rollicking, reddish-gold hair. I sit up from where I'm digging a trough in the sand and wave to her. She turns back towards the house and I call after her, *"Mommy, Mommy, let's go to the dunes, let's go to the dunes!"*

"I'll just be a minute," she calls.

I keep digging my trough, waiting for her. I tire and scoot over the sand, poking at jellyfish with sticks. I dig out their jellied insides and scatter them about the beach and gaze at the sky and at the white feathery underbellies of clouds. I wait and wait. I must've slept, for I open my eyes to a ratty dark cloud covering the sun and I'm shivering with cold. Something black and fat and shapeless is hurtling down the beach towards me. It is Missus Louis and she is shouting my name and she wraps herself around me in a rustle of hemlines and bloomers, crying, "Oh, *macushlah, macushlah,* my poor *macushlah."* She sobs and snorts and sobs and sounds like water choking through a clogged brook and I am afraid.

She takes my hand and sees the ruptured jellyfish splattered like blood clots over the sand and she crosses herself and smothers me again in her arms, crying, "Poor little lamb, poor little lamb." She leads me up the beach towards the outport. She is wiping her eyes and blowing her nose into her sleeves and I no longer want to walk with her. I want my mother. I start to cry. I try to yank my hand from hers and she lifts me and carries me all the way to her house and sits me on a cushioned bench by the window and wraps a shawl about me as if I'm cold and I say nicely, "I want to go home." She nods and feeds me canned peaches. Her eyes wrinkle into tears and she starts sobbing and a sickness grows in my belly. I want to sit on my pot. I want to sit on my pot and cramp down hard. Mister Louis comes in through the door and takes off his cap when he sees me and lowers his eyes. "We'll wait for her father. He'll be back by morning," Missus Louis whispers and he shakes his head and then nods and they both look at me, tossing and shaking their heads like fidgety horses. Missus Louis gives me tea and cookies and coddles me, murmuring *macushlah, macushlah,* and the sickness in my belly tells me to stay quiet. It tells me to change into a too-big nightdress when it gets dark and not to cry when I'm put into a little cot with a smelly stuffed rabbit.

It is another morning and another and it is scarcely light, the air ringing with birdsong. I steal out of the little cot and put on my clothes and creep outside Missus Louis's house. The air is cold and the beach banked in with fog. I run through the marsh and the grass is high and cold and wet against my ankles and I am afraid that I am lost. I keep running through the tall grass. I am breathing too fast and I call out to Mother when I see the house.

There is no smoke coming from the chimney, no lamplight in the windows. Perhaps Father is home too. I want to get in bed with Mother and put my cold feet on her warm legs. I go inside the house and it's cold, a terrible cold, as though the outside cold has entered it. There is a smell I don't know, not a bad smell, but one that makes my stomach sick again. Tabs scoots from Mother's room and I shriek with fright and then with glee and run into her room.

I stare for a long time. The bed is shoved back against the wall and a long white box sits across three chairs and Mother is lying inside of it and her eyes are closed but she is not sleeping. Her face is white and stiff and her eyes are sealed and I shiver with fear.

Tabs squirms about my legs and I topple back against the wall. There is a smell, a new smell that comes from the box. It smells clean, like detergent. It is the smell of rain on dune grass. I look to the white of her brow, her nose, her fat pouty lips. I start forward—the hair, it's brownish, there is no reddish gold, it's a dark brownish, it could never be my mother's without the reddish gold that gleams in the sun. Tabs presses hard against my legs and I pick him up and smother my face into his fur and look to the brown hair that is not Mother's. Within the cold silence of this broken moment I know that nothing will ever match onto itself again.

The faint guttural cry of a cat sounds from far away. It pulls me back, pulls me from the darkness, pulls me into my rocker where I sit by the picture window. Willaby meows up at me as I sit digging at my palms, digging out nuggets of stories Mother seamed into my bones. I chink them into being, like a miner, and they fall onto my lap like ill-fitting pieces that fossilized before truth set them right. I search amongst them for the girl cloaking herself against a too horrible truth and who curls now inside the silence of an old woman's heart, her feelings too deep to be told.

THREE

The cat cries out again. With shaky hands I pull aside the drapes and look into the wild eyes of the old tom crouching in the snow near my gatepost. He's back, his pelt more matted, rattier, his one ear shrivelled from frostbite. Willaby leaps onto the windowsill with flattened ears, gurgling deep in his throat. Behave yourself, I try to say, but I cannot speak. I close my eyes, but quickly open them to escape the stone-white face and sealed eyes of my mother. Holding onto a stomach rumbling with nausea, I rise on knees that wobble, sucking back air that smells like rain on dune grass. I hobble to the kitchen. The tom needs to be fed; he only comes at the point of starvation.

Rummaging through the cupboards, I search in vain for another can of food. The shopping, I forgot, I have to do the shopping. I dig out a bowl of rolled oats, it'll have to do, and the last of the milk, and go outside. The temperature has dropped; water seeps cold from my eyes. The tom scoots to the shrubbery near Gen's and I whimper like a cross youngster. It's been years and he still comes no closer to my threshold, despite the delicacies I lay out for him. Trenching my way through the snow, I set the food near the shrubs and bend to stare in through the branches, into the wild eyes of the old tom, and I am alarmed by their dulled look.

"You're sick, old boy. You'll be dead by morning. Come … come here … *pusss pusss* …" He hisses, neck fur rising. I rest my hands on my knees, pursing my mouth to breathe easier, damn asthma. Gen's footprints from this morning catch my attention and I peer closer. They lead straight to the cedar shrubs. I'm caught again by her lie—and what was it she hid in her pocket?

I make my way to the shrubs. Curiously, they're not shaken free of snow, as they ought to be if she was rooting through them for a hockey puck. I check the basement door; it's securely latched from the inside.

A deep shiver cuts through me, sending me scurrying for the house. Inside, I smell again the odour of souring cabbage. The garbage, I thought I'd put it out. I tie up the bag and put it by the door, then sniff again. I still smell something—kitty litter? But I cleaned the litter yesterday. Or was that the day before? The basement. Perhaps I forgot the kitty litter in the basement. Yes, the smell comes from there, but I've no mind to clean just now, I don't feel well, the dreams, the memories. And Gen, her boy—ahh, not a good start to the day. And what a day. Already it feels like two days in one. I circle about the house and come back again to the smell of kitty litter. What's this, what's this now, it's too much trouble to clean a bit of kitty litter?

I return to the porch and slide the bolt on the basement door. Lifting the flashlight from its shelf on the wall, I creep down the steps and smile as the kittens leap around my feet, their tiny claws tickling my ankles. Such little things. I flick the flashlight around, searching for the litter. Where is it—where did I put it? I sit on the upturned bucket and look about; the boy must have moved it. The mother cat stares at me with translucent eyes. I look at her toughened, scarred paws and wonder what stories they tell. I look at her body curled in comfort around herself, her head scarcely lifting off the floor as she continues to hold my stare, and I see how she is in acceptance of this moment with no thoughts or worries of tomorrow. I envy her that, for already this day has filled me with deep unrest. Unlike the old queen lying here before me, I am shamed that I grew old without seeing it, that I missed some knowing she must have accrued along the way, some knowing that allows her such acceptance.

She closes her eyes, shutting me out. A sense of aloneness envelops me. The absolute aloneness of not even having myself for a companion, for I don't know myself as old.

What's this, what's this now, I sit here moaning like something half perished? There, there it is, the mind slipping. But I shan't fear it, I know the tricks of the mind. I wasn't old till I saw myself old. I'll burn that damn picture of myself. It's what's causing me unrest, causing my mind to wander, stirring up old stuff, and I'm getting heartburn, it's what's giving me heartburn as well. And I'll speak to Gen about that lie. I'll go to the hospital, too, and sit with Ronny, and then go to the nursery and sit rocking those babies and changing them and making their formulas and being of help to the little mortals, as I have been for the past sixty years. I'll not let a silly old picture detour my step.

"I'll be back with supper," I assure the queen, and take myself back up the steps, holding onto the wall as a slight dizziness overtakes me. I look at the clock: half-past three. It is the one designated hour for naptime, but today I've been napping like the cats. I make my way back to the living room and sit wearily in the rocker. I don't like this day, I don't feel well. I reach behind me, flicking on the lamp to ease the dreary light.

The tom meows from outside. Shifting aside the drapes, I see greyish sky through windows sheeted with ice. The temperature has dropped severely. *You'll die out there, old boy.* He meows again, a crusty, fearful sound that disturbs me. My chest pains—the asthma. I tense, feeling an attack coming on. Instead a rush of heat suffuses my face and I lean to the cool of the iced windowpane. Two fish eyes glisten back at me. They glimmer like tears, frozen tears, the girl's tears, and I try to look away but she's here, pressing hard against me, squeezing my heart. I see her eyes shining through mine in the frozen window, catching me with the heat of a forgotten memory, my mother standing atop a rock outside the graveyard, her hair streaming out behind her and burning in the sun, her arms splayed like wings. I see her over Father's shoulder as he bends to pin a black ribbon to the sleeve of my red coat, his head shiny without hair, without his fedora. He looks into my eyes and his are dry as bone, his jaw slack as though struck by surprise. "Her heart just stopped," he says and he repeats his words louder as though trying to penetrate my glazed look.

He pats my shoulder and nods to the people wiping their eyes, their noses, murmuring softly to him. He lets go of my hand to shake another's and I run towards Missus Louis who I see standing by the lilac bush near the side of the church. Her dark cloak is fastened tight beneath her chin and her hat is askew as she blows her nose into a tissue. "I warned you, I warned you," she says to a thin woman whose face is buried in her gloved hands. "You should never have left it so long. I warned you about leaving it so long."

The thin woman removes her gloved hands from her face. It is Grandmother Creed. She cries out to Missus Louis, "You'll not tell. You swore you'd never tell."

Missus Louis turns abruptly, blocking the grandmother from view as Father approaches and takes my hand. I trot to keep up with his stride as he leads me through a huddle of people and towards a black hole and the long white box sitting beside it. I look for my mother outside the fence and she is smiling at me, her hair a burnished gold. I smile, reaching for her, but am encased in shadow as Grandmother Creed appears, crumpling onto her knees before me. Her cheeks are pale beneath their spots of rouge and her eyes are bits of sky fused with tears.

"The boat, it was held back," she whispers. "I couldn't get here, I couldn't get here, little one." She draws me to her shoulder, she smells like powder and she keeps saying, "The boat, the ferry boat, it was held back, I couldn't get here sooner." She isn't talking to me, she's talking to the white box and her face crinkles all over as she breaks into sobs, pressing gloved hands to her mouth. *"I must see her,"* she pleads to Father, but he shakes his head and the minister is shaking his.

"We kept her as long as we could," says Father, and his voice is scratchy like he wants to cough. The grandmother sobs bitterly, "Blessed child, my blessed child," and I feel her hurt as she reaches towards the white box near the black hole. "Mother isn't there," I want to say, but there's a sickness in my belly. Yet my heart knows something, it knows my mother isn't the cold, brown-haired woman in that box, my mother is hiding amongst the dunes on a sunlit beach and waiting for me to come find her. These are the words I try to say to Grandmother Creed, but they lump in my throat. These are my thoughts as I stand beside Father, my eyes fixed on the spot outside the fence where she'd been standing. These are the thoughts I whisper to Tabs that evening, nestling with him in the grass, stroking his ears, stroking his crown, searching the beach, searching the ocean, searching through the dune grass for Mother who is hiding. She is hiding somewhere and waiting for me to come find her.

It is morning and I sit on the sofa holding onto Tabs, looking to where Mother used to stand cutting bread in the kitchen. There is no sense of her, no scent, no shadow, just a stark emptiness that suctions my breath. Father comes out of his room rubbing his head, wiping his nose with a handkerchief, and he stops, staring at Mother's spot. He, too, sees the emptiness. Slowly he moves into it as though it intrigues him. Pouring water into the washstand he washes and rubs his scalp with a towel and pours more water and shoos Tabs from my lap. His forehead shines as he stands me beside the washstand with a bar of soap and a comb. He tries to speak but he coughs instead and I know there are words choking him and he coughs louder to get them out. "You'll get used to it, everybody gets used to it," he says to me. "It'll be hard for you without her. Be still now, I washes your face, you've a dirty face and behind your ears is dirty."

He puts a soapy cloth on my face and it burns into my eyes. I try to pull away but he holds tighter, scrubbing my face; I can't breathe. Soap gets in my mouth, it tastes bitterly bad, and I bite his hand. I bite it hard and he shouts and I bolt out the door. "Bloody animal, bloody little animal—wait—*Livvy!*" He chases after me. He catches me by the arm and drags me back inside the house, forcing me onto a chair, and I yell and kick. Grandmother Creed comes out from the small room where nobody sleeps. She's wearing a thin pink dressing gown. She sits like a skinned rabbit on Mother's chair and her eyes are puffy and reddened.

"So like her mother's," she whispers, touching my hair.

Remembering Mother's mouth puckering like a hurt baby over her mother wearing her clothes, I kick the grandmother's leg and dart to my room with Father stomping after me. I scrabble under my bed with a cry of fear, but he doesn't come into my room, merely closing the door. I keep crying and kicking the bottom of the bed. The floor is cold beneath me. I want Mother and I kick and scream and a huge shivering seizes me, chattering my teeth and stuttering my cries. I hold my breath to stop the chattering and hear the grandmother shouting at Father, sounding eerily like Mother: "You won't trust her to me, oh no, you won't trust her to me. Listen, Durwin, I'll do good by my word, I swear." Father answers in the same snappish way he spoke to Mother, "You'll not have her, by God, you'll not cheat me again." They start whirring the same strange words at each other as they had that first time I heard them fight: *manifest, lading, insurance, lloyds, cargo.* I shiver and shiver.

A rare shaft of sunlight catches me as I sit amongst the shadows at the back of Father's store. I am wearing one of the puffy-sleeved dresses with bows and buttons and a ruffled pinafore he has brought home from his store for me, and I am quietly practising my A's, B's and C's on a piece of brown wrapping paper he has laid out—to ready myself for school, he says. I suck on peppermint knobs, keeping a bowed head to the jangling of the bell above the door and the outporters coming and going, offering sympathy to Father in French, in English, in Mi'kmaq, in Gaelic and in the broken and mixed languages of a people borrowing generously from one another. They smile, reaching towards me with their work-chapped hands, their touch so gentle it dispels the language of tongues and nearly touches my hungering heart.

Father's heart hungers too. But not for the well wishes of his customers, no matter how deeply he returns their smiles. I watch, intrigued by the ease with which he speaks so effectively in their broken and borrowed languages, writing up orders to the satisfaction of all. When he smiles into their eyes and shakes their sympathetic hands, his starched white cuffs momentarily equate to theirs all frayed and shiny. But the second they leave he withdraws behind his counter, tallying and adding up their orders in his credit books with a dissatisfied look tightening his jaw. Digging his hands into his pockets, he jingles coins the way a baby might a rattle and stands by the window staring outside—at the post office, it seems, for he knows instantly when the mail arrives and turns to me.

"They've sorted it by now. Go get the mail, Livvy."

Remembering Mother's words about never being allowed to pick up the mail, I am surprised the first time he sends me. He's at the door each time I return, his hand held out for the envelopes. He flips through the letters, and never finding what he's looking for, angrily tosses them onto the counter and paces the store. Sometimes, when there are no customers, he counts the money he keeps in a drawer behind the counter or sorts through silver in the big glass jar he hides beneath a bottom shelf.

"Go outside and play," he snaps, his mouth ticking with annoyance those times he feels me watching. I bend my head over the sheets of brown paper. I don't want to play. I feign absorption, and when I'm tired of practising letters and words I simply sit there, staring at the molasses barrel, at the bolts of fabric I once hid behind, at the counter where Mother wasn't allowed to work. Father repeatedly tells me to go play, but warns

I'm *never* to venture near that Irish woman and her brood. I go nowhere. I am tired, too tired to walk or play or scoot like a crab along the beach. I simply want to sit. I am tired. I am tired from wanting Mother.

Rain taps against the roof, dripping with an echo into a galvanized bucket Father has put beneath the leak near the molasses barrel. It is a month before the beginning of my first school year. Father sends me across the road to the post office and watches as I return, hopping around the muddied puddles cratering the road. He takes the envelopes from my hand and flips through them, pausing before the last one. He rips it open and pulls out a folded sheet of paper. His jaw tenses as he reads, then grows more tense and I fear he's going to bust the buttons from his collar. Slamming the letter onto the counter, he lets out the growl of an angry dog. He kicks open the store door, grabbing the bell and choking its jangle, and steps outside. The flat of his back rises and falls with each angered breath and I know there is a wind that can bend him.

He orders me out of the store, throws the lock into place, and in the middle of the day and without his jacket or fedora, he starts for home through a drizzle of rain. I scrabble to keep up as he bashes the muddied craters with his shiny shoes, splashing mud up his pant leg. He halts beneath the knoll upon which Missus Louis's house stands and stares at Mister Louis who is sitting in the window staring back at him, white puffs of tobacco smoke rising furiously from his pipe. They keep staring at each other and I lower my eyes, the air between them foul with strife. Snarling like a dog again, Father lunges along the path through the marsh.

I follow quiet as a rabbit, and later I nibble at the beans and bread he sets at the table for my supper and watch as he goes to his shed with a bottle of whisky.

The next morning Father slouches over a mug of coffee at the table, his eyes reddish, his face pasty. I wander outside towards his shed and see that the door has been left open. Peeking inside, I note the clean floors, the wrenches and stuff hanging in orderly rows on the walls. Firewood is neatly stacked by a small barrel cut in half and used for a stove. A wooden chair sits sideways by a rough little table that holds the half-emptied whisky bottle from last evening. For the first time I enter the shed and sit, looking at the shiny rows of tools and a neat stack of books and papers on a shelf by a lantern. My leg itches from a fly bite and I pick at the dried blood, not hearing Father as he suddenly appears in the doorway. He is surprised to see me, and looks disgustedly at the dried blood I'm picking off my leg. He orders me to the house to wash. I run from his shed and through the thatch of woods and down the beach, crying for Mother.

It is evening. Father comes to my room and kneels beside my chair and looks at the fly bite. He lays his hand on my knee. It's warm and I'm surprised, I would've thought it cold. He looks into my eyes and then looks away and coughs the bitter odour of whisky into my room. "You want to be a good girl, don't you?"

I nod and Tabs jumps upon my lap and Father tries to speak quietly but his words distort into a harsh whisper instead. "You remember when I brought him?" he says, touching a finger to Tabs's head. "It was Christmas, you were sick with the mumps. I brought you the kitten and put him on your pillow. You lit up like the tree bulbs. It was me that give you the kitten, not your mother, do you remember that?"

I say yes and he leads me to the table and feeds me leftover beans and burnt toast and then goes off to his shed. Rain pounds on the roof all night and the wind snatches at the door like some beast wanting to get in. Come morning it seethes at the window as though trying to claw back Father's shoulders that are wet and slumped over the table like a great hound. He raises his eyes, reddish and swollen, and stands unsteadily, pointing me back to my room.

"The store, get ready for the store." He sits back down, holding his head in his hands. He stares about the house, at the foul-smelling dishtowels beside the sink and the plates yellowed with dried yolk, at the table cluttered with yesterday's supper dishes and our muddied boots piling up by the door, and his face becomes a sickening white.

Not out of hunger, but perhaps because Father is sick and he is my keeper, or perhaps because I'd once seen him pad quietly into that great emptiness of Mother's kitchen, I too now walk into the kitchen, and pick up the bread knife from the counter to cut bread for breakfast.

"Put it back, put it down," Father orders. "You'll have cheese at the store. Get ready, go." Then, holding his stomach, he bolts for the door.

A stout wind swipes through the deepening summer evening, rustling the trees outside. A knock sounds on the door, a rare knock, and Father rises as though expecting it. A young woman stands on the doorstep. She is younger than Mother, and tiny, but with big curves. Her eyes are big too, and flowery with thick lashes. Father, I quickly learn, has hired her out of the orphanage in Corner Brook to come live with us and keep house.

"Oh, the wee little thing, we'll get along, luv," she says upon entering the house and seeing me. Hearing the Irish lilt to her words, Father scowls.

"I said *English,* I said I wanted an *English* maid."

The woman's mouth dimples into a bold smile. "It's the Irish nuns that raised me, sir. I can't help what they did to my tongue. But you'll find more Irish in the Queen than you'll find in me." She dimples another smile and tells Father that her suitcase is at the train station, and that she was guided here by a French boy called Henri. "He had the look of a rogue, sir, but I had to trust him as you weren't there to meet me," she says accusingly. "And unless you're accompanying me back, I'll start work while you go fetch my bag."

Father goes to the train station for her bag. Her name is Etna. She doesn't hear well, which irritates Father as he loudly sounds out her orders the next morning before leaving for the store.

"Look at me when you speak," she tells both Father and me. "I hear better if I see your mouth as you talk." Father nods impatiently, then directs most of his words to me. I am to stay with Etna, and if I misbehave I'm to sit on the chair in my room. He leaves and I am glad not to be accompanying him to the store. I like looking at Etna's pretty face and bright eyes. I like how her dark hair is tied at the back in a bunch of little sausage curls, and I like how she smiles at me and calls me "luv," just like what Missus Louis called Mother. And I like how she hums when she cleans.

It is another day and it is many days and Etna smiles and hums while she sweeps and mops and cleans the floors, and empties out the cupboards, washing all the dishes, even those that are never used. She says the same words every time I ask her why: "Aye, germs, luv, germs." One day I ask her to show me one and she shakes her head. "Wee little things, they're the wee little things, luv, I saw them in a doctor's book." She shivers as though they are crawling up her sleeves and scrubs the dishes harder.

"What's a doctor's book?" I ask, touching her arm so she'll look at my mouth as I speak.

"A Bible for medicine," she replies. "It tells you everything that's ailing you."

"Did you clean in the orphanage?"

"Clean, chaste and honest, that's what the nuns preached. First thing God sees is cleanliness. We scrubbed the rooms and then the children. We scrubbed their faces, ears and necks, and then they says their prayers. Did your mam read you the Bible, luv, about cleanliness being next to Godliness?"

I turn from her mentioning of Mother and she quickly puts her arms around me, hugging me against her soft bosom, her hair and dress smelling like soap. "I'm sorry, luv. I bet you had a real clean mam. I can tell because her cupboards mightn't be too tidy, but there's no scum around her water taps. Here." She gives me a small piece of cloth and invites me to help her clean. I help her some. But I am soon bored and simply sit, listening to Etna hum as she dusts and wipes the tiniest of things throughout the house. "It starts with the small stuff," she says, "good housekeeping starts with the small stuff, else there's no sense to any of it." She laughs as I stare at her without understanding and continues with her cleaning, her smile more contented than Tabs curled into his sunspot beneath the kitchen window.

"Now, there's a thing," she says, shaking her head at Tabs. "There was never an animal in the orphanage. They carry fleas, luv. Can we keep him outside? Perhaps we'll talk with your da," she adds as I shake my head.

"He gave me Tabs. He won't ever keep him outside. He don't have fleas."

Etna doesn't hear; she isn't looking at me, she's busy wiping the chrome on the stove.

Missus Louis comes to our door bringing a present, and Father stands stiffly, blocking her entrance. "Her Grandmother Creed wrote me, asking if I would deliver it," says Missus Louis as though talking to a stubborn youngster. "Durwin, you forbid the child a present from her grandmother?" Brushing past Father, she hugs me, whispering "*Macushlah,* my *macushlah,*" and presses a little package into my hand. "From your grandmother—keep it somewhere safe. It looks expensive."

Father watches as I unwrap the package to reveal a thick silver chain with a heavy square locket that snaps open. Inside is a tiny photograph of two young girls, one dark and stern, the other blonde, pretty and smiling. "The blonde one is your grandmother when she was young," says Missus Louis. "And the dark girl is her cousin." She turns to Father. "Her grandmother isn't well. She begs a visit from Livvy."

Father squares his jaw and Missus Louis gives me another quick hug, looks crossly at Father and leaves.

"Let's have a cup of tea. I'll cut us some cake, eh?" says Etna with a sweetness to Father. He ignores her and goes to his shed, where he goes most every day after he comes home from the store.

"She seems like a fine woman," Etna says. "Why does your father dislike her?" I shrug and she wanders to the window, looking thoughtfully towards the shed. "Perhaps you can take your father a piece of cake?"

I shake my head.

"It's a cold scarf those arms will make for his neck," she chides, and cutting a piece of cake, she takes it on a plate to Father.

Father starts smoking. He begins sitting at the kitchen table long after supper is finished, smoking and twiddling a glass of port or whisky, seeming not to hear or see anything Etna might say or do.

"Poor man, he's grieving hard," says Etna to the sympathetic parishioners when she takes me to church. Father no longer goes. I am glad, for now Missus Louis stops each time she sees me and hugs me. She smooths my hair, her eyes dark as raisins as she looks into mine. "She's in your heart, little one, be brave, *macushlah,* be brave." Etna hurries us through the marsh, slowing her step each time we pass Father's shed. Those times when she sees Father looking through the window or standing in the doorway, her mouth pretties with smiles, no matter the cigarette burning low to Father's lips and the reddish fuzz charting his jaw.

Each morning Etna leads me to school and I am stiff like Father's collars in my new dresses, with their tight waists and full skirts and puffy sleeves, and my new buckled shoes. There is a Depression, Etna says, and people all over the country are starving, without food and work. I am lucky to be dressed so nice. The other girls wear rough blouses cut out of flour sacks and dyed in ochre or lime or dandelion greens. They stare at my new dresses and keep a wide berth and I feel like a crocheted bed doll. Esmée's girls, Suzie and Colette, walk on the other side of the road, too, and stare at my dresses. Once, when I smiled at them, they smiled in return, then ran. "Because the nuns are watching, luv," Etna says as I verge on tears. "They're Catholics, they're forbidden to speak to Protestants and you're a Protestant, land of the holy, don't you know that?"

She tells Father about the encounter over supper and Father taps the table with his fork.

"If they were bloody saints from heaven, you don't speak to that crowd," he says loud enough that even Etna flinches. Suzie and Colette must've heard him too for they always pretend not to see me after that. I don't like school. There are sixty-seven pupils of all ages in the one room and three quarters of them speak only French. The teacher calls them *Frenchies;* he speaks only English. Whenever he hears someone speaking or muttering or whispering in French, whether inside or outside the school, he cracks the ruler across their knuckles. Despite my being one of the few English-speaking students, I do more poorly than the Frenchies in copying letters and writing numbers.

Missus Louis brings a birthday cake from Grandmother Creed, whispering in my ear that the grandmother sends her love. Since the day Father received that letter from the post office, he's been drinking late into the evenings, sometimes spending the night in his shed, but come morning he is dressed inside his collars and marching off to his store. It is his eyes that he can't hide. They no longer shine like new nickels, but are dull, bleary from lack of sleep and too much drink. When Etna calls him from his shed for supper, he eats quickly, breathing the stench of whisky over the table.

Etna wrinkles her nose and turns her head. After the meal she cleans the dishes and the sink and then sweeps the floor and polishes the stove. She keeps inviting me to help her clean, but I always say no.

"Haven't you killed all the germs yet?" I ask one morning.

"You can never kill all of them, luv. They lay their wee little eggs that are always hatching. You can't see them but if you don't clean, they'll be everywhere, oh yes, luv." She nods, her flowery eyes sombre and alert. "Oh, yes, luv, they'll crawl all over your food, and over you, too. They can hatch in your skin. You have to clean the little buggers before they hatch."

"Are you scared of them?"

"It's the nuns, they made us scared of everything. They showed us pictures of germs. Ugh," she shivers, then smiles. "But don't be foolish, lass, that's not the only reason I like to clean. I like making dirty things clean. It's like I'm making it mine. I cleaned the kitchen so many times in the orphanage it used to feel like mine. Comes from having been in so many foster homes, I suppose. When I finally settled into the one place, it started feeling like home, even though I shared it with fifty others." She starts humming again, then stops, her eyes resting kindly on mine.

"Most orphans never had a mam or pap. Perhaps it's harder having a mam and then losing her, even if you do live in such a nice house. Are you sure you won't help with a bit of housework? You mightn't feel so sad if you were busy."

My lip near quivers at her look of kindness. Father comes in at that moment, and Etna makes him tea, chattering like a songbird as she serves us hot, molassey buns heaped with butter. "It's not that I need an extra set of hands," she says to Father, sitting with a cup of tea, watching us butter our buns, "but it would do her good to take a broom to a mat or scrub the dishcloths on the scrub board. Housework has always felt like playing for me." She smiles at Father. "When I was a girl, I'd rather sort through a basket of odd socks than play with a silly doll. Such a good feeling when everything's nice and sorted and put where it belongs." She brushes a stray sausage curl off her forehead as Father looks at her. She always has that stray curl and is always brushing at it whenever Father is looking, or when she's leaning over the table, placing a plate of food before him.

"Even when I'm dreaming I'm working," she once said, partway through supper. "I'm always dreaming about organizing the forest—okay, all you pines over here, and all you spruce over there, and get away you silly old alders." She tinkles a laugh as Father's brow rises in amazement. "Oh, yes, I'm always sorting and organizing the trees while I sleep—truly," she adds, her face flushing a pretty pink as Father gives a loud laugh. I stare at him with astonishment; it is the first—and will be the last—time I ever heard Father laugh out loud.

It is winter and it is summer and I do homework in my room, my books awkwardly positioned on my pillow. Tabs stretches beside me; Etna is skittish of him so Father orders he's to be kept in my room. Father has taken to lingering at the kitchen table long after supper is done, drinking whisky or sipping port. Etna chatters as she cleans off the table, dimpling her smiles even more. When she runs out of chatter, she hums. She hums and hums, the one long note that never dips or rises as she swishes shut the curtains for evening, refashions the linen cloth on the table and steps lightly across the floor with the broom, sweeping tufts of dust out the door.

A light grows in Father's eyes. He watches the round of her neck as she bends over, polishing the table legs, the curve of her arms as she irons his collars and pants. Sundays, when he doesn't go to the store, he strolls through the house, watching through the doorway as she leans over his bed, her slender hands pressing the sheets to his mattress, her face flushing as she sinks to her knees, tucking in corners and undressing his pillows and plumping them into slips fresh from the clothesline and honeyed with sun. Straightening, she sends him sweet smiles and struggles to keep her nose from wrinkling at the smell of his whisky and cigarette smoke.

Rising from my pillow, I tug back the curtains to a window dusty with dawn. The hallway floor creaks and through the slim opening in my room door I see Etna run from Father's room on bare feet. I watch as she stands, looking around the living room as Mother often did the sea, as though it is the first time she's seeing it. Clasping her hand to her heart she wanders to the table, smooths the white cloth, then whisks it off the table and goes to the door, shaking it to the wind and letting it bellow about her shoulders like the veil of a bride. She catches me watching her and abruptly closes the door, folding the cloth into the drawer as though it were a guilty secret.

Father comes out of his room, buttoning his shirt. He, too, stops abruptly when he sees me standing there, looking from him to Etna. He clears his throat, and with a sense of discomfort, walks past me to the washstand, splashing water on his face and over his head.

After breakfast—where Father resumes his brooding look and Etna contents herself with caressing her china cup and pouring

tea for Father—I walk through the thatch of woods, then along
the shore. Tabs finds me sitting amongst the dunes and I nuzzle
his crown, looking through the thin light of morning at the water.
I think of Mother. I always think of Mother. But it is different
now. Without the whispers of her voice, without the warmth of
her hand, her memory is dulling. The embers cool in my heart,
leaving it more cold and sterile than the bleached floors beneath
Etna's mop.

Missus Louis brings another cake and more best wishes from my
grandmother. I am thirteen and my mother has been gone for
seven years. It feels like one year, it feels like forever. Etna continues
to visit Father in his room after I'm in bed, but she's always in her
own bed when I awaken in the morning. They neither touch nor
speak any differently than they always did, when I am about. Nor
is it any different when I'm not there; I know this because I watch
through the window sometimes. I stay in my room a lot. I watch
the leaves turn from green to red and swirl through the air, baring
branches that soon snap like ice candles under winter's breath as
the snow piles high outside. Etna gets a vicious red sty on her eye.
She comes home from the doctor's, her face white with fright.

"It's an infection, I've germs in my eye." She looks nervously towards my door beyond which Tabs sleeps, then at me, her
dark eyes fraught with fear. "I'm sorry, luv, but the doctor says it's
caused by bad nerves. I'm always nervous of your cat."

"But he lives in my room."

She looks pleadingly to Father who grunts and goes to the
stove, rooting at the fire. "Keep him outside," he says to the quiet
following him. "I'll make him a place beneath the house."

"But it's cold, he'll freeze."

"He'll stay outside," Father argues. "I'll make him a door into the shed. He can sleep in the shed if he's cold."

He steps irritably away from Etna, who's following him, trying to read his lips as he speaks.

"But he sleeps in my room," I yell at her. "He's not hurting you when he sleeps in my room."

"I'm sorry, Livvy, I'm so sorry, luv, I wish it wasn't this way with me."

We both look anxiously at Father, but he won't look at either of us. Laying down the poker, he leaves the house for his shed. He builds Tabs an opening into his shed but Tabs refuses his new home and keeps coming to the door, sitting outside for hours, meowing to be let in. Sometimes at night I sneak him in through my window and put him out in the morning before Etna or Father awakens. Then he resumes his watch by the door. The second it opens for one of us to enter or leave, or to toss out a pan of dirtied water or a handful of scraps for the crows, he darts inside, sometimes slithering his cold, wet body against Etna's legs, which brings forth a scream like that of a broad-winged hawk. After one such scream that sends me flying from my room and Father's hands to his ears and Tabs scurrying beneath the sofa, Father hauls open the door and stands angrily beside it, his eyes hard on mine. "Get him out of here," he orders.

I go to the sofa and pull Tabs onto my lap. Etna stands on a chair staring at him as if he's a giant rat. "You encourage him, Livvy," she cries in a hurt tone.

Tossing Tabs gently outside, I go to my room and already Tabs is leaping onto my windowsill, his mouth opening with wide, angry meows. I giggle. I giggle without thought. I giggle and giggle, feeling the urge to run outside and wrap my arms around the stubborn cat and plop down with him in a snowbank and laugh and toss him about as I did when he was a kitten and we both felt light as snowflakes. Making sure my door is tightly shut, I open the window and Tabs leaps onto my bed and we burrow beneath the blankets.

Etna's sty worsens. It is meaty-red and near swollen shut. It causes such pain she can't be in daylight and so the windows are draped. "It's the cat, the doctor says it's the cat," she says piteously to Father after returning from her appointment with the doctor one day. She looks fearfully towards the window, beyond which Tabs sits, his shadow outlined on the drapes. "It's my nerves, I'm nervous of the cat and it's making the infection worse."

"But he's outside," argues Father, loudly stoking the stove as he always does when he doesn't want to listen to something.

"He springs on me every time I goes out. And he's always in the house at nights. I'm sorry, luv," she says to me, "I don't want to cause trouble for you."

Father looks at me irritably. "Is it true?"

I shake my head.

"She lies," whispers Etna, her good eye darting over me as though one might leap from my pocket. "I'm sorry, luv. But it's my eyes, I have germs in my eyes. They can spread through my body. I'll have to leave," she ends in a fearful whisper to Father.

I run to my room and close the door, barring my ears against anything else that might be said. Etna stays in her room throughout the next day with a compress on her eye. Come Friday I sludge through snow that is heavy with water towards home. Disheartened by the darkish room and stench of rubbing alcohol and Etna sitting in fright on the sofa, one eye swathed in a compress, the other following me accusingly, I lay down my books and go back outside.

"Wait, where you going?" Etna calls. She sounds nervous. I think she's worried about Tabs darting in, so I don't answer her, I simply close the door. She raps on the window to get my attention, but I don't care. The sun is warmish and I walk through the thatch of woods towards the beach. Snow bows the branches and clumps coldly about my face and shoulders as I push through them. I see Father standing at the water's edge, which is crumpled and grey with slob ice. He is heaving big, flat rocks at a brown paper bag floating on the sea. The soggy bag breaks apart and Tabs's head bobs to the surface and he paws at the water and I scream. I scream and scream as Father heaves another large rock and it smashes down on Tabs's head.

"Leave him out there, you leave him out there," Father orders as I tear past him and plunge knee deep into the icy water. Grasping one of Tabs's paws, I drag the weight of his water-soaked body into my arms. I sob bitterly, scarcely hearing Father as he says in a sullen voice, "Had to be done. Better than giving him away, he would've just come back." I turn on him as Mother did the time he raised his fist to her in front of Missus Louis's house. His mouth tightens but he says nothing. He drops his gaze heavily onto Tabs, the furball he'd laid upon my little-girl pillow and now drowned by his own hand. He starts to cough and then turns from me, hurrying up through the thatch of woods. And it is me now who stares accusingly at him, the brunt of his betrayal a soggy dead weight in my arms. Lugging Tabs down the shore, I carry him to our old nest in the dunes. My teeth start to chatter and I will for the blaze of Mother's hair to rise up from the rocks, for the heat of her smile to warm my chilled heart. But I see only the waves being sucked offshore, leaving strands of seaweed clinging like black roots to the rocks. My fingers stiffen from stroking Tabs's cold, wet skull and they begin to ache, nailing my attention onto the pain and keeping my thoughts from roaming about the shoreline. A pain starts up against my face, it feels like fire yet it stings the back of my neck and my mouth is numb. Opening my eyes, I find myself sitting in my rocker, leaning sideways, my forehead resting against the iced windowpane. The old tom meows hoarsely. It has grown darkish outside and he crouches in the whisper of light from my window, his dull gold eyes staring fixedly into mine.

FOUR

Shivering, I sit back in the rocker and pull the blanket up over my shoulders. Goodness. My goodness. Pressing a warm hand against the numbed side of my face, I breathe deeply to fix myself in time. I think of Father, but push him away. The girl, she's here, I feel her, she frightens me. *What do you want?* I call out, my voice harsh. I close my eyes and try to shiver the cold from my body, but I'm chilled through to the heart. *Girl,* I rasp, and am startled by a sudden urge to cry. *Foolish. Foolish old thing.* I swipe at my trembling mouth but I cannot wipe away the girl. She hovers, stirring my heart, and I am seized with a need to see her, to look into her eyes.

Brushing Willaby to the floor, I get up slowly, my knees creaking worse than the rocker, and go to the big leather-covered Bible sitting atop the cabinet. Tucked inside its pages is a class picture taken from my last year in school, with me sitting on the edge of my seat at the far left of the front row. I am tiny, my face wan and whitish, my shoulders huddling beneath a scarf that looks cold to the touch. I remember it was green and silk-heavy and serrated along its edges like a frond of seaweed—and that is what I look like in the photograph, a frond of seaweed that's been torn from its roots as it swayed and whirled in the sea and now lies limp upon a rock. *Hello girl,* I say, and wonder how it is I can't see my breath, that it isn't chilled white from the child I carry like a frozen embryo in my heart. Bringing the picture almost to my lips, I breathe over her with my hot breath and take her back to the rocker. I sit, rocking her as I rock the babies at the nursery, relishing that full feeling it always gives me in return, as though I'm holding the beginning of something new and pure and that through rocking it I'm helping to feed it with the love it will need to begin its mortal growth. The cats prowl around my legs, meowing loudly. They are hungry. I must feed them. I must lay the girl aside. "There, there now," I say, taking her back to the cabinet and laying her on top of the Bible with trembling hands. "There now, you be warm," I whisper. "A moment, please, a moment," I say to Willaby, and feel a tug of guilt. It's past supper-time; I heard the shrieks of children awhile ago on their way home from school, and it's quite dark now. I'll go to the store for cat food. There then. That's what I'll do, I'll walk to the store and buy food for the cats.

I look at the photograph of the girl once more, and walk from her on legs that are stiff as cardboard. I glance at the iced window. It will be cold and my asthma won't like it. Fetching the puffer from my room, I shoot three sprays down my throat and then pocket the cylinder and wrap a thick scarf around my head and mouth. Putting on my coat, I go outside, gasping in air so cold it stings my face. There's a truck pulled up at the curb, the same rusty red truck Gen's brother drove away in the other morning—or was that this morning? Gen is leaning inside the truck, tugging at something.

"No, stay, stay in there," she's commanding someone. "You go home with Stu now. I'll call you in the morning, you can come to the hospital with Stu in the morning. Oh, for God's sakes!" She pulls back from the truck and slams the door, and then sees me coming slowly down my steps. "Livvy, where are you going?" she yells, irrationally loud.

I ignore her tone. She's a right to be irrational, or whatever it is she's feeling towards me. "The boy?" I ask.

"Ronny!" she snaps. "His name's Ronny. And he's fine. Go back inside, it's bloody freezing out."

I am down the steps now, shuffling to my gate, breathing through my scarf to keep from coughing. "I'll sit with Ronny tomorrow," I say, my voice muffled. "I—I was sick today."

"I've already found someone, go back in. Where do you think you're going?" She walks over to my gate as I try to push it open.

"I can manage."

"It's frozen. Let me do that."

She gives it an extra tug and I step out onto the sidewalk, muttering crossly, "I'm not so weak I can't open my gate."

"Where you going? For God's sakes," she exclaims as I slip. Holding onto the fence, I brush her hand aside as she tries to take mine.

"Go about your business," I say sharply. "I'll be on my way."

"On your way where? Livvy, if you don't tell me, I'll follow you."

"To the supermarket. I have to tell you where I'm going now? What's wrong? What's wrong with you?" I ask again, for she's shut her mouth and is standing before me, staring mutely into my face. When she speaks, her voice is gentle.

"Livvy, it's past midnight."

I stare at her confusedly. "No it isn't. I heard the children. My dear, I heard the children. They were coming home from school—" I lapse, taking in the empty street bereft of cars, horns, people, the darkened windows of the corner store.

"Were you dreaming?" Gen asks. "You must have been dreaming. Were you napping?"

I look at her. I feel dizzy. Without the grip of time, I feel dizzy.

"You must have fallen asleep in your rocker," says Gen.

"How do you know where I was sitting?" I ask. "Are you spying? Is that what you were doing in my yard this morning, spying on me?"

"I have to spy? Every day you sit rocking and looking out your window, and I have to spy? Now you're really scaring me."

"I looked in the bushes, the snow was still on them, you weren't searching for anything there, but you hid something in your pocket, you hid something, what was it?" My voice verges on hysteria. There's a fear growing in Gen's eyes, whether from my confused state or some state of her own. She's spared answering by the truck's passenger door swinging open, followed by a low moan.

"Ohh, gawd," Gen mutters as an old woman, not too unlike myself, lurches out and stands wobbling on the sidewalk, a fur cap lopped sideways on her head.

"Whesh my boy, whesh Ronny?" she cries out drunkenly.

"My *mother*," says Gen.

Despite my sense of confusion, I hear the resentment in her tone. I watch as she goes to the old woman, who's now glowering at me through the dark. There now, I think, there's that shaft of night darkening Gen's eyes.

"Who'sh zat?" the old woman asks Gen. "Who'sh that? Why ish she zaring at me— *Why you zaring at me,*" she calls out in a shrill voice, flailing her arms as Gen takes her by the shoulders and tries to manoeuvre her back inside the truck. The old woman frees herself, raises a fist towards me and then slips sideways, taking Gen down with her onto the ice-crusted sidewalk.

I hurry towards them as Gen struggles to pull herself back up, her mother limp as a noodle in her arms. "Where's your brother?" I ask crossly. "Shouldn't he be helping?"

"He's inside the house. Stand back," Gen orders as I grasp her mother's shoulder, trying to help. "Oh, hell, just what I need, two broken hips to cart around this evening. Will you just go inside, Livvy?"

"Where's your brother?" I ask again, then catch sight of a dark shape with spiked hair hurtling across my yard and jumping into Gen's. "What're you doing? What're you doing in my yard?"

"Sorry, I needed to piss."

"You needed to piss in my backyard?"

He comes through Gen's gate, scoops up his mother as though she were a child and lays her inside the truck, across the seat.

"Take her home, honey," says Gen, closing the passenger door. "Livvy, let's go inside. Livvy," she pleads as I push away from her, staring accusingly at her brother who's now bending to examine the front of his truck.

"I needed to *piss*," he says irritably. "Sorry. Your backyard was darker than Gen's."

"*Now* you care what people think?" I ask, staring at his spikes.

"He's not thinking properly, he got a fright," says Gen. "He just hit a cat. He was driving us home from the hospital and nicked a light pole back there, trying not to hit the old tom."

"You hit the old tom?" I ask with alarm.

"Just nicked him, I think," says Stu. "He'll be fine."

I tighten with anger. "Fine? If he got hit by a truck he's not fine, my son. He's got broken bones, I can guarantee you that."

"I'll drop by in the morning," says Stu.

"He could be dead in the morning."

"He scooted under the steps of the bike shop. Moved too quick for anything to be broken."

"We'll look in the morning," says Gen. "It's too dark to see anything."

"But the cat—"

"We'll look in the morning, Livvy. You're wheezing and it's late. I don't mean disrespect, but he's an old cat, and wild. Unless he wants to be found, there's nothing we can do. Least, not tonight."

An old cat and wild. There, there it is, no more than that. A life wrapped up in words, dispassionate words from yet a passionate heart. As if the old hadn't lived, had never padded across hot yellow sand and licked the salty tears of a girl, had never crouched fearfully in the grass, listening to the split second of silence between lightning and thunder, had never felt the lethargy from time withering their bones to dust.

I walk away from them both, back through my gate and up the iced steps, ignoring Gen's soft tones following me. I want to question her further about why she and her brother have suddenly taken to sneaking around my house. It upsets me, why are they doing that? But other things disturb me more right now—my sleeping through the day, and the old tom.

Inside, I find my asthma pills, take double the dosage with a glass of water and then, shaking the puffer, fire a good shot down my throat, sucking it in. I sit by the window in my rocker and wait till Gen's lights are out. Then quietly I open my side door and step outside. The houses lining the street are dark, their moonlit windows a membrane of frost. Carefully descending the steps, I push open the gate and start down the sidewalk, the moon shadowing my bent body and spindly old legs that wobble inside their oversized rubbers.

I hang onto a fence post to catch my breath. Across the road is the side street with the spruce tree on its corner, and I see now why it was odd for that car to have been parked there while Gen was driving off in the ambulance. There's a fire hydrant near the spruce and no one parks there. Then something comes to me. The man who'd been standing by the car had looked familiar, and now I realize why: he was the driver of the red truck that had picked up Stu this morning. There was something odd about the way he was staring after Gen, and then at her house like that.

A rustle of wind sweeps snow fine as dust into my face. I swaddle my scarf more tightly around my mouth and start walking again. The greenish light from the bicycle shop shines eerily upon its front steps and the snow banking its sides. I turn off the sidewalk and climb the left bank already trodden with footprints, probably Stu's. There is an opening of sorts tunnelling beneath the steps.

"Are you in there, boy?" I grope around the opening, my fingers numbing through my cotton gloves. "Tom—pussss, here pussss." Bending down on my knees, I reach further beneath the step, iced snow scratching against the bared skin of my wrist. I touch something soft and then snatch my hand back as something sharp lacerates my wrist. With a demonic hiss, the old tom shoots out past me and vanishes around the side of the building.

I sit back, holding onto my wrist. It smarts like hell, and I can see a dark trickle of blood growing thicker. I rub it against the snowbank and near weep from the sting. *Fool, old fool,* I mutter to myself as I pull myself onto my feet. Prowling the streets at midnight, looking for an old tom. This will give Sunderland something to blather about, and everyone else on the street. It's giving *me* something to talk about, fool, old fool, chasing after cats like a witch woman, trying to rescue poor old Tabs, dead for seventy-something years.

Ahh, the tricks of the mind.

Stuffing my hand in my pocket, I start up the sidewalk, tilting my chin down so that anyone looking mightn't recognize me. The street darkens in front of Gen's house, but I won't look up; perhaps she'll think me a spectre of her dreams. I make it to my gate and manage to keep my shoulders erect as I go slowly up the stairs and step with relief inside.

Shedding my coat and boots, I trudge to the cupboard, eat a handful of crackers and drink some water, then hobble wearily down the hallway to my room. My shoulders are still erect and I wonder if perhaps I might have inherited a bit of Father's pride.

Father. His voice comes to me, faint but stern: *Look at me. Look at me.*

I turn from it. He's been circling my thoughts since this morning's dream, trying to get in, but I've not let him. I reach beneath the blankets, rubbing my cold feet, wrapping them in my hands to warm them as I had that night of Tabs's drowning and I near lost them to frostbite. *Look at me, look at me.* I close my ears. I touch my wrist; it still stings. *Look at me,* shouts Father, and I look wildly around the room. It's dark and I become frightened; my dreams are frightening me and I lost time today.

"What do you want?" I croak, and the sound of my voice frightens me more, for surely it's madness to speak out loud to ghosts. I close my eyes and see the accusing eyes of the girl. Her hair is tightly clipped behind her ears, yet it glows a burnished gold like Mother's the day she stood outside the graveyard, her arms raised like wings. This is the memory that burned itself the deepest in my girlish heart, the one I curled inside of those cold days I stole away from Father's house and crept into the grass searching for Mother, searching for comfort, stroking Tabs. I should have looked then, when its blaze was the brightest, to find a different path to place my feet. But I was a girl, I want to shout. I was just a girl in whose world the sun had darkened. I hadn't learned how to grip onto a rock with my toes and face down the wind and see which way to go. Even now, lying here on this pillow with ancient eyes, I can see no clearer through that dark cloud that diverted my girlish steps. Perhaps that's why my heart beats with fear now. It's frightened of those other paths, the ones I might've missed when my sight was frozen in grief, paths that might have led me towards a brighter doorstep than the heavily shrouded house of Grandmother Creed's.

But this is where the girl leads me, to those dark corridors of memory. Her hand is gentle and she is not afraid. I am shamed and I let her lead me to that little straight-backed chair in my bedroom and to Father, who stands looking down at me, shouting, *Look at me, look at me.* I will not. I am fourteen and sitting at a desk, struggling to do percentages, to understand the dance of numbers spreading across the page.

Look at me, look at me, Father shouts, and I'm cold and shivering with the same cold that has chilled my bones since the day of Tabs's drowning, a shivering I can't get rid of no matter the cardigan and scarves bundling my shoulders. I stare harder at the page of numbers that holds no pattern, like a hen's track on gravel. "You're daft, you're daft like your mother, you can't learn, you're daft like your mother," shouts Father, and he leaves my room with a spew of hot breath.

Fog dulls the school windows, greying the gaunt face of the skinny man-teacher loudly telling me I have failed the same geography test twice in a row. The others lean with lowered eyes onto their pencils, but the teacher yells at them anyway, calling everyone dumb for barely making their fifty percent.

Outside the school two English girls my age call to me, but I'm two grades behind them and too weighted for their light step and ready laugh. I try to think why it is I keep failing other subjects besides arithmetic. I hate numbers, I hate figuring sums. But reading and understanding and remembering are easy, and yet I keep failing those subjects, too. Somehow it's the writing. When I write out answers to questions I work so hard trying to spell right and to remember where to put commas and periods and to stay on the lines that I forget what it is I'm writing about and get everything mixed up and then there's no time to start all over again. It's gotten so that I dread going to school. I dread sitting at the table and having Father watch over my shoulder as I struggle through homework, through writing out simple things that I know fully in memory, like the names of clouds and rocks and planets. I want to quit school as Suzie has done. I want to be Colette who now runs ahead of me with a group of French girls, waving her test with a coveted sixty percent at her brother Henri, who has quit school too and fishes offshore during the summers.

Henri ignores her. He's standing before the dirtied windows of the pubhouse. He spits on his knuckles and hoists them towards a group of boys staring him down. Dark-skinned, with a sheen of black hair sweeping his brow, he charges the boys and they scatter like gunshot down the road. "Wharf rats," he calls after them, and then he swaggers back to the pub. Mister Louis pokes his shaggy white head with his rounded blue war cap out through the pubhouse window. "You kick their Proddy asses," he roars, and then laughs, saluting Henri with a mug of ale.

Henri catches sight of me and grins. "Hey, curly locks, where you been? Come meet me by the *rivière,* eh? I'll teach you to swim."

The store door opens, bell jangling, and Father stands beneath it with a bristled look. "Trash," he mutters to me, yet loud enough for Henri to hear, "stay away from trash," and I hurry along the road towards home.

Father slides his chair over to where I'm sitting at the kitchen table, struggling over a page of long division. Smelling of whisky and tobacco, he puts his face near mine. He scratches his stubble like a dog scratching fleas, and grips my pencil so hard it imprints on the next three pages as he starts working the sums.

"My mother was a *fool,*" he says, his voice hard yet low, as though guarding his words from the deafening Etna mixing up biscuits a few feet away. "She streeled the streets, blathering like a fool to other fools. She left me sleeping in piss-soaked beds with the younger ones and fed me stale bread and yellow tea in the mornings. My father—he was the captain of a ship—he stole me off the street one morning when he was ashore, took me from Liverpool to London on a train and put me in a boarding school. I never saw my mother again—a God-given blessing."

I stir uncomfortably. He's never spoken to me this long before and I listen intently as he tells of his father who told him to call him Captain, and who put him to work on his ship during every holiday. He says he kept sitting on the ropes of the schooner looking up at the sails. They stood so far up he thought they scraped the sky, were so billowed with wind he thought they'd lift the schooner off the water and sail through the heavens. "But it never scared me," he says gruffly. "I would've sailed to hell and back for a chunk of beef or chicken to chew on."

I smell his soured breath. I feel the heat from his face as he talks. I'm tense that his cheek will touch mine and I both yearn for and shrink from the thought. He pours another whisky from a bottle in the cupboard and sits back down, gripping the pencil with a malice incurred from the crib. He explains how to work numbers and wanders with the whisky into more talk of Captain, his voice growing growly as Captain's must have as he tells me about sailing a schooner in screaming winds that rolled the sea. "And when I got sick, Captain took me aloft to the bow and straddled me across an anchor and roared over the wind, *Now pretend you're riding a horse, and you ride them bastard rollers coming at you, and you spew sideways from the wind till you got nothing left to spew.*

"Lots of times after that I was sick," said Father, "but I never showed him. I swallowed vomit and kept right on walking beside Captain. Came the day I never got sick, no matter the swell, and they ran deep. So you stay with them sums, and you'll learn them. You'll not be a fool and spend your life blathering."

He turns the page of my scribbler and plies the pencil through more long division as he talks of the boarding school, where all the boys his own age walked quietly through big darkish hallways whose stair rails and floors and ceilings shone with varnish. He learned everything they put before him. When he finished school, Captain took him to the French shore on the west coast of Newfoundland. "Right here in Sables d'Or, this is where he and my grandfather brought me. My grandfather was a captain, too, from the Queen's navy, but was too old and arthritic to cling to a gun. But he was spry and mixed in good with the Frenchmen living here, and he and Captain built the store from nothing, little more than a fishing room. My grandfather died when I was about your age. Captain gave that store to me, the first of more to come. But your mother's damn Frenchman got in the way of that." He puts the pencil back in my hand and turns his big-jawed face towards me, his metal-grey eyes scraping against mine. "Luck kept me from a son. It's you who's got to keep what's mine after I'm dead."

Pussy willows weave a silvery swath along the roadside and I hide another failed report card in my books. Missus Louis stands on the steps before Father's store holding a green-dyed egg in a little basket of straw. She smiles at Colette who is waving her report card excitedly, then turns a haughty look onto Father who's standing in the doorway, the overhead bell tinkling as he tightens its hook into the header. Colette runs off and both Father and Missus Louis are looking down at me and the report card partly hidden between the pages of my book. I say nothing. Father's cheeks splotch red as he turns from me in anger.

"Ahh, it's the teacher, he's stun as a gnat, luv," says Missus Louis. "Let her come to me," she says to Father. "She's smart, I'll find the problem. It's probably something simple like how she hears and writes. I've taught her kind before."

"She'll be educated the proper way, in a school," says Father without looking at Missus Louis.

Missus Louis sniffs and turns to me, saying kindly, "They don't know how to teach you, luv, that's all. Take this, it's an Easter egg from your Grandmother Creed," she adds, tucking the painted egg inside my hand. "I told her you're a young woman now, too big for such things, but she made me promise to make you one." She looks at Father. "Her grandmother writes often, asking about her—as she should," she mutters, and takes her leave.

"I want to go with Missus Louis," I say to Father, the words pushing from my mouth like moths from a cocoon. They hover on crumpled wings before the gleam of spite in Father's eyes. He takes my shoulders, twists me in through the store door and sits me hard on a stack of flour bags.

"Nothing, you've heard nothing. You're daft like your mother. They *drowned* your grandfather! Does that mean *anything* to you? And that's just the *half* of what they done to your grandfather and your *great*-grandfathers. They burned them out. They burned them out and stole their river. If your grandfather was here now, he'd tell you stories, how the Irish are worse than the French. *We* brought them here, my forefathers. They were eating rotting spuds and we brought them here. For that they turn on us, they spy for the French. Least we'd see the French coming on the tides, hear them tramping through the woods with their guns. But the Irish—knife you in the goddamned back! I'd square off with a musket any day, least you can see what got you. You *never* enter that house. You'll learn your school lessons, you'll learn them like I did. And you'll *never* let an Irish mick and a French traitor have a say in your life. Look at me, are you listening? Are you listening? *Look at me!*"

I'm staring at the dark grainy floor of his store, I'm hearing his words and staring at the dark grainy floor and he shakes me, *Look at me, look at me!*

I look into his eyes and see the hatred smouldering beneath his strife, his hatred for all things, for Mister Louis, for Missus Louis, and for Mother. And me too, no matter that I'm his child who's done no harm. He's fuelling a rage against me too, for it's easier to hate me than learn the wrong he's doing me. But it is Father now who's doing the looking. He's looking into my eyes and he sees a deep, burning rage, and he sees that it's for him. He recoils, his hands falling away from my shoulders, because it's fiercer than what he feels. For mine is an anger newly born and fuelled by love. While his has been filtered through time and wisps of history already diluted by tongue and the whispers of ghosts.

Father is seized with a fit of coughing, and he won't look at me. He lifts a knife off the counter and says something about supper, then cuts a thick slice of cheese from the round and wraps it in paper and tucks it beneath his arm. He opens the store door, I step past him and he shrinks back so we don't touch. I feel giddy. I would've thought anger a poisonous, heavy thing, something to abhor, and yet I feel proud of it, protective, my step feels light.

Father catches up with me and then adopts a one-step-ahead stride. He begins talking again, a politeness to his words now, like Mother's those rare times she tried to make amends for some ill thing she'd said or done but couldn't admit to. "Your great-grandfather was one of the first Englishmen to put down roots around here. The French kept us back a hundred years, kept us from settling, from making laws, tying up our land rights with their claims to these shores. They cared nothing for this land. They wanted a beach to dry their fish, and for that they kept us back a hundred years with their outdated treaties."

He coughs, trying to cover the bitterness in his voice, but I hear it and I'm surprised. Aside from Mister Louis, he's never spoken ill of the French; almost all his customers are French. "But they were no more than pirates back then," he says, "burning out the English whenever they tried to settle, robbing their tools. But my grandfather, he was like Father: iron fists. He sat in a dory once and faced down one of their warships. They were strong men, your father and grandfather. They didn't back off, they fought for their right to live wherever they damn well pleased. And they did. A lot of those Frenchmen here were traitors to their own flag. They abandoned their own ships and hid out in the woods, and wouldn't serve the English flag either. Hooligans, most of them, hiding behind the Indians, hiding behind the Irish, marrying their women and hiding behind their names. In 1904 the last treaty was signed. You remember that date, 1904. The French were finally bought off by the English and we took what was ours."

I listen as we keep walking. I think of the boy taken from a piss-drenched bed and a blathering mother and then placed before men groomed with captain's hats and jackets, facing down the sea and warships with iron fists. I wonder how much vomit he swallowed, how many white horses he whipped, how many riggings he climbed to harden his fists like Captain's, like his grandfather's. I listen hard and I hear his words, but it's the pride strutting through them that keeps me from feeling them.

He clenches his fists now, and squares his shoulders in the same prideful stance as I imagine his father stood, and grandfather. And yet, looking up the thick length of his arms, past the width of his shoulders and onto his jaw, I see the same peeved look curling his mouth as curled Mother's whenever she scorned Grandmother Creed. I see a puffiness from too much drink and too little sleep padding his eyes, and a pucker from too much brooding marring his forehead. How come you're not happy then, you're walking so big, I think to ask. But I don't care to know. I'm more curious about the boy in his piss-drenched bed. How might he have fared,

I wonder, if he hadn't been stolen from a mother who dressed like a streel and blathered with fools?

Father orders Etna to accompany me to the doctor's, and I'm given glasses and more time at the kitchen table for homework. I study till my eyes water to the darkish evening light and my head aches. I study till Etna blows out the lamp to save oil and sends me to bed to save firewood. I light a candle beside the bed and get head-aches from straining to its light. I read about stuff I already know, stuff every teacher who ever sat before a school desk preached daily to us youngsters about the British and French battling for years, battling for the earth, battling themselves, battling three hundred years now, over the fish and the Newfoundland shores. The English sought settlement as well as bounty, while the French sought only a summertime shore to dry their fish and to make use of their yearly commutes to season their seamen for warships. *Nursery for seamen, Livvy,* Father keeps saying, *are you listening, that's what this shoreline was to the French, nursery for seamen, cradle for their sailors. Are you listening, Livvy, are you listening?*

I listen. I listen and read. I read and read about the French shore, trying to understand Father's harshness towards the French and Mister Louis's harshness towards the English. I read about wars and treaties and colonies and I learn that the strife between Father and Mister Louis has nothing to do with flags, that most settlers up and down the shoreline, whether they were French, English, Jersey, Scots or Mi'kmaq, get along just fine. While it tells me nothing about Father or Mister Louis, I feel proud of this knowing, and come time for tests, I strive as hard as I can to put these thoughts onto paper. But when the marks are passed down

I have done poorly again, passing some subjects with meagre marks and failing others. I'm always the one most surprised by my failing, and Father the least. But he doesn't yell anymore, not since the day he looked into my eyes. And with my feelings of dread becoming more and more crippling as I attend school, my writing and my report cards become more dismal. Father stops talking to me. He acts like I'm not there, that I am invisible. It is a strike that hits me harder than his yelling, harder than his anger.

A new teacher comes to The Crossing and tells Father quite simply that I can't learn and Father takes me out of school. It is a relief. I am fourteen and in grade eight, a far lower grade than the others my age—at least those few who continue with school. Most drop out by the age of fifteen, and I tell Father I'm old enough now to be hired out as a serving girl. He thrashes me with a look and says, "We *hire* servants in this family, we don't *make* them," and orders me to help Etna with her cleaning.

It is a cleaning that never ends. Etna's germs can never be swept, scrubbed or washed away. *They lay wee little eggs, luv, they lay wee little eggs.* She smiles at me all the time, but since Tabs's drowning, her smiles are more sympathetic than sweet. I don't blame her for what Father did. I don't blame her for fearing germs. I understand how fixing one's mind too strongly on something can hatch fear and dread. It's probably what kept me failing in school, the dread of failing. So I smile back at Etna and we sweep and scrub. I sweep the floor and Etna sweeps it again. I wipe a countertop and Etna wipes it again. Her growing deafness keeps her from chattering as much, but she hums all the time, humming her way through her cleaning, scarcely noticing she's redoing what I've already done.

Suppertime, when Father joins us, we all three sit in a polite silence that serves each of us: Father and I with our brooding thoughts that are as obsessive as Etna's about her germs, and Etna with her deafness, since she doesn't need to study our mouths to hear what's being said and can concentrate instead on passing around the matching tea things with the smile of a girl playing dollhouse.

It is summer, it is warm and I settle for the outside chores: beating mats and bringing in wood and water and polishing windows and hanging out clothes. I neither like nor dislike Etna, for she inspires not enough passion within me for either, and aside from her humming, we share the rooms in a comfortable quiet. Oftentimes I read or flip through the catalogues. Most times I cannot sit. It is the aloneness that undoes me, the terrible aloneness of feeling defeated by one's self. I want only to walk.

This place where I live is called Sables d'Or because of the gold sand beaches scattered along the shoreline. It sits open to the winds on a wide, flat flood plain beside the shifting blue waters of St. George's Bay. Behind it, not too far in the east, is a long range of mountains, green and grey hulks shouldering the sky. It was the shoreline that drew Mother and me, but since Tabs's stoning, I no longer feel comforted by the yellow sand, and the dune grass cuts me with its sharpness and the sea hisses at my feet. I now walk inland around little ponds and towering hillsides that make me feel small. Easy enough to avoid people with Father's house off to itself. People talk. They think Father never got over losing Mother, that his drinking, his giving up church, his sullenness are all part of his grief at being widowed. They offer me invitations to Sunday dinners and gatherings at the church, but I've never gone. Like Mother, I don't have a knack for languages and would rather be alone. More than that, I feel distance from their big, overflowing families of uncles and aunts and cousins, and that deepened sense of belonging to each other, and to the shoreline too, as though they were spawned out of the ocean with the fish that fed them. And Father feels more like a visitor, a strange bird that lit upon their rock and built a misfit nest for his come-from-away wife and their child.

But mostly it's the failing grades I received in school that keeps me to myself. It confuses me, foils my step, and I understand better now Mother's keeping to *her*self. She failed, too, in becoming the businesswoman she thought she'd be with Father, and in leading the colourful life she'd painted for herself when she first met him.

Aloneness becomes my companion. It allows me to curl into the tuck of a breeze and track its scent across bogs and stunted tucamores and climb the highest of hilltops, gazing for hours out over the sea till I sometimes feel myself sifting into a flake of snow, a fogbank or a drop of rain. In those moments I am blessed and freed from discontent.

Etna is fluttering nervously around the kitchen as I enter the house late one evening after one of my walks, and Father is dousing port into a glass. Grandmother Creed sits calmly on the sofa, wispy thin inside a tweed jacket with big lapels, a small hat tilted smartly to the upsweep of her yellow hair. She reaches for a cane and rises towards me, her eyes the same crisp blue that I remember, her bony cheeks gaunt beneath their tinge of rouge.

She grasps a lock of my hair with a withered hand. "You're more and more like her. How quickly you've grown," she exclaims, her tongue so English it's as though she just stepped off the boat from Liverpool. "My dear, I've so wanted to see you." She turns to Father. "You mustn't begrudge my coming, Durwin, she's my *granddaughter,* after all." She looks back at me, her voice dropping to a whisper. "My dear, you're all I've left in the world."

"And all *I've* left," Father cuts in meaningfully. His words are not for me but for Grandmother Creed. They are still fighting beneath their civilities. I take myself to the kitchen but keep a keen ear to my grandmother, who's altered her tone now, meekly apologizing to Father about not giving notice of her coming. When I return she's scrutinizing the room almost as sharply as she scrutinized me as she talks, and her eyes linger deliberately on the worn arms and saggy cushions of the old mustard-coloured sofa. Meanwhile Father prowls the floor like a poked dog.

"Who thought the Depression would last this long," says Grandmother Creed. "It's quite beastly, I've given much to the soup kitchens. I imagine you've had to cancel many debts," she adds as Father sits gulping his port, the glass clicking against his teeth.

"I've kept my head," he replies. "Do you have the tea ready, Etna?" Etna skittishly places tea and fruitcake on the coffee table before Grandmother Creed, and I quickly bid good evening and escape to my room.

After Etna—her room given over to my grandmother—tucks in beside me and her breathing steadies with sleep, I listen to my father and grandmother talking in low voices. I hear Father's tone, boisterous with blame and anger, and my grandmother's, placating, pleading. *Stop punishing me, Durwin. It was your father who foiled things. I'll make it worth your while. I've a right. I'll send her back.*

I sit up in alarm. She's come for me. The grandmother's come for me. Springing to my feet, I press my ear against the door. *You'll never have her,* says Father. I cling to the doorway with relief and their words garble again, but some I catch—those I vaguely remember from their old row: *manifest, lloyds, lading, cargo.* I wonder now at those words, but there is a wicked sense of pleasure stealing over me from the rage between my father and grandmother, and it dawns on me that I hold them both responsible for my mother's dying.

Their vileness creeps into my dreams and I awaken before dawn, unable to sleep. Rising carefully so as not to awaken Etna, I go to the kitchen for a glass of water and am startled to see Grandmother Creed, wrapped tightly in a silken dressing gown, leaning against the sink. She is fingering the teapot, her face drawn with sadness.

"Will you join me for a spot of tea, dear?" she asks, eyes brightening at the sight of me. She looks to Father's door and puts a finger to her lips as though we're being naughty. Stealthily, she opens the cupboard doors. "Did your mummy have a special cup?" she half whispers, and looks disappointed as I shake my head.

I sit at the table, watching as she makes toast and pours tea, her fingers dawdling over the knife handles, the cup handles, the spoons, the countertop. She is looking for Mother. She places a mug of tea before me and sits with one for herself. Her eyes squint disapprovingly as I heap three teaspoons of sugar into my tea.

"It's how Mother had hers," I say.

She grimaces but giggles cutesy like a girl. "She was a bugger for sugar. And messy, my goodness, getting her to comb that hair. Tell me dear, tell me some things about her. What did she like doing the most?"

"She brought soapy water to my room," I say. "She always

watched over me while I washed. She always fixed my hair, and she made my bed without wrinkles. She liked sweeping and mopping and starching Father's shirts and collars."

The grandmother's face goes quiet. She knows my lie, yet feigns ignorance and carries on with her own lie. "She always loved ironing clothes. That was the only housework she liked doing. My goodness, she loved clothes—her pretty frocks and matching ribbons. She liked it when we dressed up and went out for walks together. I've kept all her things and her room is the same as the day she left it. You must come for a visit. Did she tell you about her room, dear, how I let her pick her own colours and furniture?"

"I'm sleepy." I push away from the table and take myself back to bed, wondering what dirty thing pushes my grandmother to lie about such simple truths.

The thorny bramble of a raspberry bush pricks my ankle as I stand near Indian Head, looking out over the sea. Dark clouds are rumbling from the east. They bring fear and an excitement that stiffens the backs of men and curdles the hearts of mothers. "Europe is at war," Father announces, and he too takes to walking the road, grouping and talking with others beside the post office, the train station, the pubhouse.

Coming out of the store with a parcel of flour and raisins for Etna, I pause, watching Mister Louis coming stooped-shouldered and stiff-legged towards Henri, who's leaning drunkenly outside the pubhouse doorway. Henri hops off the steps, looking stiffer than Mister Louis in his new dark-blue jumper from the Canadian navy, a round white hat stamped in gold letters above his brow.

A bunch of his mates crowd the doorway behind him, chuckling loudly.

"Stand right there, *Grand-père,* you stand right there," Henri orders, his voice the same lazy, deep rough as when he was a boy. "Bloody hell," he mutters as Mister Louis keeps marching doggedly towards him. "See that, lads?" he shouts, pointing to Mister Louis's leg wrappings and blue cap. "He's still fighting the last war, gawd–damn. *Grand-père,* go home."

Mister Louis raises his fists and Henri jumps sideways to escape being barrelled over as his grandfather charges him. His cap falls from his head and he curses as Mister Louis stomps on it. "Ahh, feck," he mutters as Mister Louis keeps stomping on the hat, shouting, *"Traître, traître!"*

"Give over, *Grand-père,* give over." He watches with a bemused look as Mister Louis kicks the hat in a perfect arc, landing it in the dirt near my feet.

"Traître, hey—you damn *traître,"* shouts Mister Louis at me and I gasp in surprise. But it's Father he's shouting at, Father who's come out of his store and is now standing behind me. "Goddamn *Anglais!"* bellows Mister Louis, shaking his fists. "Churchill, hey, that fat *bâtard!* That bullet-headed, fat *bâtard,* he rescued his own men from Dunkirk, hey—he *abandonne* the *Français* for the Nazis! I tell you, he left them on the beach to be slaughtered by the Nazis!"

"He rescued the French too, you old fool," says Father contemptuously. "Those who weren't already kowtowing," he adds nastily, but Mister Louis is marching towards the pub. Pushing through the guffawing sailors, he vanishes inside. Henri shakes his head in resignation. I want to reach down and rescue his cap from the dirt, but he's already sauntering towards it, grinning up at Father.

"Eh, bugger the old fellow, he's blind when it pays him." He picks up his cap, dusting it against his leg. "How does it look?" Flashing a grin at me, he flips the now squished, pie-shaped hat on his head. His eyes are darker than I remember, slanted and gleaming with fun. His words neither curl like the Irish nor roll nasally like the French; he talks now with the flattened-out brogue of the English-speaking fishermen he's worked with who often tie up at the wharf, looking for supplies in Father's store.

As if knowing the strain of Father's presence on my tongue, he looks at him with a nod. "Yes sir, old fool *Grand-père* is. No back doors with him, though: says it like he thinks it. Tell me, sir," and he takes off his cap, trying to reshape it, "I was too small at the time, and folks have stopped talking about it—well, most folks. But that night of the *false light* so to speak, when was that—1924? Some sixteen years ago now, was it? Something I've always found interesting is that you were right offshore here when trouble struck. Almost home, so to speak. Yet you were sailing from Halifax to England, is that right? That's what *Grand-père* claims, but you can't trust everything that crazy old man says."

"You'd do well to trust nothing the old fool says," replies Father.

"But if you were sailing from Halifax to England, how come you were just off our Newfoundland shores? I've got to admit, sir, I must be as stun as *Grand-père,* but I can't figure a storm would take you that far off course."

Father drops his hands into his pockets, fingering the coin he always has there, and I think he's not going to answer. Neither does Henri, and he's about to move off when Father's voice detains him. "You start figuring too close, and your old *grand-père* might start smelling like a rat."

"Perhaps I'll leave it be, then, sir. You have a good day now."
Looking at me, he tips his hat and tosses a smile as one might toss
a bouquet of wildflowers, then saunters towards the pub.

"Supper's waiting to be cooked," Father says to me, pointing
me homeward like a wayward youngster.

Clutching the parcel, I start down the road towards the marsh.
I know nothing about that night of my grandfather's drowning,
except for Father's belief that Mister Louis and his father, Theo,
shone a light through the fog, tricking Captain Higgs into
believing he was a safe distance from the rocks. I think about
Henri's questioning Father about his positioning on the seas, and
why he's so curious about it. But mostly I think of Henri, and
continue walking home, stroking the petals of his smile.

Winter of 1941 banks the land with snow and muffles the sea
with ice. Father listens to the radio, his face twisting with worry.
He wrings his hands and paces the floors and pummels pathways
to his woodshed, looking skyward for answers to his deep unrest.
Others look skyward too in anticipation of the hundreds of planes
that will soon be roaring overhead as the Americans pour into
Stephenville, a town of five hundred on the other side of the
hills from Sables d'Or. They're building an airbase as a fuelling
stop and jumping-off point for Europe, and everyone's specu-
lating that the Americans will soon be joining the war overseas.
Overnight the town swells to six or seven thousand with military
and labourers and the war is everyone's talk. Father grows more
and more restless, and the Japanese bomb Pearl Harbor.

Sometime during the night of September 5, just offshore from
St. John's, the rock-rugged hearts of the Bell Islanders tremble in

horror as a German submarine torpedoes two freighters anchored at their wharf, firing up the night sky, killing twenty men and spawning rumours of U-boat sightings up and down the coastline. Several weeks later an old woman picking berries not too far from Sables d'Or spots a long black U-boat on the surface of the sea and four soldiers onshore with a dory, filling containers with water from a small brook. Some of the outporters are frightened off the shorelines, while others scoff. The scoffing turns to terror as that very night a smoke-belching passenger ferry sailing from Sydney to Newfoundland is slammed by a torpedo that rips a hole through its belly, drowning a hundred and thirty-five men, women and children and leaving others screaming in horror and clinging to rafts and bits of wood in the ice-cold waters. A month later, Father rubs his hands in angst as another U-boat torpedoes two more freighters anchored to the wharf at Bell Island, blasting the wharf, killing a couple dozen more men and sending frenzied rumours through the outports about spies and further attacks.

Snow melts into the spring waters of 1943 and Henri has been gone for three years. Father wrings his hands over a war of a different sort happening inside his door: Etna's fear of germs is worsening. She's taken to cleaning herself as she does the house. Her hands are pink from washing them over and over with soap and rubbing and rubbing them dry. She's washing her clothes separately from mine and Father's and hanging them at the far end of the line off to themselves. At the supper table she sits at the furthest corner, shielding her food with her hand should Father or I lean too close, reaching for bread or salt.

"Ask for things," she says to me one evening as I reach past her for the salt. "Ohh!" She leaps to her feet as Father sneezes.

"It's not right, the way you are," says Father irritably as she scurries to the sink, dumping her tea.

"I'll just pour another cup," she says apologetically. "I was about to anyway."

"You need to see a doctor." Pushing aside his plate, Father walks out the door. It's been some time now since he dawdled at the table after supper, smoking and admiring the clean floors and tidied sink, for he's no longer allowed to smoke inside the house. *It hurts my eyes, the smoke hurts my eyes, the sty will come back.* Those times he comes in from his shed with the smell of wood and cigarette smoke on his clothes Etna cowers from him, trying not to grimace. She follows him with a mop, wiping his tracks off her polished floors. Once, watching his look of discomfort as she followed him with a broom, sweeping outdoors those bits of him shedding to the floor, I felt a twinge of sympathy for him. He caught my look, and for one startled moment we were sitting back at the supper table when I was a girl, he staring pityingly at my dirt-grimed nails. "What, am I a germ?" he now rails at both Etna and me. "Am I a germ in my own house?" He stomps out, thudding the door behind him.

Before bedtime he returns with an armload of kindling for the morning's fire, dropping several sticks on the way to the woodbox. I pick them up and he snatches them from my hands without looking at me. I sense his deepening resentments. He senses it too and perhaps he can't bear the hatred of another wrong towards me, or perhaps he can't bear another day of Etna's germs, or perhaps he finds a more deserving battle to fight, for a few days later he announces, in the overly loud voice he uses for Etna, that he's leaving for Halifax. He's joined the merchant navy to help deliver goods to England.

"You've nothing to worry about," he tells us. "The Randall brothers will run the store and they'll bring groceries every week. Give them a list of what you need." Straightening the lapels of his tweed jacket, he draws back his shoulders and circles the room picking up his things, his tobacco pouch and matches, his razor and shaving brush and comb, then walks briskly to his room. He pulls a suitcase from beneath the bed and empties his drawers, his movements decisive. The war has given back purpose to Father's step, but taken it from Etna's. Watching him pack, she starts to cry. She doesn't understand about the war, for no one has explained it to her, but she's lived and worked amongst orphans most of her life and understands goodbyes. I try to explain but she either can't or won't hear.

I go to my room, taking Father's latest copy of the newspaper with me. I read more about Great Britain on the brink of losing the war for need of food, fuel and arms. I've been reading and listening to the radio for four years now about the formidable work of the German U-boats sinking millions of tonnage of ships in the mid-Atlantic before they can reach England. I know about the convoys of merchant ships loaded with goods leaving Halifax for Great Britain, and how the outcome of the war depends heavily upon them arriving. And I read and reread today's headline about one of the worst naval defeats in United States history. U-boats have blasted tankers and cargo ships along a U.S. shoreline and strolling Americans are recoiling in horror from dead soldiers washing ashore at their feet, their ships burning hellishly in the night sky.

That night I close my eyes to a barrage of images of merchant ships crossing the Atlantic, becoming easy targets for the U-boat wolf packs lurking beneath the waters, torpedoing their bellies and leaving naught but the fleeting foam of whitecaps marking their watery graves. Come dawn, I hear Father quietly moving about the house. I slip out of bed and go to him. He is bent near the door, putting on his boots.

"It's safer with the navy than the merchant ships," I say.

He looks up, more startled, perhaps, at my knowing such a thing. "It's a man's duty," he says. "I should've gone before now. I hadn't thought it would last this long." He shakes down his pant leg and cuffs and looks about the room, his face becoming murky with thought as he looks towards Etna's door. "You'll take care of the house, and her. You'll need her for company," he adds, his voice thinning with discomfort. He rubs his jaw and I feel his tiredness. The anger and all the other things fighting for dominance inside of me are pushed aside and I'm discovering something else within me, something that isn't the love I feel for Mother, but it fills my heart and in this moment I want only to give comfort to Father's fatigue. But he's gone, his hand lightly touching my shoulder as the door closes behind him.

I run to the door and open it. The air is still snappish from winter. A full moon shoots whitish light through dark, swirling clouds over Father's head as he nears a bend in the path. His fatigue is gone and he's walking hard as though he's angry with himself. And I want to run after him, for I've grown wrapped in his anger; since Mother died it's the only cloak I know. I try to call his name but it sticks in my throat. *Look at me, look at me,* I try to shout, but I cough instead. I run back to my bed and burrow into the dark of my blankets. A great shivering seizes me, as when I was a girl under my bed, shivering and kicking and screaming from the cold, hard swipe of Mother's death. And I know now it wasn't cold that consumed me, but fear, that terrible, terrible fear of abandonment, the same fear as consumes me now as I huddle under the blankets while Father walks off to war. So violent is my shivering it frightens me and I pull myself back from the dark of my blankets and look to the window instead. It is dark, the moon beyond struggling free of cloud. I will my cold self towards its faintish light as I used to will myself into the blaze of Mother's hair. The whitish light grows brighter, filling my window, it is the sun, an early morning ray of sun that glitters through the ribbed ice on my window. The phone rings sharply beside my bed and I grasp my blankets with fright.

FIVE

"Did I wake you?" asks Gen. "I'm sorry, did I wake you? You're always feeding the birds by now, I figured you were up."

I struggle to keep my voice calm. "I—what do you want?"

"I saw you through my window last night. You shouldn't be out at night, I can hear you wheezing. Did you see the cat? I went down to the bike shop just now, he's not there, so he must be fine. We probably didn't hit him, just scared him. I felt sick when I thought we struck him. I don't want you thinking we didn't care."

"I—I don't think that."

"I was snotty last night. I'm sorry. I'm worried sick about Ronny, and then with Mother showing up— Christ. She lives in New Brunswick, she wants to move here. Look, are you sure you're all right? I'll bring you over some soup. Why don't I take you to your doctor, I can't remember the last time we went— three or four weeks ago? It's past time."

I rub my temples; Gen's talking too much. "I don't need a doctor."

"I'll bring you your soup, I'll be right over."

"Wait," I say, but she's gone, and I hang up, annoyed. I don't want to get up, I feel tired. My dreams, I want to go back to my dreams, there's so much there. I shift for comfort, I can't lie still, I am astir. I think of my father, of his swallowing vomit and riding the white horses alongside Captain. I think of his gloating over his grandfather sitting in a dory, facing down a French warship. And how proud he used to be of his store, his house. I wonder at his anger, too, and how it was mixed in with his pride, but mostly I wonder about his pride and how it reigned so long. Perhaps his pride brought him more pride. Perhaps pride grew like a cancer into his spine, stifling his anger with its false sense of pleasure, like sugar in a sour broth.

I tuck the covers beneath my chin, closing my eyes, seeing again the stiffness of Father's back as he walks from me through the night. I hear his tired-sounding "Ahh" and the feeling it evoked in my heart and I'm feeling proud too, for I know now it was compassion that filled my heart, and what is compassion if not the darling of love. Ahh, I am grateful for this moment, grateful for this ember of memory that tells me my heart wasn't always shrivelled in anger and shrunken and dried like a prune, that it was once ripe and firm with flesh that was red and sweet. And your heart, Father, what of yours, I want to call after him. But he can no longer hear me, he is walking away from me. I watch him again and again walking away from me and I will him to turn back, even in fantasy I will him to come back, but he does not and I'm saddened. A heart cannot feel both compassion and anger, for one does away with the other, and it is that tiny whelp of a girl that does me proud because she chose compassion over anger, whereas her father chose his anger.

I thrash the bedding, struggling to sleep. But it was anger, not compassion, that ruled in the end. I can't think of that now. I can never think of that, yet I am astir with thought, with memory. Let them come, then, I'm not bothered. I'm in bed where most old folks belong this hour in the morning, and isn't this where the old mostly live anyway, in their minds? Am I not old?

I tut-tut out loud, remembering the fears that had consumed me last evening before sleeping. How foolish to be frightened of ghosts, of memories that need no connectedness to time, merely a mind to receive them. Sit for a while then, let the memories flow if they wish. Let them drop by like old friends for tea.

Eh, I'm feeling cocky. For all the night's turmoil and stiffness of joints, I'm feeling good.

Getting out of bed, I quickly dress in yesterday's clothes and pad down the hallway, cursing my lungs that won't let me take a full gulp of air. Serves me right, prancing about the streets at night. I switch on the kitchen light and glance at the clock. It is eight-thirty. The cats are pacing the kitchen, licking their chops with hunger. "Wait you things, I must eat first." I search through the cupboards, but there's no bread. No eggs. The cereal boxes are empty. What's this, what's this now, I put empty cereal boxes back in the cupboard? Willaby meows, and Tuff echoes him. "Go, wait your turn," I command. They're like Gen this morning, in my face, wanting, demanding. "Oh, fine then."

I go to the closet and pull out the bag of dried cat food only to find that it too is empty. Yes, that's right, I remember now, I'm out of cat food. I must shop. And take out the garbage, the bag is toppling over. And the kitty litter is taking on that acrid smell.

Ahh, the whole house needs airing, but it's winter, it's bloody winter. Too cold to do anything properly. And I told Gen I'd done the shopping—why did I do that?

Fine, then. So, now I do my own shopping!

I go for my coat and pause. Something's scratching on the

basement door. The mother cat? Of course, it's the mother cat. She's hungry, too. When did I feed her last? Yesterday? No. I changed the litter yesterday—bands tighten around my lungs. I pat my heart. Quiet, now, quiet, but there's a fear growing. What's this, what's this now, why am I feeling fearful? A couple sacks of food is all I need. The cabbie can bring them into the porch. Why is my chest tightening? I'm feeling frightened— what's this, what's this now, I'm not used to a little tightening in my chest?

Shuffling to my room, I find the puffer and shoot three hits of spray down my throat and hold it. I sit on the bed to wait for things to right themselves, to rest for a moment. Then I make my way back to the kitchen and look about—what was it? What was I doing? The cats. Yes, the cats. They're hungry. I have to shop.

Pulling on my heavy fur coat, I search through the closet for a pair of decent walking boots. A knock sounds on the side door and I look towards it irritably. Who is it? Who's at the door this early? I'll not answer, then. No one's a right to knock on my door this early.

"Livvy! Livvy, are you up?"

Gen. I'd already forgotten, the soup. I open the door to a draft of cold air. Gen stands in her puffy red coat, her eyes big and wettish with morning and smudged makeup.

"Bit early to be up and about," I say with a mite of contrariness.

"Aren't you the picture of grace," she replies in the same contrary tones. "I brought your soup. Here, I'll put it in the kitchen."

She makes to enter, but I block her way. Although the smell of the soup has set my mouth to watering, I'm not wanting her to see the garbage and the dirty kitty litter; she'll start talking about doctors again, and I'm not wanting the trouble.

"What, I'm not allowed in now?" she asks. "What's wrong, why're you looking at me so strange? You think I'm the Gestapo or something?"

I take the chicken broth, faint with hunger. "I'm grateful, but I'm not ready for company."

"Company? What, I'm the city's social committee now, coming to visit? Be careful, it's hot," she says as I take the cloth off the bowl of soup. "I heated it up for you. Not exactly breakfast food, but the broth's good for you—medicinal. Where you going? You need something done?"

"I was just about to feed the pigeons."

"I'll do it, it's minus ten this morning. And there's a storm coming, do you need anything? The stores might be closed tomorrow. Are you taking your medicine?" she asks as I start coughing.

"It's the cold air."

"Right, it's my fault you're coughing. Go inside then, have a fine day." She starts back down the steps.

"Thank you for the soup. I—I'm about to have a nap, is all." She's coming back up the steps, her foot keeping me from closing the door. "You're having a nap?"

"What, a soul can't have a nap, now? Go, get your foot away."

"You just got up. Why're you having a nap when you just got up?"

I stare at her confusedly. "I'm tired. Can't a soul have some privacy?"

"I'll be a licensed social worker in less than three months, and I'll call social services in less than two minutes if you don't stand aside and let me in."

"I'm tired, the asthma's keeping me up," I protest, but she's shaking her head, staring at me. "The gall of the young," I mutter,

and stand aside for her to enter. I go to follow, but this morning
isn't done with me yet. The blast of a horn brings my attention
back to the street. A darkish blue car careens near the curb, its
horn still blasting. A thin figure with an ancient face hunches over
the wheel, a stiff, coppery brush of unnatural hair cloaking his
head. Reverend Wright from the hospital.

"Hold on there, Livvy," he calls through a partly lowered
window, and leaving his motor running, he unfolds his long,
thin body from the car and reaches back inside, dragging out a
large straw basket covered with a soft flannel baby's blanket. "The
nurses sent you some soup and fruit, and lozenges for your throat.
How are you?" he asks, coming through the gate, his long skinny
legs comical looking beneath the mushroom shape of his short,
fat parka.

"What, am I dying, now? I need palliative care?" I ask more
roughly than I intend, taken by surprise with the basket.

He laughs heartily. "Always charming, dear lady. And I
should think you will be if you don't get in from the cold."
He nudges me aside with the basket and lays it inside the door.
"How's your flu? You look a bit peaked, you're getting your nourishment, I see." He gestures to the bowl of soup I'd forgotten I
was holding.

I look down at the basket and into his kind eyes, nearly
hooded by drooping lids. Water seeps from his nose and he sniffs
it back, and I retreat a few steps guiltily. "I'm not so sick. Just a bit
tired of late. I'm certainly not needing a food basket—give it to
somebody more needy."

Reverend Wright isn't listening, he's pulling from an inner
pocket of his parka a creamy, oblong card, dotted with little
sketches of sleeping baby faces. "The nurses were talking," he says.
"They've calculated how many babies you've helped care for over

the years. About two hundred a month for well on sixty years, now. That's a lot of feeding and rocking, dear saint."

"Saint! Heavens forbid." The words burst from me and I gratefully relinquish the bowl of soup to Gen as she appears by my side.

She introduces herself to the reverend, saying expressively, "She'll need a few days adapting to sainthood. And if we don't get her fed and warmed, we'll soon be looking at a corpse. Come— have some tea with us," she invites the reverend, but he's already out on the step, hunching inside his parka from the cold.

"I've more baskets to drop off; this weather has taken down half the city. Good day, Livvy."

"I'll see you to your car," says Gen, placing the soup bowl back in my hands. "Go, drink it, it's cold by now."

I take myself to my rocker, knees buckling from hunger and the blasphemy of being called a saint! Trembling, I lift the soup bowl to my mouth and drink. Gen comes back in, stomping her feet and closing the door. She drapes a shawl around my shoulders and then props the baby card on the cabinet. "What a caring man, bringing you the basket. And you *are* a saint, all the work you've freely given to that hospital."

"I'll not hear no more about that," I say crossly.

"You've cared for thousands of babies, you've not taken a penny, what do you think makes a saint?"

I set aside the soup bowl, unsettled with this talk. Gen remains quiet, for once, yet I feel her eyes trying to prowl through my past.

"I won't ask a single question," she says. "The fact that you're not grabbing for the saintly crown makes you a saint right there. Now, then, why'd you lie about having your shopping done? Why?" she repeats, and I look at her, feeling flustered and smothered with all the attention this morning.

"You threw me off with your lying," I say to her.

She has the grace to look away. Surprisingly, she nods. "I've got some stuff going on. I'll soon have my degree, things will be fine, then."

"It's that brother of yours, he's got you in trouble, hasn't he?"

"Oh, give up on Stu, he's an angel. He spikes his hair and everyone thinks he's Charlie Manson."

"His friend was spying on you. He was parked down the street, spying on your house. The fellow who drives the red truck," I add as she stares at me with alarm.

"Sandy?" She gropes after my words as though she's missed something, then waves them away. "Sandy is Stu's best friend, they play hockey together."

"He's up to something, he didn't like my seeing him."

"Why? Why do you say that? Are you getting paranoid?"

"And he was driving a nice car, not his truck."

She rises and goes to the window as though expecting the car to still be there.

"What kind of stuff?" I ask.

"Nothing. Nothing worth talking about. You're making me paranoid like yourself." She sits again, lacing her fingers and staring at me like a problem she has to fix. But her mind has been taken elsewhere and she jiggles her foot nervously.

"I'll not be put in a home," I say. "I'll walk out the door first chance I get and drown myself."

Her mouth drops, her eyes widen. "Where's that coming from? Holy freaking Christ, you think we're out to turn you in?"

"I wouldn't be the first tucked away somewhere."

"Oh my God, Livvy. You don't ever have to worry about that—I'll move in with you, comes to that. Cut your toenails, dose out your meds." She grins, then slips onto her knees before me. She reaches for my hands in my lap and cups them in hers, her great dark eyes searching my face. "You're such a curiosity. So shy of people. Makes me feel special to be sitting here with you like this."

It's been so long since anyone stood close to me in intimacy that my mouth starts quivering with nervousness. "I'll bring you some groceries this afternoon," she says quietly. "You stay there, I'll let myself out."

I scarcely move as she leaves. I touch my hands where she's cupped them, and close my eyes to Henri's as he knelt before me many times, holding my hands, warming them with his.

Pulling the woollen wrap around my shoulders, I rock. Saintly, indeed. It's what Henri often said, but only Henri. I feel him. I often feel him as I sit here rocking. I hear, too, the other sailors marching down the street, hollering and taunting and threatening as they prowl like pack dogs through the night, bored, hungering for some kind of action. I think of the girl but I'm not feeling her presence this morning. Like all ghosts she picks her own times to haunt. This morning I don't need the girl, I'm leading myself. I'm cold and I'm leading myself through the soggy spring morning in Father's wake. The sun pales the moon, chasing night from the woods, and I'm walking hard like Father through wet, shivering marsh grass towards Missus Louis's house. I feel emptied. I feel emptied of all things, of Father, of Mother, of Tabs. My heart echoes through a hollow chamber. I run madly through the marsh, feeling a sense of myself hovering slightly behind, watching me as I run. It feels as though I'm caught in a terrible dream and am unsure if the dreamer is the one running or the one hovering behind. I run harder, trying to escape them both, and arrive winded and cold and frightened at Missus Louis's door.

"*Macushlah!*" Missus Louis grasps me to her and I feel my knees strengthening. She leads me into a room filled with morning and fraught with contrariness as Esmée, her lips trembling, shouts at her father, Mister Louis, about Henri, her poor boy Henri.

Mister Louis walks away from her, shaking his grizzly head and muttering, "Little *traître. Bâtard soldat Anglais*, what! *Mon grand-père, mon père* and *moi*, we fought them all, the *Anglais, Portugais, Spaniards, Anglais*—did I say the *Anglais*? Ahh!" He turns back to Esmée. "We *battre* their white asses off the *océan*. Now the little *bâtard*—he wear their flag, ahh."

"You! You and your French flag," shouts Esmée. "They have all surrendered, no? The French have surrendered. Here, take this." She crumples a white cloth off the table and throws it in his face. "That is your flag, no? So white it hurts your eyes?"

Mister Louis grabs the cloth with a growl. "You say that about your *drapeau*?"

"My *drapeau*," she sneers. "I care nothing for *drapeaux*. I care nothing for men and their wars."

"You care nothing? You care nothing?" Mister Louis's eyes pop. "Who fight for you? You care nothing for your country that fights for you? Here, you take this"—he grabs a dark towel off the washstand—"you put this on the *bâtard's* arse to hide his shit next time he sees a gun!"

"My soul, he's a coward too now, is he?" cries Missus Louis. "He gets blown up by a torpedo and that makes him a coward? Ahh, go to bed, old man, you've gotten stupid like a rock. You've a tongue to cut wood." She turns to me. "It's Henri, *macushlah*. Poor Henri came home last evening with a wounded leg. His ship was blown up by a submarine two weeks ago."

"He suffers terribly," Esmée says accusingly to Mister Louis. "His ship was *torpedoed* and all this time he didn't let us know so's not to worry us. How is that for a brave man, *Père*, how is that, hey?"

"Poor fellow, poor little fellow," moans Missus Louis. "He nearly drowned, it's a blessing he's alive. And he wrote not a word of it to us. The sainted fathers, he never learned silence from you!" she shouts at Mister Louis who is cracking the bowl of his pipe against the woodbox, muttering loudly to himself. "Pay him no heed, Esmée. He got a fright. That's why he howls like a wolf. He got a fright over poor Henri."

Esmée yanks on Mister Louis's beard. "You say nothing to him, you hear me? You say nothing, else he'll never call you *Grand-père* again, I swear to it," she threatens, and walks out of the house.

"Never mind them, luv, they're always at each other," says Missus Louis. "Here, sit and tell me what's happened."

"Father's gone to war," I say breathlessly. "He left last night, he'll be sailing on a merchant ship to England."

"Is that so? Your *père*, he is finally gone to war?" asks Mister Louis. "Four years before he takes himself to fight?"

"He thought it wouldn't last long," I find myself trying to explain, and Mister Louis squints his black eyes and then taps his fist into his palm with a laugh. "The Germans, they got the *Anglais* by the *balles,* no? Ahh, the *Anglais* have the big planes and the big boats, but the little black fishy boats got them by the *balles,* ahh."

I nod and he grins, splaying his hands to Missus Louis. "See? She agrees!"

"Go spy through your window," Missus Louis scoffs. "He thinks he can see through hell's fire across the seas," she says to me. "He would've made a good Jesus, eh? He would've made a good Jesus with them eyes. Go, *macushlah,* go see the girls and help them with the butter, they haves their fun churning butter. And go see Henri, go see poor Henri."

She ushers me outside and I run the short distance to Esmée's house. Inside, Suzie is ladling out porridge to chattering youngsters crowding a long wooden table that takes up most of the room. Colette butters toast and pours milk into seven or eight mugs lined up across the sink. I'd not noticed before how tiny both Colette and Suzie are. They're a year or two older than me, perhaps eighteen and nineteen, but they look older with their aprons and pinned-up hair.

They fall silent as I enter, casting curious looks at each other and back at me as I stand cold and shivering before them. Perhaps they're noting too how much I've grown since I've last been here, and no doubt they're wondering why I'm choosing to visit them now. Behind them Henri is partly covered beneath a blanket on the daybed, his bare arms gripping two squalling youngsters against his hair-blackened chest, and I am dumbfounded by his nakedness.

"Well, hell, we've got company, scallywags." He sits up, grunts as one of the youngsters pokes a fist into his eye, and I look away as a hairy black leg kicks out from beneath the blanket.

"Come, Livvy, sit," invites Suzie. She pours a mug of tea, hollering at Henri to stop his roughhousing. He stands, a sheet wrapped around his waist and youngsters tumbling to the floor and yelping like pups as he balances himself on his good leg, the other swathed in bandages. He is not so handsome with his hair clipped to a dark sheen on his head. It fattens his face, and his lips are shaped like a girl's. I stare at his chest and he laughs, his face dissolving behind square white teeth, and I avert my eyes from his nakedness. Quickly I take a seat at the table amidst the row of dark heads slurping tea, their greedy pink tongues licking cream off their spoons, and I drink deeply from the mug of milky tea Suzie has placed before me.

It is another day and I chase the early morning light as it spreads across the marsh, arriving winded at Missus Louis's. She waves to me from the field as she plucks the last of the turnip with Esmée and a couple of young ones. Inside, Suzie is skimming cream off the top of a large aluminum pan of milk sitting on the stove and Colette is peeling spuds for the soup pot, the both of them shouting orders at the younger ones who are milling about, searching for boots, a cap, begging a glass of water before scuttering out the door.

"So he's gone, eh," says Suzie in her Irish-French accent, her dark eyes dancing over me curiously. "Your feyther is gone, is that good, no? Arseholes, are they not? Feythers are arseholes?" She smiles her gratitude as I peel a wrestling little girl off her legs and plop her at the table.

"Aye, she'll sit for a minute. She's the plague, that one," says Colette. "We've not seen our feyther for three years—since the last one was popped in the oven, hey Suzie."

"He is a good for nothing, a hangashore," says Suzie. "We hope he never comes back. Perhaps he is drowned."

Colette laughs. "He cannot drown, he's got seawater for blood, Mam says. He floats like cork, he's beached on some island and his ship lost to sea."

"That is true," says Suzie. "He's trampling trenches through sand dunes, Mam says, praying for rescue, his gullet dry for want of rum."

"Pray he's never found. Pray the crabs pinch his bones clean." They laugh, their eyes full of light.

"Perhaps they pinched off his pecker first," says Suzie.

"Yeah, they pinched off his pecker. He is sitting in sand, bawling over his pecker."

"He lives with a whore in Glasgow," says Henri, limping

through the door on his crutch. "Isn't that a shame now, he's found comfort elsewhere." He looks disgruntled as the girls clap their hands with glee. He's wearing a thick sweater that fattens him out. He's not much taller than me and limps about the kitchen, kicking outside the rooster that has fluttered, squawking, in behind him. He closes the door with a thud.

"What's wrong?" asks Suzie, and she curls her mouth like a mother soothing a pouty youngster. "Ohh, you miss your daddy? You miss your daddy, no?"

"It's not so funny," he says, his tone deepening with angst. "I drank a barrel of rum with him. He's not looking so pretty— yellow to the gills with piss and his whore is ugly. Oh, did I tell you?" he asks with a nasty smirk. "He's got two more daughters."

Colette claps her hands. "Grand, grand, maybe he'll not come again."

"I would've thought him too pickled to father a tadpole," says Suzie. "He is ugly, yes?"

The girls sober as Henri clumps with his cane to the window, brushes aside the flimsy scrap of curtain and stares outside. Suzie goes to him. She touches his arm, but hastily withdraws as Henri shrugs away from her.

"Why do you look like that?" she asks quietly. "Henri." Her voice verges on tears. "What is wrong, tell us what is wrong, please."

"I buggered his face with my fist," mutters Henri. "That make you feel good?" He keeps looking out the window, his body taut like wire. "I bloodied his snout and sliced off his balls. They're in my bag—I made little coin purses for you from Papa's balls. They are just tooo cute." He turns back to them, wiping a mock tear from his eyes.

The girls stare at him, then scream with laughter. Colette

grabs the spoon out of the cream and splatters his face. He chases her around the table, but it is me he grabs around the waist from behind. He is big and soft against my back and something hard pokes at me; I know enough to know what it is and I shriek, scrabbling away from him.

"Henri likes you, watch out for him," teases Suzie as we hasten to the river with a bucket of cream.

"Yes, yes, I think he likes you, I can tell," says Colette from behind us, dragging the young one. "Aye, you watch out for him and his pecker."

"What pecker," says Suzie. "He's been mauling it since he was two, hiding behind the stove and mauling it. Nothing left but a peephole."

The girls bust out laughing and I bust out laughing and we scamper down the bank to the river as when we were youngsters. I crouch with Colette near an ice-cold stream gushing out of a cliff. She scuffs a shallow pool with the heels of her boots and sets down the five-pound bucket of cream that hardens as the spring water sluices around it. She beats and beats the cream with a paddle, beating the milk out of it. Suzie joins us, and we take turns beating the hardening ball of cream and keeping watch over the young one wading in the river. The girls keep teasing me about Henri and they laugh and I laugh and it feels like warm soup in my belly.

Etna polishes the doorknob behind me as I dash outside, waving goodbye. I race through the marsh and Missus Louis calls from her back door as though she's been waiting for me.

"Come, *macushlah,* the doctor is changing Henri's bandage. Here, be off, scallywags," she calls to the younger ones huddling on Esmée's stoop. They let us through, then huddle in the doorway again, trying to see past the thickly bearded doctor who's bent over Henri's leg and asking him questions in English.

I falter at the raw smell of blood and antiseptic and hang back with the young ones, listening, as Henri talks to the doctor about his ship being torpedoed and most of his mates hove into a sea of burning oil. "You can imagine, *docteur,*" he says, his voice tensing with pain as the doctor probes his wound, "one minute I'm riding the swells and then, *sonofabitch,* this blast flattens my ears and sends me flying like a bird through smoke and fire. And then this smoking hot spear jabs me—*aahh*—yeah, right where you're poking. Brought me down like a busted balloon. Hit that water dead centre in a ring of flames." He flinches as the doctor pokes some more, sweat speckling his brow. "How's it going there, *docteur,* near done are we? It's fine, Mam, it's fine," he soothes as Esmée covers his brow with kisses.

"A wonder he lives. Men and their wars," says Esmée. "Is there a cure for men and their wars, *docteur?*"

"How is his leg, will he heal?" asks Missus Louis.

"Good, good, it is good," says the doctor, nodding at Henri. "You'll be steering your ship again in a couple of months."

"Damn, *docteur,* stick some poison in there and let's make that a couple of years."

"No, no, he will not sail again," cries Esmée. "Tell him, tell him, Henri, what you did in that ring of flames."

"I done nothing much, Mam. I floundered about, gaping like a landed fish in that water. You can imagine, fire sucking all the air."

"But you dove down deep," says Esmée.

"That's right, Mam. I dove down deep like a gull and come up to the outer side of that fire ring. And that's when I near met my maker, in the lifeboat. They caught hold of my collar and near strangled me. They hauled me aboard, near crushing my ribs on the gunnels. They dropped me face down in bilge water, I near drowned before they hauled me back up. Thirty of us in a lifeboat built for ten. Squished like sardines, you can imagine. We sat on each other's shoulders to make room for bailing—*owwieee*, jeezus, *docteur*, how's she going down there?" he hollers as the doctor touches a sore spot. "All right, Mam, stop that, now stop that," he pleads as Esmée peppers his sweat-riddled brow with kisses. Missus Louis holds his hand to her bosom, darting dirty looks to the doorway as a muttering from Mister Louis swarms through like a buzz of nasty hornets.

"*Grand soldat, grand soldat*. One day with a gun and he is home, crying to the women."

"Ah, the Arse-Commander's taking a stroll," groans Henri. The doctor turns a grim look to the window as a loud belch sounds from Mister Louis.

"His ulcers are acting up," says Missus Louis, without pity. "He always belches when his ulcers act up. Come, *macushlah*, let us go start the washing."

I follow her outside, dawdling behind as she accosts Mister Louis about his haranguing Henri. "Small wonder you belch, carting that gutload of foul air, you old fool. Why don't you shoot the maiden here? She's *Anglais*, would you shoot her? Ahh! Crazy like your father and your old grandfather." She scurries ahead and Mister Louis winks at me.

"You tell her this happens when you marries shit, eh—you spend the rest of your life batting away flies." He laughs and I laugh and run after Missus Louis.

Inside her kitchen she starts to make tea, beckoning me to the table. "Don't mind the old fellow out there. He's not as bad as he lets on," she says. "He's just old and stupid like a rock. Get the jam crock from the pantry, luv. Poor Henri, I thought he would faint. You'll not catch him back on a warship too soon. What is it, luv, you've a look of torment."

I stand indecisively for a moment, then ask in a small voice, "That night of the drowning. Did Mister Louis—or perhaps his father—put out the false light?"

Missus Louis draws a deep breath that makes her bosom quiver. Her soft white hair falls forward like a girl's, shrouding her mottled face. "No, luv, not your man Louis out there. I would've had it out of him by now if he had. But I won't lie to you; nobody knows for sure whether Theo—that's his father, Theopold—we don't know if he done it. There's truth in what he says. Your grandfather was the only merchant here in Sables d'Or and he didn't trust that Theo would pay him with his furs come spring. That's the way it was back then, the English didn't trust the French. So he gave him only flour. He was a heartless bastard, luv, your grandfather. He watched Louis and his father near starve. Perhaps Theopold did trick your grandfather ashore to get his goods. Or, it's as Louis says—Theo and he just happened to be walking by that evening of the drowning. Murderer or a saviour, girl, only the good Lord knows that one."

She brushes aside her hair and her eyes are brown and moist like planting soil. "It's old strife, *macushlah*. It should've been buried along with the old fellows. But your man out there, he can't let go of it, it's all he knows." She adds a spoonful of sugar to my tea and, as with my mother and father when they lapsed into tirades, she pours forth Mister Louis's story with such emotion that it feels like it's the first telling. I feel her sorrow for the boy Louis, who, from the time he could hoist ten pounds over his head, was taken by his father—like my father was—aboard a wooden-hulled frigate somewhere in Normandy and taught to polish cannons, run sails and walk bow-legged to the swell of a warship.

"When Theo was too gnarled to man a gun, he brought himself and Louis ashore, not too far from Sables d'Or. They spent winters by themselves, guarding fishing outfits for the French who were gone during the winters. It was just Louis and Theo, half starving through them long months and Theo spying on whoever was coming and going. Spying on the English, spying on the French too—those who were jumping fishing boats and warships alike, looking for an easier lot onshore.

"I think it was 1903 or 04 when the French signed their last treaty with the English and took their fishing boats and warships home. Mattered nothing to Theo. He kept right on spying, threatening both French and English settlers. Nuisance to everybody, luv. We were all living together just fine, but my soul, that old geezer would've kept the whole shebang going if he could've. He was a relic, everyone laughed at him. Louis was jeered and banished along with his father and most likely would've been shipped back to Normandy if I hadn't married him and given him my name. He's since took his own back. Like Henri says, he's still fighting the old wars, *macushlah*. But he's not mad, I tell you this, girl, he's not mad. He's just stuck on what he believes. If it was the Bible he was flouting, they'd be calling him a saint."

Missus Louis brushes the damp from her eyes with her apron. She wipes her mottled face and rubs her arms, shivering from a sudden cold. "It can make you low-minded, muddling through the old stuff."

"Father said they stole his river."

"Your father said that? The saints be praised, he's like the old fellow out there, the both of them stuck to their past like leeches sucking bad blood. It was after your grandfather near starved

Theo. They both laid claim to the same river, one burning the other's shack whenever they come across each other. Thousands of miles of beach and your grandfather and Theo near murdering each other over the one rock, the one river. They burned each other out any chance they got. The government finally made it law—no one can own a river, and that was the end of the burning. But not the strife. I tell you this, there's no worse strife than that between two warring men, for they finds a face for the hate that's been bred in their bones. They'll fight to death then over a rock or a river. Tell that to your man out there, and your father—that it's hate that drives them. Not their flags or rivers. Ahh, they'll take it to their graves. Good then, begone with them both and perhaps that'll be the end of it."

"Do you think it odd Father was so close to his own shores that night of the false light? He was sailing from Halifax to England."

"Now, there's a question," Missus Louis exclaims. "Who's been talking to you?"

"Henri asked Father the day he fought with Mister Louis down by the pubhouse—before he went to war."

"*Henri?* He's never let on he thinks about this stuff." She slaps the flat of her hand to the table and laughs. "I bet that took Durwin's eyes out, ah! Sorry, luv, I'll not pretend fondness for your father. Henri's question is the other side of it. Theo and Louis was blamed, but not by everyone. There's those who question your father. And your grandfather. It's a bit off that they were so close to home that night. Just a bit too cozy. But nothing could be pinned on them. The Lloyd's were here, they asked their questions. They wondered too— What's the matter, luv?"

"Lloyds—who're the Lloyds?"

"Lloyd's of London. They're an insurance company, from England. They insure the ships and their cargo. They had a suspicion too about your father and grandfather that night of the storm. But we've not heard the outcome of it. At least, as far as we know, they haven't settled the case.

"It was a hard time for your man Louis out there—people thinking him and his father thieving pirates and the cause of three drowned men. But there's as many think it's your grandfather who was at fault that night." Missus Louis shakes her head. "Let this be our last word on it, Livvy. It should've perished along with them poor men that never made it to shore." She slaps the table again and grins. "I'd liked to seen Durwin's face when Henri took a poke at him. Ah, I'm sorry luv, I keep forgetting he's your father." Her face becomes sombre. "Tell me. Durwin, is he a good father to you?"

I try to think. I close my eyes. He is too big to think about. He is this big, sulking thing that rages and snarls from a long-suffering wound. He sees me only through the ravages of his pain and I've grown twisted and bent around his feet, trying not to be trampled.

Something comes to me. That night I was sent outside while Mother and Father and Grandmother Creed argued, and later Mother lay on my bed, smoking and bleating like a hurt lamb: *They'll burn in hell, I pray they'll burn in hell.* I remember the violence of her words, how her body jolted. *They done something, Durwin and my mother, they done something.* Did she finally learn? That night she fought with Father and Grandmother Creed, did Mother finally discover what it was they did?

I think to tell Missus Louis about the fight, but something stops me. The way Mother lay in my bed that night, gazing at the moon. Quiet. Scarcely moving, her heart no longer thudding like a beat drum, but fluttering like a moth caught inside a fold of cotton. They took something from her. I remember now, things lost to me: her sitting pale with a bluish mouth on the sofa after the grandmother left the following morning. How she wrapped herself in a blanket and stared red-eyed at the door that Father never walked through for days after he took the grandmother to the train. He slept in a little backroom at the store, he did, like he was hiding, and sent home food—lots of food and peppermint knobs, too, like he was trying to please her. But she wasn't pleased. And when he started coming home again, she took to sleeping in my bed. I'd forgotten. I'd forgotten about that.

"*Macushlah,*" says Missus Louis sympathetically. "That I would ask you such a question. You've more than a father, remember that. You have all of us and you have Julia."

"Julia?"

"Your grandmother, luv. Her name is Julia."

"I've only known her as Creed. Grandmother Creed."

"Creed's her last name. Julia Creed. I've always thought it a lovely name, do you?"

"It's just a name."

"Yes. You are right. What use is a name that calls forth nothing but its own charm. '*I have no name: I am but two days old. What shall I call thee? I happy am, Joy is my name. Sweet joy befall thee!*'" She smiles. "The poet, Blake. I used to read his words to Mam, and to the old ones dying in the orphanage, where I used to work. That is my wish for all of us, Livvy, that we will once again be Joy. And there is none so needing of joy right now than your Grandmother Creed. She writes more and more often, asking me to pass on her wishes to you. She's crippled in both legs now. And she's sick at heart from not seeing her daughter's child. Would you go visit her, luv, if I was to help with the travelling? Before your father comes back—you're old enough now, you don't need his permission to visit a grandmother."

"Why do you care about her?" I ask.

"I know loneliness, Livvy, even though I got such a crowd around me. I seen enough of it while teaching in the orphanage. And she looks to be so lonely. She keeps hinting, too, that things aren't right. I think she needs to put things right before she dies. I'm old like her, I think about these things. Perhaps you can help her fix things right. Don't you feel something for her, *macushlah*? She's your mother's mother. Aren't you curious? Maybe you'll find something of your mother there, in her old house, where she grew up."

"My mother is dead. I will never go."

Missus Louis grasps my hands, her tone growing intent. "You think I'd just send you off, *macushlah*? You think I'd just send you off without reason?"

I stare into her eyes. They are unwavering. I see something that searches, something dark—a secret sorrow that begs me to touch it. She turns from me and starts putting away the tca things, as though I've seen enough.

"That day in the graveyard," I ask. "When Mother was being buried. You were arguing with Grandmother Creed, you were warning her about something, you kept saying *I warned you, I warned you*. What were you warning her about?"

Missus Louis looks surprised. "That was such a long time ago. I don't know. I think—I remember warning her not to frighten you. She was taking it so hard that Cecile died. Such a horrible day. I scarcely remember any of it, except for the frightened look on your little face. Now then, go to the cellar and get me some potatoes for supper and I'll start the washing."

I remain sitting. "I thought I'd find my mother here," I say quietly. "It's the only place she liked to be. Can I stay here? I'll work. I'll work hard."

"The saints be praised, you know you've a home here," exclaims Missus Louis. "But you'll go home at night and sleep. Etna needs company. Yes, yes, she does," she argues over my protest. "I told you, I know about orphans and loneliness. Now, take the pan and bring me some potatoes from the cellar, I got a terrible rapping in me skull."

I run to the cellar for spuds, and the days run faster than me. They are filled with work and I take to it like thirst to water. I try not to think of Father and Grandmother Creed and Lloyd's insurance, and not of Etna and spies and U-boats and war, and not of tomorrow and not of Mother's fading heart as she lay upon my pillow those remaining nights, gazing at the scrap of moon that was fading, too, upon its star-pillowed sky. I fight to lose myself in the moment, the one long sustaining moment of scrubbing and cooking with Missus Louis, pickling and churning butter with Esmée, scraping and peeling turnips and spuds with the girls. We tease Henri with sticks and pebbles as he hobbles about on his crutch. Suzie and Colette and I sneak into the loft above the cellar and shove aside the sheep's wool and lift the latch, raining potatoes down on Henri's head. He hobbles outside with a mutter of oaths and gives chase. Despite his crutch he catches us, but it is me, it is always me, he grasps around the waist. He swings me around, pressing his self hard against my backside. I don't mind, he's not so ugly with his hair starting to grow, but with his thick brows and black eyes and big nose he looks fierce when he topples me to the ground. I scream, his breath is hot on my neck, his big bear body wraps around mine and my heart beats hard from running and wrestling and this is how I always want to be, tightly held and warm, with my heart beating hard and the sun pressing hot against my eyes.

※

Kneading down a galvanized pan full of dough at Missus Louis's, I swat at Henri's hand as he pops inside the door and slaps the firm, creamy mound. "Like a woman's buttocks, eh," he says, and I can feel my foolish face turning pink as morning sky as he pinches off a wad and shuffles outside. Within a minute I hear him squabbling with Mister Louis.

"I've already stacked the wood, *Grand-père*. Hey—come back, don't you go in there, get the hell out of there!" A loud rumbling sounds from the woodshed, followed by yelps and curses from Mister Louis. I dart to the window and see Henri tugging at the shed door, nearly falling backwards as it suddenly swings open and there Mister Louis stands, stoop-shouldered, mouth drawn, shaking his fist.

"You! You stack everything crippled like yourself!" he yells.

"Get out of there, what did you do?"

"Get out, get out, I smash your teeth, *Anglais bâtard*! The *enfants* will stack it—Esmée! Esmée, send me *les enfants*! Where you going? You come back, come back here," growls Mister Louis as Henri leans on his crutch and limps away with a reddening face. I run to the pantry window, watching as Henri rounds the corner of the house and kicks at a rotten fence post. He leans against the post and I see his chest heaving with each angered breath. Pulling back, he smashes the post with his fist and turns towards the woodshed.

"I'll crack your feckin' jaw, see if I don't!" he yells, and I run back to the kitchen window as he marches up to Mister Louis, shouting, and I listen to Mister Louis shouting back, and I hear their anger giving way to muttered threats and then to grunts from Henri as Mister Louis threatens to *battre* his arse, then more squabbling as more wood founders, and then grunts of laughter from them both as a goat pokes its head between them and starts bleating.

Their laughter is the sound I take with me that evening, running through the marsh towards home. It is the sound that makes me slow my step and touch that tender spot where Mother burrows. I pull her fully from that cold, dark corner of my heart where she curls like night. I pull her into the deepening dusk alongside of me as I face into the brisk wind. I think back on her kissing me and stroking Tabs. I remember her laughing and crying with Missus Louis, and shouting at Father, and ranting and ranting as she walked the beach, and it heartens me now to know she wasn't always bleating like a hurt lamb; that she, too, washed anger through her veins with a good douse of yelling and ranting and laughing with Missus Louis. She didn't suffer that great aloneness of a blocked heart as Father does. Till that night of the fight with Father and Grandmother Creed. *They done something, Durwin and my mother, they done something.*

The grass rustles loudly ahead of me and I halt my step, frightened of late by more sightings of U-boats and spies lurking in nearby woods. The grass shakes again and I scream and Henri limps with his crutch onto the path, his finger to his lips, beckoning me to follow. I creep behind as he moves slowly down a pathway to a good-sized brook flowing rapidly through the woods towards Harry's River. He points up the brook, I stretch past him to see and he tussles me to the grass beneath a thickly branched black spruce.

"You devil!" I shout and kick and he yowls, grabbing his hurt leg, and I'm all apologetic and he falls back again, pulling me against him and I feel awkward to be lying so close to him without Suzie or Colette or a wailing youngster or a goat or a sheep grazing nearby. Rolling onto his side, he tucks my head onto his shoulder, his hands gentle. He smells like cut grass and I lie still, my awkwardness soothed by his sense of ease and his fingers stroking my hand.

"Does it hurt?" I ask.

"What?"

"Your leg."

"Yeah, where you kicked it."

I grin and he tickles my ear with his nose. He strokes the soft flesh of my inner arm and we fall quiet, watching light wane through the trees.

"What're you thinking about?" I ask.

"Shit, little girl, if I was to tell you that you'd turn me over to *Grand-père*."

"I'm no little girl."

"Got the same skinny butt you had ten years ago, swimming naked in the river."

"You didn't see it."

"Two white doughboys floating on the water." I slap his hand and he laughs. "What're you thinking about, baby doll?"

"Baby doll?"

"Come on now, let a fellow have a little love talk."

I smile, pleased as anything with his love talk. A breeze stirs the darkened branches of the black spruce spreading above us, a needle tickles my cheek.

"Not hearing much," pesters Henri.

"The time you fought with Mister Louis outside Father's store, why did you ask Father that question—about his being so close to home that night?"

He coughs, clearing his throat like I dropped something in it. "There's a fine dose of loving. Best you can do?"

"You asked what I was thinking."

"Your father. You're thinking about your father." He leans on his side, his face shadowing mine. "You mind if I take offence?"

"Please," I whisper.

He grunts and rolls onto his back. "Didn't like him standing there, sneering at *Grand-père,* that's all."

"You think my father done something wrong that night the boat foundered?"

"I think he's like his old man: a cold bastard looking for profits and don't give a damn how he gets them. But no, I don't know if he done anything wrong that night." He strokes my arm like a youngster with the edging of a favoured blanket.

"I think you hate my father. I wonder you don't hate Mister Louis, too. Always yelling, calling you a bastard."

"*Grand-père's* a bit impatient, is all. Them damn ulcers give him pain."

"He calls you a traitor."

"He likes reminding me that my old man's a miserable Limey bastard that ran off and left Mam alone with her brood."

"Why does he like reminding you of that?"

"So's I don't run off and leave someday too."

"Does it bother you, being English?"

He snorts a laugh. "I got too many bits to be any one thing: a bit of Brit, a bit of French, a bit of Irish mick, Protestant, *bâtard,* traitor. Feck, I wear more colours than one of Mam's quilts. And they're all bleeding into the good ol' Royal Blue of me navy jersey." He snorts another laugh.

"You always make jokes about everything?"

"Picking a flag's no joke, Livvy. The minute you settle on

one, you spend the rest of your life serving it, else you're a traitor or a coward. Which fecks me good because I'm everyone's feckin' brother, uncle or cousin. Gawd-damn," he ends in wonder.

He stops stroking my arm and falls quiet. I look up at his face and it's the most serious I've ever seen it. "Nothing human in it, Liv. Nothing human in war, seeing a man's entrails spreading out on the water, wrapping around his neck like a bloodied scarf. More respect shown a pig before slaughter. And there's a reason for slaughtering pigs." He grunts, flexing his hurt leg. "Old limpy here, he's not such a bad thing, he'll keep me from ever pointing a gun at another man's guts." He nuzzles my hair. "English as the rose," he murmurs. "Your British, Proddy-dog pap's not going to look kindly on you mending and scrubbing Mam's sheets."

"With all that strife out there, your mam's sheets is the only flag worth fighting for."

"It sure is, Livvy, it sure is. I'd like to be there when you tell that to your pap."

I pull myself up; it's dark now. "You better walk me home, Henri. Case there's spies about."

Henri groans, and I feel his body stiffening. "Just a minute, just a minute."

"Is it your leg?"

"Yeah. It hurts there." He puts my hand on his inner thigh, the one that isn't wounded, and presses it tight.

"You trickster," I try to say, but he's kissing my mouth. He strokes my belly and I've never felt anything so soft as Henri's fingers. A warm glow spreads through me and I push away, startled by a fierce desire to press harder against him, to fall into the rhythm he's kneading into my belly. Scrambling to my feet, I run through the marsh, straightening my clothes and wondering if this is love.

A soft light shines through the dark. Etna is in the window, peering curiously at Henri who is a step behind me and now taking my hand, kissing it good night. I flush at the softness of his mouth on my skin and try to keep the smile off my face as I enter the house and Etna stands before me.

"Aye, I thought it was the old woman who captured your heart," she says with mischief in her eyes.

"He walked me home, there are spies about," I say, slipping off my shoes.

"A gallant man, eh, kissing the maiden's hand."

I face her, moving my lips with exaggeration. "Missus Louis told him to walk me home. There are spies about."

Ignoring Etna's silly smile, I fill the washpan with warm water from the kettle.

"My first day here, he walked me home too," she says, keeping her silly smile. "I thought he had the look of a rogue. You have to watch these fool boys trying to be men."

The scorn in her tone catches me. "Did you have boyfriends?"

She tightens her mouth. "Good boys don't want poor deaf orphans, luv. Nor do I want boys, I helped raise enough boys."

"Did you turn from love?" I ask her.

She laughs. "I turn from everything I can't touch and clean."

I awaken to the squawk of a crow and dawn sifting through the curtains. Dressing, I hurry into the kitchen, where Etna already has the fire lit and the kettle humming. "It's a nice day," she says, going to each of the windows, opening the curtains to a brightening sky. She flits about the living room, touching things, brushing the arms of the sofa, straightening its cover while she waits for the water to heat up enough for washing. And after she's finished the washing she'll fold back the crochet tablecloth, lay out the checked tea cloth, take two cups and saucers from the top cupboard, their rattling breaking a silence she doesn't hear, and her fingers will go on to flow as repetitiously through her morning tasks as her humming flows through the house. I wonder now if her humming isn't too unlike Mother's ranting, a way of sieving hurt from a wounded heart.

"I don't want tea," I say loudly, and she looks at me.

"Did you wash? You can't go without washing." She roots the fire, hurrying the kettle to boil. I want to go to her. I want to take her hand, to run with her from the stagnancy of polished floors and sinks where she tries to wipe clean the ills of her past, to usher her over different thresholds.

"Come to Missus Louis's with me."

"Don't be foolish, luv, I've enough to do here without chasing after cows and sheep." She gives a mock shiver. "You run along then." She resumes her humming, eyes brightening onto the steam oozing from the kettle, and I leave her protected within the clean confines of the life she daily creates around herself. And I run through the marsh towards mine. If Etna's is to stave off germs, mine is to continue what Mother had been doing during her last months: coupling her uncoupled heart through immersing herself in Missus Louis's brood, helping them with milking cows and goats, sluicing down pig pens and stoops and feeding hens and feeding the youngsters and all the while feeding herself upon the bounty of this great, sprawling family.

It is Saturday, washday, and I hurry the bigger girls outdoors, their arms piled high with blankets to air on the line. The boys help turn over the heavy feather mattresses and we straighten and beat them into shape, sneezing from the dust. I pile sheets and pillowcases on the kitchen floor where Suzie scrubs them in one tub that smells of bleach and Colette rinses and blues them in the other that smells clean like soap. Their hands wrinkle white from the water and I run to hang the wet garments on clotheslines already dancing with sheets, stockings and pantaloons.

The barn door bursts open and I hear the guttural moan of a cow late with giving birth, the raw smell of its birthing water sweetened by stewing currants sifting through Missus Louis's kitchen window. She hollers from her back door to Esmée who's coming out of the cellar with a pan of pickled herring, and behind her hobbles Henri with the scythe. He winks at me as he passes, then holds the scythe threateningly towards Mister Louis's neck who's railing at the youngsters for flattening the hay with their play. He looks back at me and winks again and I quiver with excitement and hurry to the house for more laundry.

Dusk thickens the air as I run through the marsh path from Missus Louis's. Henri waits for me as he has done the past several evenings since we first lay together, and this time he leads me deeper along the riverbank and into a rickety structure made out of boughs that he uses for trout fishing. Inside the bough whiffen he lays his sweater on the dirt floor and we both lie with the river that surges beside us. My head rests on his heart and his cheek nuzzles through my hair and his breath warms my neck. He strokes my cheek and strokes my belly and I pull back, looking into his eyes. They are dark, they are deeper than the river, and I fall into them as he smiles and keeps his hands from prowling too far over my body.

The next evening Missus Louis calls through her kitchen window, "*Macushlah*, it's getting late, run home now. Here, come, take some supper to Etna."

"She'll not eat anything unless she cooks it herself," I say, kicking the muck off my boots before entering Missus Louis's kitchen. She's sitting at the table, spooning a thick stew into a bowl. "Can't I just stay here? I don't want to go home. I can help you sew," I add, noting her darning basket sitting atop a pile of laundry.

"You have to see to her, luv, we care for our own." She looks worriedly to Mister Louis as he staggers in from the outhouse, bent like a wishbone, heading for bed. "Drink your ginger, Louis. Did you drink your ginger? Silly old fool," she says with a worried look as Mister Louis grunts, the room door closing behind him. "He thinks if he throws up deep enough, he'll throw up the ulcer. How do you help someone like that?"

"Won't he see the doctor?"

"He'll have to, he's getting worse. Least he'll have a bit of rest with winter coming and everything hatched down. Bad as winter is, it's a time for resting."

I feel a tiredness coming from her. I stare into her old woman's eyes. They are deep and dark from looking inward, and embedded on a face strong with flesh. She smiles at my scrutiny. "You're such a curious thing," she says, and beckons me to fetch her sewing basket as she sits at the table, cutting undershirts for the boys out of sheets of cotton.

"Can't I help you sew?"

"Shut in the hens, and get yourself home while there's light.

My word, the time falls back next week. We'll be in darkness afore we gets out of bed."

"But I don't like to go home."

"The girl needs company."

"She won't ever leave the house. I ask her to come with me, but all she thinks about is germs and cleaning."

"She seems content, though? Long as she's not fretting."

"She used to wash her hands a lot, but not since Father left. I think it was his smoking she didn't like. But she's not right."

"We're all drunk on something, luv. Some of us a bit more than others."

"She says it makes things feel like hers when she keeps cleaning them. I think she pretends the house is hers."

"Some people spend all their lives pretending," says Missus Louis. "It's easier than what's around them sometimes." She knots her thread and weaves the needle through the piece of cotton in her hands. "These old eyes, can hardly see. Have you never pretended, luv?"

I am quiet. I remember those days when I sat amongst the sand dunes, searching for my mother. "Perhaps," I say. "Did you?"

She laughs. "Mary and Joseph, I've never had time. But I've never been an orphan. I would think they pretend harder than others. Perhaps it's the only thing they have sometimes, their made-up world. You lost your mother, but you have a home, luv. It's not a nice place, the orphanage: dreary grey rooms, grey walls, grey bedding, leaky bare windows and washed-out clothes and cold hard floors. Easy enough to start making up other worlds."

"I remember you said you worked in an orphanage …?"

"My da died a young man. My mam took herself to an orphanage and worked to have a place in which to raise me. We had a nice room and enough to eat and I was educated by the nuns. I was lucky to have a mam. I seen what it can do, not ever having one."

She keeps sewing, her face calm yet her eyes anxious upon her needle as she weaves it in and out, hemming the cloth with perfect little stitches. "I remember this little thing being born one night," she says. "I was only ten, but Mam and the nuns let me help with heating the water during her birthing. They let me hold her. I can see like yesterday, those blue eyes rolling open and staring into mine. It's the closest I've ever felt to God, looking into those eyes just born and yet full of knowing—like God himself staring up at me."

"What was her name?"

"Neave. Brightness. I named her. From the day she was born, I was the one who took the most care of her. I tell you, girl, she grew to be the prettiest thing: her hair blonde and soft as cotton. And her eyes, so big on that tiny face she looked to topple over any moment. She'd sit for hours in the window seat, letting me twist her curls into whichever shape I wanted. Blessed be the saints, when the sun caught in that fluffed-up hair and her eyes shone like stars, she was the picture. I used to sit with her like she was my own, keeping her soft and pretty. Keeping her from fading to grey like everything else around her."

"And did you? Did you keep her soft and pretty?"

"Yes. Perhaps too pretty. Heat the iron for me, luv. You got me muddling through the old stuff again."

"What happened to her?"

She glances at me, her eyes mournful like an old sleigh dog's, and beckons me towards the stove. I grasp the wooden handle of the flat-iron from the range and lay it heavily on the stovetop. Giving the fire a good stoking with the poker, I lay it aside and sit quietly on the edge of the woodbox.

"Did she get adopted?"

"Kind of. Run home now, Livvy."

"But was it a good family that took her? How old was she? Oh, please tell me," I beg.

"You can be as stubborn as she was, when you've a mind. I was fifteen and was hired as a teacher by a wealthy couple living outside St. John's. They had an eight-year-old daughter with no one to play with, so I brought Neave along."

"What was her name, the daughter?"

"Frances. Her parents, the Crenshaws, quite liked Neave as a playmate for their daughter. They had their servants bathe and dress her as they did Frances. They became great playmates, and Neave was happy there. Ahh, it was a wonderful thing, watching Neave being dressed like the little lady and learning her lessons. She was so smart, Frances could never keep up with her in their schoolwork.

"We were there for near on five years, going back to the orphanage on Sundays. I tell you, girl, that orphanage looked bleaker and bleaker each time I returned to it. But I had my mam there. Neave had nothing. A little grey bed in a row with twenty-five others. Was only natural she'd start fighting against going back. Only normal."

"Did she stay with Frances?"

"Yes. Yes, she did. Mrs. Crenshaw finally let her stay. Now then, you get yourself home, it's getting late."

"But what happened to her?"

"Nothing happened to her, they lived together like sisters. And then I met Louis on one of my return trips to the orphanage and moved here. You remember this, when you're sitting home this evening," says Missus Louis intently, "Etna's an orphan. She had nobody to teach her about trust and love. All she's ever had is herself and her made-up world. Anything you take from that, you take from her. So, let her be. The most we can do for anybody is try and understand them and love them anyway. You think you can do that, *macushlah*?"

I give a contrite nod, and taking the covered bowl of baked beans and mackerel for Etna, I hurry along the marsh path, looking back for signs of Henri. He's camping overnight on a birding trip, and won't be back till late tomorrow, but still I look, hoping to see him.

The house is brightly lit as I approach. Etna peers through the window, then quickly drops the curtain. The door opens and Father comes charging towards me. The mortified twist to his mouth tells me that he knows about my being at Missus Louis's, and more, that Etna has told him about Henri. He comes before me, his eyes stony with repulsion. "You've outdone yourself this time. Your things are packed. We're leaving for your grandmother's, that's where you belong."

I stare back at him. I feel no fault of wrongness, but only an awakening of the anger I had thought gone. It is not so dark that he cannot see. "Go, pack the rest of your things," he orders, but I don't move. He raises his hand to strike me as he had with my mother that time outside of Missus Louis's, but she had stood her ground and I know now that she wasn't afraid of him and neither am I. His hand lowers. Perhaps, as with my mother, there's nothing to be had by striking me. Or perhaps, as with my mother, he fears that I too will laugh at him.

Mute like a fish, he starts back towards the house, the thud of his footsteps blunted by a scream of crows erupting like a black cloud from the trees. They flap over his head and I see their darkness settling into his eyes as he turns back to me. "You'll leave," he says tightly. "You'll leave, else I'll cut their credit. I'll starve them like Grandfather did. I know every merchant here and I'll blacken their name like a winter spud. They'll be eating salt fish and cowhide before the winter's halfway through."

I stand rooted in shock. I turn from him, walking stiffly inside the house. Etna stands by the window, her face ashen. "I'm sorry, luv, I didn't know he was coming—his ship docked in Port aux Basques. He—he threatened to send me back if I didn't tell where you were. It slipped out about your fellow, I'm sorry, luv."

Inside my room my drawers are emptied, suitcase already packed and sitting on the bed. Whether to Missus Louis's or my grandmother's, I am being tossed from Father's house. I sit, choked with such rage it muffles my breathing. Evening swirls its darkness through the window. The trees sigh and the first stars blink pityingly down on this ruinous moment.

Etna knocks on my door, her voice thin and anxious. Then she knocks on Father's door and he yells something, his voice gruff. I strain to hear; perhaps he is relenting, but only silence follows. I think of Henri, his eyes deep as river water. Pushing open my window, I slip out into the night and race back through the marsh to Missus Louis's. I stand on her back steps, looking in through her screen door as she still sits, sewing garments, straight pins nipped between her lips as she peers at her stitching through the dim glow of her lamplight. Mister Louis coughs, and I hear him as he squeaks out of bed and goes to the bucket at the end of the darkened hallway and spits.

"Did you finish your ginger?" Missus Louis calls, the pins sticking to the dryness of her bottom lip as she speaks. A deep gargling sounds from Mister Louis—he's throwing up again. Missus Louis lays aside her sewing and rises, the floor creaking, as must be her bones from her manner of groaning as she rubs her hip. I step back from the screen door as she lifts the lamp and trudges wearily down the hall. Brushing away mosquitoes whirring about my neck and ears, I sit on the step, listening to Esmée calling out to her boys who're squabbling over whose turn it is to bring in the firewood. I hear Suzie calling out to Colette that she's off down to the river to empty the slop pail. I think of Henri and his wounded leg and the sheep and cows and barrels of cod and herring stored in the cellar, and the appalling hardship wreaked upon them all should they be forced to uproot and move, for they would have to if Father cut off their supplies. And I remember Mother lying back on my bed, her heart fluttering faint like a trapped moth. I remember her sitting on the sofa the following morning, pale with a bluish mouth, staring red-eyed at the door that Father had just closed as he left for the store. *They done something, Durwin and my mother, they done something.* I see the shale rock leaving Father's hands and smashing against Tabs's thin, velvety skull and I know he would do it, he would take their homes apart. I think again of Henri. When poverty walks in the door, Missus Louis had once admonished Suzie for flirting with a useless hangashore, love flies out the window. Wrapping my arms tight around my belly, I set out for the marsh path.

"Livvy!" I startle and turn back to see Missus Louis, who's shuffling towards the door, still holding the lamp. "*Macushlah,* what are you doing? I thought you left."

Hope lifts my heart. I look at those warm, dark eyes lit by her lamplight, and a trembling starts up inside of me, as when I was a girl, frighted out of sleep and sobbing from a bad dream, and Mother would be rushing from her room and holding me till I calmed. "It's Father," I say. "He's come home unexpectedly, he wants to take me to Grandmother Creed's to live."

Missus Louis's hand goes to her heart. "My soul, the Lord has his ways," she whispers. "I've been trying to find a way, and now He's done it Himself. You must go, Livvy. You must go to your grandmother."

Hope vanishes like a falling star. "I don't know that I want to go."

"You think I don't know that, *macushlah*? You think it warms my heart to lose you? It won't be long, you'll be back. Go, Livvy. I've told you, there's something there for you, luv, there's something there for you."

"Then tell me, just tell me," I demand.

She shakes her head. "This is God's way. I couldn't have done it, but who am I, a mere mortal, to speak up now?" A breeze flickers the lamplight, hollowing her eyes with darkness, hiding them. I feel them holding onto me, not wanting me to leave any more than I want to. But she stands resolute.

I step back. I try to speak, to tell her goodbye, to ask her to say goodbye to Esmée and Suzie and Colette. And Henri. Instead I turn back to the path, towards my father, and rage wraps itself cold around my bones. *They done something, Durwin and my mother, they done something.* And Missus Louis's words, *There's something there for you, luv, there's something there for you.* I start walking. I walk fast. It is dark, I cannot see. I trip on a root that snakes across the path and start running to keep from falling, my hands flailing at the tall grasses on either side of me, keeping me straight, their night-wetness splashing cold on my face, my arms, and I'm cold, shivering cold. I trip again and am falling, falling and I open my eyes and I'm lying, shivering, beneath my blankets. Willaby meows from outside my room door, and Tuff joins in harmony. I hug the blankets tightly around me. My chest feels so tight I can scarcely breathe. The cats keep meowing, they scratch at my door, there's something wrong, they never scratch at my door. I try to move but the weight of my dreams holds me back, the weight of the girl's anger. I feel it thumping through my heart and I am awakened further with the knowing that the girl's anger didn't release itself through her veins with a good pumping of the heart as it did Mother's, as it did Mister Louis's and Henri's. It laid itself low inside of her all those years. Till that moment. That moment with Grandmother Creed.

I turn from the girl's anger. I push my fist against my heart as though pushing her back inside, and look to the clock. It is four in the afternoon. I sit up with alarm. It was morning when I sat down, early morning. I've slept through the day, the whole day!

SIX

A heavy gust of wind rattles the window and shakes the house. There's a storm on. And nothing feels right, the air, the quiet. And the cats, they keep scratching at my door, meowing. I swing my legs over the side of the bed, then become still. What's this, what's this now, *I'm in my bed!* But I didn't go to bed. I was in my rocker by the window. I remember clearly: Gen had just left. She had knelt before me, cupping my hands and stirring up thoughts of Henri—did I sleepwalk?

The floor creaks beneath my feet as I stand—what's this, what's this now, I'm wearing my slippers? I'm wearing my slippers to bed? I shuffle down the hallway, my back too stiff to stand upright, confusion blurring my step. "Quiet, be quiet," I say to the cats. They're hungry, and I'm hungry too, I must go to the store. Hobbling to the drapes, I open them onto thick, gusting snow, silvered beneath awnings of streetlights. It's quiet, no cars. I look back to the clock and grip the back of the rocker: it's the *a.m.* It is four *a.m.*

A different cold wraps itself around my chest. I count backwards: eighteen hours. It's been eighteen hours since Gen left. When did I go to bed?

I close my eyes to the stillness of this moment. I wait for it to righten things around me, to fit things back onto themselves, as they were this morning before I sat in my rocker, thinking of Henri. I hear a *thud,* a soft *thud* sounding from the porch. It sounds again, *thud, thud.* I stare at the door, fear trickling through me.

What's this, what's this now, I'm afraid of a thump in the night? I go to the door and open it to a draft of cold air. *Thud, thud.* It's coming from the basement. Fear muscles its way back. I want to run to my room, but my eyes are locked onto the side bolt. *Thud, thud.* I reach forward, scraping back the bolt, and the door swings open. The black mouth of the basement gapes before me, the dankness of rot fouling its breath. A sharp hiss sounds: the queen. The cat. I'd forgotten the cat. She's probably tipped something over.

I reach for the flashlight on its shelf and flick its yellow beam down over the stairs. The kittens start mewling, scampering into the circle of light that shines on the floor like the sunlit mouth of a dark cave. The queen gives a throaty warning as I draw nearer. I keep the light from the glassy glare of her eyes, then nearly drop it as another *thud* sounds, louder this time. From over there, by the door that leads outside. *Thud, thud. Thud.* I hear a cry, a soft cry sounding through the thick oak door. "Who's there, who's there?"

I move closer, straining to hear a faint voice. It sounds like Gen. "What are you doing out there?"

"*Open the fucking door,*" she screams, and then her voice falls away and my fear is pushed aside by a wallop of anger.

"What are you doing at this hour? Go to the porch door."

"Livvy! Please. Please let me in." Her voice cracks like thin ice on a shallow pond. It splinters through my anger and I drop the flashlight, darting to the door. The light goes out, I grasp for the deadbolt in the darkness and tug it open. I pull on the door but it's stuck.

"Push on it, push on the door," I call.

Thud. Thud, thud. The door swings in and a swatch of snow swipes my face. All is dark and I stagger backwards as Gen tumbles in through the door and pushes it shut behind her. She's sobbing, and she grasps at my legs, trying to feel her way around.

"A light, a light, don't you have a light?"

"I dropped it. What's wrong, tell me, what's wrong?"

"Nothing, everything's fine," she cries, her voice full of fear—and pain.

"You're hurt." I grope around for the light, but can't find it. "Follow me upstairs."

"Where? I can't see—my wrists, oh my God, my wrists."

"Give me your hand. Here, give me your hand." Her fingers are stiff with cold. "What were you doing? Why are you in my backyard? Stand up, why are you crawling?"

"The stairs, get me to the stairs."

The queen hisses like a cornered demon and Gen screams. "It's just a cat. This way. Careful, there are kittens."

"How many fucking cats do you own?" moans Gen. "Oh, God, this is weird. Are you a freaking cat woman or something? You got fifty cats down here? I can smell the stench."

"There's three kittens and they're yours," I say crossly. My foot strikes the bottom step and, overcome with fatigue, I cling to the wall, pulling myself up. Gen crawls behind, shrieking as another loud hiss sounds from the queen. At the top of the stairs I stand aside, panting for breath.

"Why are you crawling?" I gasp, impatient now, and contrary at the upset she's caused me this night. She crawls past me into the porch, and keeps crawling into the living room. Latching the basement door, I follow her inside, my hands to my chest as my lungs are besieged with a rash of coughs.

Willaby growls, neck fur rising, and Tuff leaps atop the cabinet, staring down at Gen as I do. She sits with her back to the wall, her face stark beneath the dull ceiling light. She raises her eyes to mine; they're black with wet makeup, and they're frightened. Her hair is damp and frizzled and clumped about her shoulders. She's wearing her red parka over her pyjamas and her pant legs are soaked through to the skin, as are her socks. She's not wearing boots. Something glints at her feet—I stand back with a frightened gasp. Cuffed! Her ankles are handcuffed!

"It's nothing. Please, Livvy, it looks bad but it's not. Be careful, watch it."

I've backed up against the rocker, and now sit in it gratefully.

"I was robbed," she sobs. "You were right, Sandy isn't a friend, he helped rob me. Two men broke in and cuffed me, and they robbed me. But that's all they did; they just robbed me. They tied my wrists." Her face twists with pain as she holds them out for me to see: they are reddened and raw.

"It hurts like bloody hell," she cries, and then blows on her wrists. "I burned them. I burned off the rope with a lighter after they left. It looks so fucking easy on TV. Please. Do you have something—aloe vera or something?"

"Why— How come you didn't call the police?"

"I can't."

"Why not? You said you were robbed."

"Please, I can't." She's shaking her head, wiping at her nose, her eyes. "I'm not a criminal, I know this looks bad, but—" She pauses, looking to me with pleading. "I told you this morning— I told you—I've got some stuff going on. I was holding onto money for a friend. It was a favour. I got broken into. It must have been drug money or something. I'll never do it again, you can be damned sure I'll never do it again. I just need help right now. Please, something for the burns. And a saw. Do you have a hand saw or something? I've got to get these off."

"No. No, I don't." I sit on the edge of the rocker. My legs are shaky seeing her like that, cuffed and wet. It feels as if I'm dreaming. *Am* I dreaming? It all feels so strange, my sleeping with my slippers on.

"I'm sorry, I'm so sorry to frighten you. Just give me the phone, I'll call Stu. He'll come and get me."

"In this storm?"

"He's just a few blocks away, he'll walk." Her dark eyes plead with mine. She's shivering and her hands are hurting, she's blowing on them again.

"He got you into this, didn't he?"

"No, no," she moans. "He'll be freaked out when he sees me, totally freaked out." She stares at me, her eyes wide with fear. It guts me to see her with such fear. I get up and fetch her a thick flannel housecoat and a blanket from my room. Rattling through drawers in the bathroom, I find Tylenol and bring her a glass of water and a soaked towel to cool her wrists. She shivers her thanks through chattering teeth as she changes out of her wet clothes and gulps back the Tylenol. I set the phone beside her and sit back in the rocker, drawing my wrap around me and watching the wind whamming snow against the window.

"Must be the only dial phone left on the planet," she says, trying to lighten her tone as she dials her brother's number. "Hello, Stu! Stu, wake up," she pleads. "*Please,* wake up, answer your phone. I got hit, I'm cuffed. I'm at Livvy's. You've got to get here. I have to get Ronny at the hospital in the morning—and—oh, God." She replaces the receiver. "Stu's doing shift work at the hospital. I can't call him there, but he'll be off at six a.m." She looks to the clock on the wall, it's four-thirty. "I'll have to wait, I'll just have to wait. Livvy, you can go to bed. I'll wait here for Stu. Please, you look so tired and it's all my fault."

I keep watching the snow drifting through her reflection in the window.

"You must think I'm terrible. I'm not. Really. This—this was just a one-time thing. I'm almost a social worker, for God's sakes. Can you imagine if the police came? Wow. Some career move, eh? Will you please say something."

"I don't like lies." I hate that my voice creaks with old age, that my words don't sound as deep as I feel them. Yet they silence her. She stares at my reflection as I stare back at hers.

"Secrets—they've ways of shaping our path," says Gen. "You said that. You've your secrets, Livvy, else you wouldn't have known to make that comment. Can't I have mine, too?"

"I've not made lies out of mine."

She keeps looking at me in the window. She leans forward and I feel her struggling in her mind, wondering which plank will take her safe across the river. She sits back, resigned to take the least favoured. "I— Fine, here it is. The money they took was mine. I've been dealing drugs to keep myself in school. God, that must sound awful," she says, covering her ears. "And—oh, God, this is going to sound bad. I hide them in your bushes—in the back of your yard."

I look at her with astonishment.

"It's not a bad drug, nothing like that, just hash. It's like pot, only—only it looks like hard brownie dough. It's not as bad as it sounds," she says, as I must've paled. "Soft core, not like *acid* or anything."

"You hide drugs in my shrubs?"

"I'm sorry. I'm so sorry. I— Nobody would suspect your shrubs. Really, nobody would suspect you of peddling Black Moroccan."

"It's that brother, isn't it? He's got you doing this."

"Will you freaking get off Stu? He's straighter than a gawddamn priest. Well—some priests. Oh, jeezus." She lowers her face into her hands. "My ex, he stopped paying for Ronny last fall. I couldn't just quit my courses, I'm too close to graduation. Ohh, I've got to get out of this." She grabs for the phone and starts frantically dialing, and as I rest my head in my hands she tells some clerk her brother's name and the ward where he's working. I don't feel right, I'm dizzy, and my throat—it's hard to swallow. A flu. I'm coming down with the flu. Gen's voice wavers on air, *"Swear to gawd, Stewie, I'm so fucked up—you've got to get here, get these cuffs off. No, come now, please come now, I can't sit here like this. Treen! What's she doing—tell Treen to fuck off! Just tell her to fuck right off!"*

I hold up my head as she slaps the receiver into the cradle. "Who's Treen?" I ask, fanning my face with my hand.

"Treen's my freaking mother. *Trina.*"

I hold back my head and the dizziness subsides, leaving my stomach nauseated.

"Stu's coming. He knows somebody who can help. He's freaked out, I told you he'd be freaked out. You look tired, I'm so sorry for this. Did you get the Vita drink I bought you? I put it on the sink beside your pills."

I look to the sink, there's a bag there, and several cans of cat food. "When were you here?"

"This afternoon. You were napping. I knocked, you didn't answer, so I let myself in. Didn't you see the bags on your sink? I fed the cats, they looked hungry."

"Where was I?"

"In your bed, where the hell do you think you were? You're acting weird again."

"*I'm* acting weird?" I ask, pointing at her cuffed feet. "Does she always drink—your mother?" I ask, to shift her attention away from me.

"What you saw the other night, that's what I've been looking at and listening to all my life. Bah, listen to me, yakking about my mother and I'm no better." She lowers her head, brushing at her eyes.

"Ronny's happy. Only good mothers have happy children."

She sniffs and wipes her nose. "Thank you. Thank you for saying that."

"Is Treen why you're sad?"

"Shit. You can see that?"

"Social workers don't swear."

She snorts a laugh. "There's no math, that's the sole reason for my career choice. But I'm liking it. I just got to start making money—get out of this mess. Frig, I'm my own first client."

"Why does she drink?"

"Who, my mother? The same reason everybody drinks: to get drunk. Sorry, I don't mean to be rude. She just moved here from New Brunswick last week. She thinks it's time she became a mama, and a grandma. Isn't that cute, now. You know what's worse than Treen drunk? Treen sober, and blubbering over being drunk—missing birthdays, missing graduations. Ugh. Shame's so pathetic, it makes me squirm.

"What, you got nothing to say now?" she says to my silence.

"We all have our stories."

"You're standing up for her. Why?"

"Doesn't help to be angry, girl," I say, rubbing my eyes with fatigue.

"Ah! Tell that to a kid with a drunk mother."

I cringe from the anger in her tone, in her eyes. How to tell her about anger, how it sits and grows, how it's already aging her girlish eyes, how it will dull the soft pinks of dawn and deafen her ears to the whisper of a falling leaf?

"They say your husband died about twenty-something years ago," says Gen, looking at me curiously. "They say he never missed a dance. Oh, don't get peevish, I like hearing those things about you. I think of you dancing. Did you like dancing?"

"What's this, I'm your client, now?"

"I asked you a frigging question!" she snaps. "What, I can't ask you a question? I tell you things, but you're a frigging state secret, or something?"

"I've not imposed myself on you."

She looks down shamefaced at her cuffs. It shames me to have caused her shame. "I liked dancing with him," I say. "There's been little laughter since he left. My fault—I've never felt comfortable around people."

"How is it you let me inside your door?"

I think back, remembering Ronny that first time I saw him a year ago, leaning over the fence and watching me as I threw feed to the pigeons. "Ronny asked me for a cup of tea."

Gen looks shocked. "Tea?"

"I made us tea and we sat on the step, chatting."

"You made him tea? Where the hell was I?"

"Weak tea. You were still sleeping, it was about six in the morning."

She shakes her head. "He never said a word."

"We shared a few cups. Till school started. Such a sweet boy."

Gen stares at her cuffs. "If he saw this, he'd be so scared. I was always scared. Treen was always going off, coming home hours later. I was like a drool, clinging to her—scared that the next time she left, she wouldn't come back. Talk about abandonment issues."

Her words probe an ache in my withered heart. "Betrayed," I say quietly. "You were betrayed."

She looks at me with surprise. "Betrayed. That's a good word. Were you betrayed? Oh, come now, you wouldn't have used the word if you didn't know it."

"Where's your father?" I ask.

"Never knew him. Poor Ronny, he's growing up without one too. Tell me about your father. Tell me you had a father and he was good."

I rub my eyes, my face, feeling agitated.

"You're tired," said Gen. "Such an ungodly hour. Please go to bed, Livvy."

I rise and the room quivers, along with Gen's voice. I hold onto my stomach, becoming nauseated again. I start down the hallway, my father's voice coming to me from a distance. I try to answer but my tongue is thick, my mouth filling with saliva. I make it to Grandmother Creed's door and pain strikes across my chest. A loud crash reverberates around me, and Etna's voice, as shrill as breaking glass, cries to Father, "Let her stay, let her stay, please let her stay," but Father isn't listening. He's yelling through my room door, "Gather your things!" He stomps away and I hear Etna crying and I hear Father telling her we'll be catching the midnight train coming from Corner Brook within the hour.

I pack the rest of my belongings and leave my father's house for the last time. Capping my rage with pride, I walk steadily behind him as he marches along the scarcely used trail across a barren piece of land, rooted mostly with shrub brush and dimly lit by the night sky. Carrying my suitcase with one hand and his own small bag with the other, he leads me to the deserted train platform and we stand apart from each other. His face holds the same contemptuous look as it held that day on the rocks when he pointed out the splintered bones of the ship where his father had drowned and he accused my mother of betraying him. It is me now who he feels has betrayed him, and a smile tugs the corner of my mouth. *They done something, Durwin and my mother, they done something.*

The overnight train rattles and whistles out of the dark, shuddering to a stop in a burst of steam. I go without Father's ushering up the rickety steps and take a seat to myself, and for the next three hours that it takes to get to Port aux Basques, I stare in silence at the bogs, meadows and distant mountain range passing outside my window. Under a dull sky I disembark the train a few steps behind Father, careful not to touch him or draw his attention, for I am knotted tight inside and want no gesture or look from him that might undo me. On knees strengthened with purpose I climb a gangway onto a ship that smells of rust and steel.

Father leads me past the curious eyes of men hustling about the ship's decks in heavy clothing and caps, throwing about ropes and hoses as they snort and curse and laugh and holler to each other. Pulleys squeal overhead as they hoist boxed cargo from the docks and then lower them, creaking and groaning beneath their lashings, onto the deck of the ship. There are large guns mounted by the railings and I remember there is a war with U-boats gutting ships with torpedoes, but I feel no fear. Ducking into a long, darkish corridor, I follow my father as he leads me to a small, boxlike room with a musky-smelling bunk.

For two days I lie there, huddling with nausea against the long, deep roll of the ship as it plows through the seas, the room shuddering, the woodwork squeaking and groaning. A cabin boy brings soup and bread and I nibble weakly and think of Grandmother Creed. Small wonder she didn't visit more often.

After what feels like eternity the rolling and squeaking stops and we are motionless. Soon, Father comes for me. I lift my head weakly from the pillow, gather my few belongings and follow him onto the main deck into a stiff wind and the sun sinking low. Slabs of steel vibrate beneath my feet and a cacophony of foghorns and whistles and hollers blasts us from all directions.

Clutching onto the bulwark, I wait for Father and look about Halifax Harbour, stunned by the sights around me. There are ships everywhere, their hulking, grey-steeled hulls anchored three abreast on both sides of the harbour, towering over warehouses sitting on the wharves. They crowd the centre of the harbour, hundreds of them, all grey in colour, and with men swarming their decks and hollering over horns and whistles that are constantly sounding out warnings to other ships bearing down on them or chugging and jostling too close for positioning on the oil-slicked waters.

Father returns and I follow him down a gangplank that squeaks and jiggles beneath my shaky step. A bulky black man takes my hand and helps me into a small boat. I sit, gripping the gunnels, water sprinkling cold on my hands as he dips and plies the paddles, manoeuvring us among other small boats coming and going all around us, crowded with men in navy blue serge. It startles me to see fear on the faces of some of the men, and to hear their too loud laughter. A young sailor catches my eye, his face drawn with weariness, and I am shamed by the tremors of fear starting up in my stomach, for tonight I'll be sleeping in a bed on land while he, perhaps, will be clinging with bloodied hands to splintered bits of wood within the frigid curl of a whitecap.

We tie up at a quay and I climb onto a crowded, noisy dock and stare at the confusion of men in blues and khaki browns who throng the cobblestone sidewalks: some bleak-faced and silent, others yelling, cursing, laughing, jostling each other as they sing drunkenly. Yellow trams honk as they crawl through the maze of streets spiralling steeply uphill amidst row upon row of coloured wooden houses bedecked with high dormers. A massive green mound crowns the hilltop and is studded with cannons and flapping flags that appear to be saluting the thousands of soldiers roaming the streets. I think of my father and Mister Louis and their strife over each other's flag, and I wonder what strife, what unimaginable strife could bring about such a thing as this.

A stream of sailors unwittingly takes me along with them and I pull back, looking about wildly for Father. He isn't here. A rash of shivers overtakes me and I huddle inside my coat, feeling myself growing smaller amidst the swarms of people and trams.

"Are you all right, duckie? Are you feelin' all right?" asks a skinny woman with pencilled raccoon eyes and a red-slashed mouth. I stiffen my shoulders, feeling like a youngster caught with hot piss running down my leg.

"I'm fine, thank you," I say, my voice scarcely a whisper. "My—my father's right there," I add as she leans closer to hear me. "Righty-o, then," she says and totters off along the cobbled streets on two-inch pumps. I look around fearfully for Father and nearly dissolve into tears of relief when I see him making his way through the crowd, my suitcase swinging in his hand.

He orders me to follow him and I struggle to keep my hand from reaching out to cling to his as he weaves a crooked path before me, through mobs and mobs of people, more people than I could ever have imagined. A taxi slows beside us and Father bundles me into the back seat with my suitcase and climbs in front with the driver and we speed uphill, passing dozens of two- and three-storey houses on both sides of the street. The taxi stops beside a bungalow with a big front window, a picture window, looking out onto the street. To the side of the house is a door and a set of steps with a short path leading to the gate. Beyond it is a graveyard. The graveyard where Father waited for Mother. His eyes were wild, she'd said, his ears echoing with the cries of drowning men, and he had led her beneath the branches of an old spruce tree in Point Pleasant Park and seeded me in her belly.

Father doesn't look at the graveyard. He goes through the gate, up the steps and knocks on the door. Without waiting, he wriggles the knob and vanishes inside. I look at the picture window; it is afire with sun. A little wan face wavers through the flames—the grandmother, peering at me with no sign of recognition. She vanishes as though incinerated. I shift about uncomfortably on the sidewalk. A grey cat with ratty fur and a torn ear meows at me from behind a bush. She comes closer and I reach for her, kneeling, wanting to touch something warm. She sniffs my fingers, then turns and scampers towards the graveyard.

I look to the door of Grandmother Creed's house and, without waiting for Father, I go inside the gate and up the steps and quietly enter the porch. A door sits ajar to my left, leading down a steep set of polished wooden steps. Before me is another door that stands ajar, beyond which Father stands, speaking urgently with Grandmother Creed.

His tone becomes more casual as he senses me behind him, and he starts speaking of a convoy that was attacked by a wolf pack of U-boats yesterday. Five ships sunk, their crews lost, and an offshore storm now devastating the surviving ships with its icy winds.

I listen, equally as caught by the grandeur of Grandmother Creed's living room: its flowery wallpaper and green velvet drapes, its lacy lamps flaunting their light upon dark wooden cabinets and side tables with spindly legs. There is a settee with rose-carved edgings, and beside the picture window a matching rocker, thickly cushioned, upon which Grandmother Creed had been sitting, no doubt, for there is a little table at its side, upon which rests an open book and a teacup.

"My dear, you've come," she whispers, moving past Father, her hands held out towards me. No longer is she the rouged, spry figure with buttery-yellow hair; she is pale and grey now, her gaunt frame held up by two wooden canes polished a shiny black and with armrests that allow her the use of her hands. And yet the tilt of her chin as she examines my face, her perfect English accent as she apologizes for not being dressed yet, and her slender hands—creamy white and soft as feathers as she lays them atop mine—are perfectly befitting this queenly room.

"You will stay, then?" she asks me, and looks suspiciously at Father when I don't answer. As though fearful of a ruse, she points me towards a doorway at the far end of a tidy, glossy white kitchen. "Why don't you wait in there, I'll have a word with your father. Are you hungry?"

I shake my head, and go through the kitchen towards the dining room. I step inside and the door springs shut behind me. Gold-framed portraits stare stiffly from their places along the walls. The darkest of blue velvet fabric drapes the windows, and in the centre of the room is a circular wooden dining table with six high-backed chairs, their cushioned seats the same dark blue as the drapes.

Within minutes the porch door closes. I run to the window and see my father walking down the sidewalk, and it doesn't surprise me that he hasn't said goodbye. He is again walking hard. This time, no doubt, his anger is directed at me. I watch him go, my throat aching. He walks further and further away, taking with him the feel of everything familiar, and I turn back to the cold, odourless breath of this bluish room. Missus Louis's earthen eyes find me, and as Henri's low, lazy laugh sounds through the silence, regret strikes a staggering blow through my heart. The pleased smile on the grandmother's knotty old face tightens as I bolt back through the kitchen, grasping at the door handle to chase after Father.

"Do you think he'll take you back?" she cries in a thin voice. "He'll see you on the streets first."

"I can't stay here, I'm going home."

"And impose hardship on those who've been kind to you? Is that what your mother taught you?"

My hands fall to my sides as I stare at this grandmother, the gall of her words bringing bile to my mouth.

"I'm sorry, dear. I'm simply worried about Missus Louis— I've become quite fond of her, and Durwin told me he'd cut their credit if you went back."

I look to the floor with resignation. It sways beneath my feet as though I'm still standing on the deck of the ship, and I am unable to think.

"My dear, I've suffered like Job crossing on that awful ferry. Let me show you to your room. You have a rest, and afterwards we'll talk. We'll make a plan. Really, it's not that far to Newfoundland, I can get you home any time you wish. Come, let me take you to your mother's room. Would you like that?"

She leans on her canes, reaching for my hands. I clasp them behind me like a sullen child and reluctantly follow her down the hall. I'm nauseated and I need to relieve myself and I feel so tired and I want to see my mother's room—*I haven't changed a thing since she left, dear.*

Even with her canes, Grandmother Creed moves with grace. She points to a door partway down the hall. "This is my room, dear." She keeps walking. Opening the door at the end of the hallway, she stands back and smiles. "And this is your mother's."

I step past her and inside the room, dizzying with its pink scrolling wallpaper and billowy muslin that canopies the bed and floats from the windows. Gold lamps with lacy shades sit on skirted tables, and paintings of ballerinas adorn the walls. I look to the closet: it is empty. I gaze around this pink, billowy, princess room. It holds nothing of Mother.

"I was forced to give her things away," says the grandmother sadly. "They were starting to smell old, the house is so damp, especially in winter. I wish now I hadn't. I gave up thinking you'd ever come …" Her voice trails off, but I won't look at her. I really need to relieve myself and I need to lie down and I'm too tired to talk and much, much too tired to filter the grandmother's words for truths. Mercifully, she points me towards the bathroom, then makes her way back down the hall with tiny steps, her shoulders erect, her head held aloft as though it were floating on water.

Pulling myself from a fitful nap, I stare at the pink blossom walls. The cold linen pillowcase is as stiff as Etna's. The strange sounds of too many voices and car motors and horns press against the windows of this unknown house and I sit up, struck again with regret. Hurriedly I leave the room, finding my grandmother sitting at the kitchen table before a setting of little china teacups.

"These belonged to my old granny," she says as I sit, weakened by an empty stomach. "There were times we shared only tea and bread, yet she would lay out her pretty tea things and light a candle. She liked making things nice." She smiles. She's pinned up her hair and traced her eyes with dark pencil and rouged her cheeks. Her hands quiver as she pours tea and it sloshes in the saucer, but her sharp blue eyes hold steadily onto mine as she continues speaking softly. "Did you sleep, Livvy? There's so much street noise, it'll take some getting used to."

"I slept a little."

"I'm glad, dear." She moves aside a small unlit candle to make more room for a basket of bread she nudges towards me. "To this day I light a candle with supper—just me and day-old bread. Cecile hated candles. *Too dark to see the food, Mummy.*" She smiles, pouring milk into our cups. "Take a piece of bread, dear. I promise, it's fresh. The war has its restrictions, but I manage to have fresh bread delivered most mornings. Eat, now. It'll make your stomach feel better."

She nods like a pleased parent as I bite hungrily into the buttered bread. She stirs half a teaspoon of sugar into her tea and passes me the dish. "Just *one* teaspoon, not five, I'm afraid. More restrictions."

I stir my tea, saying nothing, slighting her memory of our shared breakfasts all those years ago. She examines me in my silence.

"You look so much like my granny," she says quietly. "Both you and your mother—the same colour hair, and creamy, silken skin. Perhaps I'll show you a picture of her. Her name was Cecile, too. I called your mother after her." She touches a finger to her bony cheek. "I was quite the ugly duckling, dear. Skin over bone and no nice lips to pout pretty with. I was a seven-month baby," she explains. "The doctors said I wouldn't survive. But old Gran, she took me from the hospital and warmed me in the oven like a bun of bread. I survived, and I've been flaking like a bit of French pastry ever since." She grins. A silence grows between us.

"Where was your mother?" I ask.

She sits forward as though my voice is a gift, despite the unwillingness of the giver. "My mother died giving birth to me," she says sombrely. "I know what it is not to have a mother, Livvy. It feels like I'm living two lives sometimes, mine and hers. My father left on a merchant ship after she died; I never met him. My old granny raised me. Your mother never told you? It's all right, Cecile was always angry with me. I've never understood." She sips her tea, her comment hanging like a question.

"I won't plague you about her, dear. I know your loyalty." Positioning her arms on the table, she clasps her hands like a bargaining parent with a difficult child. "I'll make a deal with you, Livvy. This city sits at the edge of a war, you saw that coming here. It's frightening being alone, listening to the air sirens, cannons blasting. They're just training, but there are times when I stand on the shore, down by Point Pleasant, and see smoke and flames from torpedoed ships just outside the harbour. They can't get in, the U-boats. But it makes for restless nights, being alone, listening to planes droning overhead—always the threat of being bombed. We've become one of the most critical points in this war because of our harbour. I'm glad we're being of service to my dear England, but it leaves us with more than a handful of dodgy fellows walking our streets. It would be good of you to keep me company this winter. Will you stay if I promise to send you home this spring? I'll see to it Durwin does nothing to upset our Mister and Missus Louis."

"Why don't you see to it anyway," I say sharply. "If you cared, wouldn't you want to help them?"

"Of course I would help them, it's simply a matter of timing. This spring I'll be in a much better position, financially."

"What happens this spring?"

The grandmother tuts with annoyance. "We've just met, Livvy. I'm not going to divulge my personal business to you, and you've shared nothing with me. My goodness, you've your mother's spirit, no doubt. I saw that when you stuck out your tongue at me. Do you remember that, the first time I met you? Cheeky little bugger. Then, the next morning you *kicked my leg.* Why *ever* did you do that?"

I shift with impatience. "Why do you *really* want me here?"

"Why *wouldn't* I want you? You're my granddaughter. You're all I've left in the world. Livvy, I have substantial holdings. My husband invested heavily and wisely. It's all willed to you. Plus this house and all the antiques Gran brought with her from England. I've not parted with a thing, they've been in our family for generations. I wanted them for Cecile. I wanted *everything* for Cecile." Her mouth quavers now with unmistakable sorrow, and she raises her cup as though to hide it.

"Cecile would never talk," she says after a slight pause, laying her cup in her saucer. "I never knew what was troubling her, or how to make things right. You're the closest living thing to her. I don't expect you to right things between your mother and me. I just want to be near you, to get to know you a little. What can I do—or give—to persuade you to stay awhile?"

I study her eyes as they plead with mine. *They done something, Durwin and my mother, they done something, they'll burn in hell.* "I have a question," I say quietly.

"Ask," she says.

"That last night you spent with my mother. What did you argue about? I was sent outside," I say to her perplexed look.

"You and her and my father argued, and you left the next morning."

She's slowly shaking her head. "It's been such a long time, dear. We—your mother and I—we always argued over silly things. I'm sorry, I don't remember. Did you ask your father? Why is this so important?"

"You asked if there was something you could give me."

"Yes. Yes, I did. It's just been so long, I've not thought about it. I do remember how unhappy Cecile was with Durwin. I certainly remember that. God forgive me, but your father can be a mean man, and *certainly* never to be trusted. What I've seen here this morning is indicative of that. Can there be a greater cruelty than turning your back on your own child?"

I look resentfully into my tea as she squirrels away from my question about Mother and scampers down this side road with Father. But she snaps me back to attention with a clatter of her cup into her saucer. "More shameful than your doings is his judgment, dear. You remember that. If there's shame to be had, it's on his doorstep. Mind, when I think of his shenanigans with that young serving girl! You need never hang your head for shame, Livvy. You're a young girl led astray. Bow to that and therein is modesty, dear."

I stiffen with anger. "Perhaps shame's something I should learn," I snap, "seeing how everybody thinks it something befitting me."

Grandmother Creed puts her hand apologetically to her mouth. "Oh, *I am sorry.* I know only what your father has told me."

"Does it serve you to believe him? You just said he's not to be trusted, and yet you believe I'm a whore because that's what he tells you?"

"My *dear!*"

"Perhaps it's you who ought to be bowing, for thinking yourself such a fine judge."

"I apologize, Livvy. You are quite right, I did take his word. I've forgotten just how insidious he can be. Forgive me, I am so very sorry. Why don't *you* tell me what happened."

"Why should I divulge my personal life to you? And isn't it *you* who's supposed to be telling *me* something?"

She nods solemnly. "Quite right again. You've your mother's spirit, no doubt. Very well, then. I'll try and think. I vaguely remember an argument of some sort—something Durwin had said. Ohh, if there's one thing I don't forget," she adds crossly, "it's the manner in which he practically forced me from his house that following morning. I walked through those horrible woods, I swear it's what crippled my knees. I've often thought back on what might have happened if I'd stayed. Or, what might *not* have happened. Ohh, what does it matter? As much as Cecile argued with Durwin, she would always take his side over mine."

Her voice softens, fading over words spoken more to herself than to me. "I just can't imagine what it's been like for you, losing her. I still can't get over it—it astounds me that she just—passed away. *My God,* we lose wallets, keys, we don't lose *people.*" Her voice breaks and she presses a wrinkled fist to her mouth. "I'm sorry, dear. Looking at you sitting there, so much like her—*I miss her.*" Tears wet her eyes. She holds out her hand to me, but I cannot take it.

"Why are you so unfeeling towards me, Livvy? Cecile was everything. She was my daughter. I waited and waited for her to come back to me, but she never did. And then she just *died*! Do you think I've not suffered?"

I remember her tears. I remember her hurt as she sobbed bitterly, knelt beside that white box. But I remember Mother's words more. *They done something, Durwin and my mother, they done something, they'll burn in hell.* I look to Grandmother Creed's eyes, half moons of blue like Mother's.

"Lloyd's of London. Missus Louis told me things about Lloyd's of London."

"Lloyd's of London? You mean the insurance agency?"

"I just want to know the whole story."

She studies my face. Perhaps she sees that I know nothing. Perhaps she sees too that I'm unable to move beyond this point of not knowing about that night, for she shakes her head like someone cornered. "God forgive me, he's your father, but I've not put myself here. Durwin and his father, Captain Higgs, they stole from me." She falters. "You've lost your mother, Livvy, I don't want to be the one turning you from your father as well."

"I must have the truth."

She nods. "Well, I say it again, it's him who's put me here. I swear, that man blames me for his father's death. It was their bad judgment—Durwin and his father's—and their *greed* that took the ship upon the rocks. And kept me from recovering any of my losses. I've never spoken of this," she says, looking uncomfortably from side to side, as though Father and Captain Higgs were each sitting there. "They offloaded five tons of dried codfish from my ship, twenty years ago," she says. "We were carrying fifty tons to England."

The grandmother continues, saying that Captain Higgs told her and Lloyd's that water from a storm had got down the hole through the hatch and threatened to spoil the whole fifty tons of fish with mildew. So they had to make a dump. Lloyd's paid for the claim, and then the exact same thing happened two years later, and another eight thousand pounds were dumped. Lloyd's became suspicious, since there hadn't been a violent storm reported in the area.

"They should have figured it out then," Grandmother Creed says angrily, "but after a bit of arguing, they paid up again. Then, when the shipwreck happened and Higgs drowned, Lloyd's took no pity on the loss of life, and simply refused to pay the insurance without an investigation. There wasn't any proof, but they suspected the same as I did—that the ship ought *not* to have been so near Sables d'Or that evening. Higgs took her there, where he was offloading fish again, just as he'd done the first two times. They had a fine business going, offloading the fish into another boat and then reselling it through their store in Newfoundland, meanwhile putting claims through to the insurance agency that the fish had been dumped into the sea. But their greed caught up with them, didn't it? They pillaged my ship till their greed caught up with them. I don't mean to sound unfeeling, dear, but they paid in the end, didn't they?"

The grandmother tries to keep a satisfied look from her face. "It's not my pleasure to tell such sordid stories about your father, even if I do dislike him. But I didn't recover *the half* of what I lost. Higgs was a greedy man and he passed on that nasty trait to his son. They'd grapple with angels if there was coin to be had. Then Durwin kept coming to me after the drowning of his father, demanding his share of the insurance money. He simply wouldn't believe me when I told him of the investigation. It lasted five or six years, and my claim was rejected. I sent your father the official letter from Lloyd's rejecting our claim, but I swear, to this day, Durwin thinks I've outwitted him. Are you sure you want to hear more, Livvy? It's an unsightly tale."

I sit still, remembering that day in the store when I'd handed him the mail and he'd become enraged upon reading one of the letters. He had started drinking that night. "I want to hear all of it," I say.

"Very well, then. That night we fought—the night you ask about—I do remember he was off his trolley. He hated my coming. He believed I would tell Cecile about his pillaging my ship to stock his store. I would never have told her. She would've blamed me for breaking them apart, and he trusted that."

Grandmother Creed falls silent for a moment, her face flushing with anger. "It was because of Durwin's hatred of me that I seldom visited Cecile. And the reason she would never visit me, I'm sure of it. I always wrote her. But she never answered my letters. Perhaps she never received them. Perhaps he kept them from her. He stole my daughter, Livvy. He stole her with lies; only God knows what lies he told her. Forgive me, dear, but your father, Durwin Higgs, is one ruthless soul."

I look away from her, seeing Father's face bearing down on mine with his crow-black eyes. *I'll starve them, I'll blacken their name like a winter spud, they'll be eating salt fish and cowhide before the winter's halfway through.*

So loud are my father's words in my head that I grimace. It is the first crumb I've tossed onto that emptied table between the grandmother and me, and she hungrily snatches it. "You've seen his hate, haven't you?" she says eagerly. "Your mother saw it too, finally she saw it."

"That night? She saw it that night?"

"His malice. The way he treated me, the way he practically drove me from his house the next morning."

"But you've not told me why you fought."

"I don't remember why we fought. We didn't, it was nothing. But she saw how he was. How he was treating me—how he was treating *her.* Not letting her work in his store." Her eyes brighten. "Yes. Yes, that's what they fought about, his not letting her work in his store. Now, I'll not say anything more against your father."

She sweeps her hand towards the dining room, the living room. "This is yours. All of it, whether you stay with me or not, I've willed everything to you. Should you sell it, there will be substantial money, along with my holdings, to last you into old age. I ask just one thing. Your Missus Louis. I ask that you brighten her house with a coat of paint, and perhaps a new roof. And fix it so she'll never have to depend on Durwin Higgs, or anyone else ever again, for her food and supplies."

"Why do you care so much? You hardly know her."

"That woman gave to my daughter and my granddaughter. I'm not long for this world, Livvy. I expect to be gone before her. I wrote to her in a letter that I intend to put things right, starting with you. And I'll fix things with Missus Louis this coming spring when my finances are in order. It would please me greatly if her last days were freed from any threats posed by your father."

Those last words are uttered deep and hard. "Will you stay, Livvy—just for a while, while I set things right?"

I stare into the grandmother's eyes and for one brief moment I see past them into that secret spot of vengeance she holds in her heart for my father. It is a vengeance that feeds into mine against them both. Other words of Mother's come to me: *Like the fox, she's like the fox,* but those words are faint and I hear myself speaking above them.

"Till spring. I will stay till spring." Unable to share in the grandmother's smile, I rise, rubbing at a pain above my brow.

"My dear, I'm delighted. Go for a lie-down, you look so tired. Shall I bring you anything?"

I shake my head and hurry to my mother's room and sink onto her bed. Her cries grow louder: *Like the fox, like the fox.* I cover my face and try to deepen my breathing. My chest, it's tight, it grows tighter, I fight to breathe. Glass splinters around me and a sharp pain reverberates through my skull. *Like the fox, like the fox ...*

"Oh, God, oh God. Don't move, Livvy, don't move, there's glass, you broke a vase when you fell. Are you all right? Can you see? You struck your head. How many fingers, tell me, how many fingers?"

My heart is fluttering like a hummingbird's. My head hurts, something struck it, something must've struck it hard, it hurts so much. "Girl!" I call out, for she's rattling nonsense about ambulances and concussions. "Girl!" I open my eyes. It's Gen, she's leaning over me, crying, her eyes fraught with fear, and I'm lying here on the floor in Grandmother Creed's room with glass all around me.

SEVEN

"Can you hear me?" pleads Gen. "Livvy, can you hear me, how many fingers?"

My chest. I touch it gingerly. It's sore, and my heart still beats like a hummingbird's.

"Livvy, speak to me. Can you see? How many fingers?"

I focus wearily on her fingers. Three, she has three fingers.

"How many? How many fingers?" she demands, her voice rising hysterically.

"You—you've lost two," I whisper, and her face breaks into relief.

"Such a clever old woman," she mutters. I try to get up, but she holds me back. "Don't move," she orders. "Wait, will you wait. Oh, hell," she cries as I try to sit up. "What happened? When you got out of your chair, you looked dizzy."

"I—I haven't been eating. It's— I'm tired."

"Oh, punish me some more," she says. "This is all my fault, damn, goddamn. And you're wheezing like a croupy youngster, don't move. Where's your puffer?"

I shake my head weakly. "My room."

Gen's off like a pup. I hear her scrabble through my room door, and within the minute she's back. "I've got it, here, I've got it. Open your mouth. Christ, you're wheezing *worse* than a croupy youngster."

I open my mouth, sucking in the cold mist she shoots down my throat. I hold it for as long as I can, and let go.

"Frig, Livvy, you knocked yourself out. You must've hit hard to knock yourself out, let me feel. Christ, there's a big bump. We need to call an ambulance."

I shake my head. "Just—just help me up."

"Wait, Livvy—here, lean on me." She's on her knees, wrapping an arm around my waist as I try to stand. "There, put your arm around my neck. And what's this about foxes? You really freaked me out."

Foxes. I sag against her. I am the fox. I outwitted myself with the grandmother. I traded my passionate heart for one of vengeance and am no better than Father. I press my face against Gen's hair, still damp and smelling of melted snow.

"Are you all right?" she asks. "You're wheezing like hell. Okay, let's walk," she says as we shuffle, stiff like cardboard cutouts, to the settee.

"Hey, boy," I whisper to Willaby, who's crept from under the rocker, tail swishing nervously as I crumple onto the settee. The wind rattles the windows and I remember that there's a snowstorm and the roads aren't plowed. Good, no ambulance. I feel breathless, my heart's still fluttering. I breathe carefully, my hand pressing against the fluttering pulse in my throat, afraid to let go for fear I may flutter away with it. I look about frantically, I'd thought death a distant thing. It is here. It has come. I feel the distance shortening between me and God. But I'm not ready, not ready. I want to walk this last mile with my sensibilities. I want the cats fixed away and the house cleaned and myself properly dressed and laid out in my bed. Gen covers me with the blanket I gave her earlier, and grabs the phone. "No!" I say with a harshness that surprises us both.

"I'm sorry, but I've got to call an ambulance."

I look to the window being pummelled with wind-driven snow.

"They might find a way to get here; we can at least try," she says, but the urgency in my eyes stalls her. She lays down the phone. "I'm afraid of a concussion," she whispers. "If anything happens, I'll never forgive myself. Tell me again what happened."

I look at her tiredly. "Please. I just need water."

She looks from me to the cuffs on her feet. She needs to believe me. But she has courage; no matter her cuffed feet, she would call. It comforts me, that gesture of courage, and I smile.

"What the hell. You're smiling?" exclaims Gen. "You near beat your brains out and we're snowbound and I'm in cuffs with third-degree burns and a social-work degree pending, and you're smiling? The past two days you've been scowling like a scorned child, and you pick this minute to smile? Kindly, share."

She's wearing me down. She's batting around words like a kitten with a ball, yet her eyes churn like a trapped feral.

"Please—make tea," I beg.

A dubious look at me and she drags her butt like a dog with an itch across the floor to the kitchen. My feet are cold. I shift about, trying to find comfort, but everything feels wrong and I'm cold, my courage ebbing. I need courage. Should she call an ambulance and they take me, I'll need courage to carry me through the turmoil and confusion awaiting like cloaked daggers outside my door. I haven't bathed in two days now, and the floors, I haven't swept them. I think of Sunderland and the neighbours peering through their windows with horror and pity as I'm carried outside like a sack of rotting sticks inside this dirty old dress.

What's this, what's this now, I lie here, dying, and I'm worried about my dress? Vanity, yes, vanity. I am not too unlike Grandmother Creed. At least she knew her vanity, whereas mine masquerades as pride. Gen drags herself from the kitchen, sliding a tray beside her with two steaming mugs of tea. A blast of wind jars the house, the lights dim then brighten again. "Wicked. Just what we need, the lights to go," she says. And then, "Listen! You hear something?"

She stands on her knees, ears perked towards the porch door, then towards my bedroom. I listen along with her, but hear nothing but the wind. "Someone's out there, I hear something," she says, a tinge of fright in her voice. "Stu. It's got to be Stu," she suddenly exclaims. "I'll go look through your room window."

She drags herself down the hallway and into my room. I hear her knocking at the window, and then dropping onto her knees and pulling herself back up the hallway. "It *is* Stu," she cries. "He's got someone with him. Listen, Livvy, we can do it here—file the cuffs—in the living room. Or would you rather we do it downstairs? I know the guy with Stu, he's, well, he's not pleasant. He's not going to hurt us. Look, we'll just do it downstairs. They've got flashlights, we'll be fine. But you can't go to sleep, you had that fall, you might have a concussion."

"Put my tea on the table there, so I can reach it," I say, as much to assure her as to satisfy any need of nourishment. Then I wave her adamantly towards the door, closing my eyes as she starts down the basement stairs on her behind, *thud thud thud*. I lift a hand to gauge my strength, and it falls limply against my chest. I try to lift my head, I cannot. I feel faint, light-headed. I

am breathless, sweating. There's a pain in my chest. Nothing. I can
do nothing. This is it, then. I am walking through the valley of
shadows. Yet I feel no fear, just a deep unrest. Willaby leaps onto
the settee, sniffing me. Tuff crawls from beneath the rocker and
lifts his nose, long whiskers scenting the air.

"It's okay, fellas," I whisper, but their instincts tell them differently. Doesn't matter that they've lived in comfort all their lives,
they've kept their instincts. I lost mine. The day I bargained with
Grandmother Creed, I lost mine. I see her now, sitting at the
table that morning, that long-ago morning, her vengeful heart
bargaining with mine.

The house shakes to another gust of wind and a cold draft
sweeps across my face. She is here, Grandmother Creed, I feel her.
She sits on my chest, pressuring my pulse. She'll not let me flutter
away before she's extracted her due, for she knows the shadow of
the valley, its path trodden with heavy heels and muddied with
confessions from the frightened and the secret hearted. And it's
my confession she waits for now, and rightfully so.

Willaby leaps to the back of the settee with a low growl.
He senses a presence, too, senses its unfriendliness. As did that
ratty little grey that I met that first morning Father brought me
to Grandmother Creed's door. She kept coming back, meowing
fiercely outside the picture window, her cold jade eyes searching
past Grandmother Creed for me, the one soul, perhaps, who had
offered to pet that tender spot inside of her not yet turned wild.

"Keep her if you can tame her," Grandmother Creed offers,
quick to encourage any sort of attachment between me and her
home. "But she must stay in the basement. I do have allergies,
dear."

I jar the basement door each day and set out food. I call her
Ashes. I can never touch her; she skirts to the side the second I

reach towards her. She's like me—I skirt sideways, too, each time my grandmother tries to touch me. And yet, like Ashes, I hungrily eat each tidbit Grandmother Creed tosses me about Mother: *She was a happy, gurgling baby, dear, with pudgy arms and legs and a dimply face. She didn't talk till she was three, and grew shy and clung to her father, who, when he wasn't fixing or pulling teeth, spent all his time cuddling with her on the sofa, telling her stories about toothbrushes and tooth fairies with bad teeth.*

"Did she cling to you, too?" I ask one day.

She is sitting in her rocker by the window with the drapes and blackout curtains drawn open. The sun brightens the first snowfall outside and chases shadows across her bony cheeks as she leans over her daily newspaper that's laid out before her on a footstool. Her hair has been freshly washed, and is swept back into a clutch of fat finger curls. Her mouth is a soft pink and her fitted, satiny dress floats in a rush of frills around her skinny calves. "It's wonderful having someone to dress for again," she'd gushed to the beautician she called in to do her hair and nails on my third or fourth day with her. "Livvy dear, are you sure you won't have your hair done?"

She had laughed along with the blonde, primped hairdresser as I vigorously shook my head and kept on polishing the spindly legs of one of her side tables. It is the bargain I have made with her to earn my keep—and to help with my snooping, Missus Louis's words haunting my ears, *There's something there for you, luv.* It helps me, too, escape the keen eyes and ears of the grandmother who is as hungry for me and my memories as I am for her hidden truths.

"Well, did she?" I persist as Grandmother Creed keeps looking at her paper as though she hasn't heard me.

"Did she what, dear?"

"Cling to you, the way she clung to her father."

"No, dear. Orrick—her father—was always home. At least, in the evenings and weekends. I travelled a lot. Did Cecile tell you?"

"No."

"She told you nothing of my travels? My work? What *did* she tell you about me?"

"I—I don't remember." I turn back to polishing the cabinet drawers.

"I would've thought she told you about my travels." A tinge of disappointment marks her tone. "But then, she hated it so much. I raised a lot of money for charities, dear. I travelled around Nova Scotia and New Brunswick by train, and took the boat to Prince Edward Island a few times as well, looking for the greatest need and sharing out the money we raised. I felt it my duty to search for the greatest need. And then, during the Depression, I became more deeply involved." She takes off her glasses, rubbing her eyes. "I saw so much, Livvy, men and women in lineups for hours for a bowl of soup and cup of tea. Right here in Halifax, just down the street, people were hungry and cold. The miseries we suffer today are pale in comparison. But it brought me a different kind of misery, didn't it? I lost my daughter."

"Why?"

"Why? I'm not sure why. Perhaps I left her alone too much. There were times I wanted her to accompany me, but she was never interested. I needed to do my work, dear—there's such need in the world and a greater need in me, no doubt, to give. But I loved being a mother. The best start in any child's life is a good mother, I've always known that. You had that, didn't you? I saw it the first moment I met you and you stuck out your tongue—protecting your mummy from that strange old woman." She grins, then swipes it from her face, holding up hands emptied like a pauper's.

"I didn't see it. With all the sickness and hunger I witnessed—and she had so much of everything, food and clothes. But she didn't have her mummy, did she? The overeating. I saw it afterwards, how she tried to make herself ugly. She knew how much I loved her pretty hair and cute little frocks—oh, she was such a pretty child. I tried telling her about the poor people, and about sickness. I showed her pictures I'd taken. I thought that if she saw my work and how little others had— But she would never look. She never told you about those things?"

I shake my head, working the polishing cloth into another darkened corner of the cabinet drawer.

"I would've thought she'd said something about my travelling. She must have shared *some* thoughts? None?"

"I don't remember."

"Well, you were so young. She probably shared lots, perhaps you were too young to remember. Or too busy playing to pay attention."

Her words lope around me like question marks, her eyes, persistent, on mine.

"She thought people who dressed up figured themselves better than others," I say.

The grandmother leans forward. "She said that?"

I nod.

"What else?"

I shrug.

She leans back with a slight nod. "Yes. Well, she always held that silly notion."

I stop polishing. "Why's it silly?"

"People dress for many reasons. I dressed every time I went serving in a soup kitchen. It showed people they were worthy of dressing for. We'd expect nothing less from a waitress in a fine restaurant, so why not dress for the poor? I kept hoping Cecile would outgrow those selfish notions."

"That's a lie," I say with anger. "My mother was never selfish. She was always helping Missus Louis."

"Oh, my soul, I'm sorry, dear, I'm speaking about her younger years. Aren't we all like that in our youth, putting ourselves first? Most certainly your mother was generous and loving.

"That was a rather harsh accusation, Livvy," she says after a short pause, "calling me a liar. You said it so quickly. Is that what you think of me, that I tell you lies?"

I've become sullen. The grandmother grins. "There's that scowly face again—just like your mother's used to be when we argued. Did I think I'd see the day when I would welcome it." She sighs deeply. "Cecile and I argued all the time, most times over nothing—like you and me just then. I bodge things all the time, Livvy. I'm just a frail soul, dear, we all are. You mustn't stay angry with me—tut tut, look at her face, I swear she's going to kick me again."

I reluctantly smile and Grandmother Creed exclaims, "Now, isn't that the sun. Be patient with me, Livvy. I've lived alone for so long I don't know how to temper my tone and watch my words. I confess, too, I fought so much with your mother, and then with myself after she left, that I've no more heart for fighting."

Later, after she's been reading for a while and I've finished cleaning the furniture, she suddenly looks up at me. "A question for you," she says. "Do you feel disloyal to your mother by being here with me?"

I dally with putting the cleaning things into the bottom cupboard. "Would you show me the pictures from your work?" I ask. "And of my mother, if you have them."

Grandmother Creed nods. "I'll dig them out of the trunk, first thing. You know, I did stop travelling after a time. I tried sorting things through with Cecile, but she wasn't one for speaking of her feelings; she kept things to herself—rather like yourself there," she adds.

I flush and take myself to the basement to feed Ashes. The grandmother watches me go. She always watches—we're like two old misers baiting each other with tidbits, trying to get at the bone of contention we each feel resides in the other. No doubt that bone of contention is Mother, and no doubt the grandmother is right in believing I feel disloyal to Mother. But not for being here. It is Mother's truth I am seeking. It is in those moments when the grandmother chuckles from deep in her heart over some comment made during tea or in passing, or her eyes twinkle with a rash of merriment and she impulsively touches my hand, that a veil drops between us, imprinted with Mother's pale face staring at me accusingly. It is then that I skirt sideways like Ashes, taking myself to the basement, sorting laundry, laying out cat food, letting myself out through the basement door and strolling through the graveyard. It's a relief to escape the grandmother's eyes, questioning me, bargaining, pleading from behind her teacups and the pages of her books as she watches me move through her house as swiftly and competently as Etna, sorting, polishing, sweeping, mopping.

I've not the courage yet to walk through the maze of city streets and its throngs of soldiers. "It's not safe," Grandmother Creed has warned many times. Listening to the constant drone of planes overhead, the sirens and ship horns and whistles sounding from the harbour and the distant blasting of cannons, I believe her.

It is the graveyard that intrigues me. It is alive during the day with wild cats, Ashes' family, I call them. They stretch across the warmed granite headstones on bright winter days—about nineteen or twenty; I've counted. They vanish behind headstones and bushes when I come near them. They pad on frozen paws into the grandmother's yard in the evening, where I lay out food for them. They are matted and dirty and crawling with worms, they are half blinded and clever. They are curious and combative. And patient. I learn, like them, to be silent and patient as I lurk through the grandmother's house, searching through drawers and cupboards for signs of Mother, of Father, and of that sorrow I saw in Missus Louis's eyes. For that, too, lies in this house.

No doubt the grandmother takes herself to her room to escape me, too, sometimes. I watch her as I shake the rugs and dust and sweep and damp-mop the wooden floors, and scrub and oil the clay kitchen tiles. She's as vigilant as Father in greeting the mailman, I note. Exchanging the latest news with him about the war, the heightening attacks on the convoys. After closing the door behind him she hobbles to her room on her canes, taking the coveted packets and envelopes along with her, shaking her head at my anticipation of a letter from Missus Louis. I try to hide my disappointment; it is word of Henri that I seek. And some other thing that I don't know, that might take me closer to learning that secret thing Missus Louis has spoken of. As with Father, I think this *thing* might come in the post, and each time Grandmother Creed hobbles back out of her room after depositing her mail, I lift my nose, scenting her face for change, her eyes for thought, her words for hidden meanings as she takes her seat by the window, speaking of some small thing, a bill, a notice. Sometimes she says nothing at all, her face quiet, contemplative as she takes her newspaper or book from its resting place on her side table.

"I can get it," I say one morning when the picture window is greyed with thick, falling snow and the mailman's steps are heard outside.

"And take my only bit of exercise for the day?" she mutters, rising, cranky this morning with the pain in her legs. She goes into the porch and returns a moment later, leaning heavily on her canes, her freed hands holding the thick, glossy pages of the Eaton's catalogue.

"It's finally come," she exclaims. "Now, this is the one thing your mother and I enjoyed together—looking through the catalogue. She *so* loved the pretty frocks. Well, before she started putting on weight. She never sat with me after that. You look perturbed, dear. Livvy, why so sad?"

"Is there still no letter from Missus Louis?"

"No. I can't think why she hasn't written yet."

"Perhaps she didn't get our letter?"

"Well, we know she received our letter, else she wouldn't have sent the note."

"She sent a note?"

"Yes, didn't I tell you?"

"You didn't tell me about no note."

"I'm sorry, dear, she didn't say anything, except that she's down with the flu and will write more later. That's all, two or three lines, just to say she received our letter and will write to us soon."

I turn and go to the kitchen.

"Don't look so tragic, Livvy," she calls out. "She'll write more. Put the kettle on while you're there, and let's look at the winter dresses." She comes into the kitchen and, putting her canes behind her chair, sits at the table, riffling through the catalogue. I smell Mother wafting from the pages and an unbearable loneliness creeps through me. I cut up cheese for the grandmother, fighting to hold back tears. Missus Louis sent a note, just a note. The swish of the catalogue pages fills my ears and I feel Mother's breath warm on my cheek, the musty smell of her cigarette smoke.

"Such lovely frocks," Grandmother Creed exclaims. "The new fashions love slender legs, we're in high style, dear, with our small bones. Perhaps I should order us something. Sit, Livvy, let's pick out a nice Sunday dress, would you like that?" *You've got the bones of a shepherd girl, you clump through the rooms like a sow, you clump through the rooms like a sow on wooden legs.*

"Such a silly thing, fashions," I remark nastily.

"Why *ever* would you say such a thing. Fashion is very important: it's being a part of our society, making good with people. There must be some things we all share, else everything would be a babble."

"It serves vanity to dress one's self in fancy clothes."

"Now, aren't you sounding like Cecile. As I told her, there are reasons to dress well. Some of us want to be liked. That might sound trite, but it helps with gathering money and things for charities when people like you. You have to put something out for them to judge you on. Jesus was a fine fellow, but his robe and sandals wouldn't do well with door-to-door campaigning these days—for one thing he'd be frostbitten," she adds with a silly giggle.

"We should fashion our minds more," I say irritably. "We've more chance of taking that with us than a flapper dress."

"The flapper dress! Good God, Livvy, that died with our old politicians. Come to think of it—the new politicians have taken us right back into the same war. I swear, the *only* thing that changes is our fashions. Perhaps it's a cover for the bodgy devils that never change, and that'll keep us warring for the next hundred years.

"Why are you so *morose?*" she asks as I place a cup of tea before her and turn back to the counter.

I feel her watching me as I spread a few crackers onto the cheese dish.

"Do you mind my chatter, Livvy? I'll be more quiet, dear. Your mother hated my chatter, too. She was always shouting *Mummy, be quiet.*" She sighs. "I swear, I can still hear her sometimes when I'm sitting here alone. I welcome it, even though she's still shouting at me to be quiet. But she wasn't always shouting. She was quiet like you. And *always* looking at the catalogues and books. She wasn't a good reader. I tried to help her with that, but she was too impatient with herself. She would've made a fine teacher if she'd stayed with her lessons. If she hadn't left with him," she ends grimly, then quickly adds, "I'm sorry, dear, I shouldn't harbour such thoughts. It's so *good* having you. Sometimes, in the early morning when I'm lying awake in bed, I hear you padding from your room and I think for a moment it's her. *I miss her,*" she adds. "Loneliness is a horrible thing. It creeps into my pores, keeping me awake at night. It is my greatest enemy."

I listen to her words with a shudder. I know her need. It resembles my own for Missus Louis, the girls, Henri's fingers caressing the soft underside of my arm. And for all those times I sat alone amongst the sand dunes, searching for Mother. And should my grandmother say another word right now, I risk throwing myself onto her bosom and baring my soul in all its shadow.

"Do you ever feel lonely, Livvy?"

"No," I say too loudly. I sit across the table from her, gripping my mug of tea, its heat near burning my hands.

"I always think back on my old granny when I'm lonely," says Grandmother Creed in a whispery tone. "And my mother, even though I never knew her. It gives me comfort to think of them walking and scuffing through this old house."

"This house?" I ask with surprise.

"Of course this house, dear. Where do you think they lived? I swear, Livvy, do you listen to anything I say? This is your old granny's home. And all these furnishings are hers. Mind you, I've put a few pennies into keeping everything upgraded, but I can still feel my granny. It's such a comfort to be living here in her house, and knowing that my mother, too, ran through these rooms. That's how I think of them: my granny chasing my mother after she just broke something. I swear, sometimes at night when I can't sleep and I think of them, I can hear the floors creaking beneath their feet. I love those moments, they never frighten me, they bring me such comfort."

I look around the room, imagining a frail old woman shuffling through these rooms with hair like Mother's. I try to imagine the grandmother as a girl running down the hallway.

"Now, aren't those smart," says Grandmother Creed, her nose near touching the catalogue as she examines a page of dresses. "Such classic tailoring. I love a tight waistline, and those padded shoulders give such an elegant look. Oh, my. Perhaps you and Cecile are right, I am utterly vain, but I just love nice tailoring."

I study her as she pores over a glossy page of shoes: her narrow shoulders, the tiny bones of her throat above the little pearl buttons on her dress collar, her wrinkled mouth and wrinkled skin sagging beneath bony cheeks.

She tips her head sideways and the trickster light shows now the smooth curve of her neck, the tips of her little pink ears, and I see the pink-lipped woman of earlier years, her smile shaped by milky-white teeth and her yellow hair curling around a slender neck held erect on her slender form. Could such a mother tuck into the curl of a sand dune? And where would the fishy-wet hands of a child grasp onto?

The shyster sun withdraws, leaving the saddened face of an

old woman looking up at me. "Your mother claimed to hate fashion as she grew older," she says chattily, turning the page. "But I noticed the catalogues stacked beneath her sofa. She had some fondness for a pretty frock, else she wouldn't have kept the catalogues.

"Well, be quiet, then," she says agreeably to my silence. "I know your mother blamed me for her unhappiness. I imagine she's convinced you of that; why else aren't you speaking to me right now? I swear, Livvy, you are the most *morose* young woman. I'll simply take the catalogue to my room and talk to myself in the mirror. It always talks back—it likes fashion, too."

She reaches for her canes and it feels as though I'm standing on the edge of a cliff with a gust of wind swiping my back. "You told her she had the bones of a shepherd girl. You told her she clumps through the rooms like a sow on wooden legs."

The grandmother blanches and then looks at me grimly. "I wouldn't utter words like those to a harlot staggering the streets. Cecile said that?" She lays back her canes, her voice breathless at first, and then crackling with anger: "Cecile had her way of seeing things. But I could never refute her for she never shared her thoughts. She was cowardly in that, in never giving me a chance to defend myself. She had her way of changing things too, to suit her needs; I saw that in her as a child. She fooled her father many times with that—and in the end that's what caused the most trouble between her father and me, his torment in never knowing what was real between Cecile and me."

She stops talking, the rapid sounding of her breathing filling the room. "I'm sorry, dear. I've worked so hard not to feel angry." She slides the catalogue towards me, her eyes blurring with tears. "Take it to your room, or put it in the trash. The good Lord's exacting another penance from this foolish mortal." Raising herself onto her canes, she hobbles off to her room, the door closing softly behind her.

                   ❧

Sunlight bounces off snow, blinding the picture window and brightening the kitchen as I add more pepper to a dipper of drawn butter for the salt fish. Grandmother Creed emerges from her room after several hours of silence. She shuffles on her canes into the kitchen and sits quietly at the table.

"Are you going to talk to me, Livvy?"

I am unsure what to say. I take a quick look; she is fondling the handles of her canes as though they're puppies. "Heaven's sakes, Livvy, will you talk with me? I'm sorry about my outburst."

"I'm not angry." I lower my head, speaking with humility. "I don't remember clearly how Mother said some things. Perhaps— perhaps she was saying them of herself," I add, thinking of some things Missus Louis once said to Mother while they sat carding wool together.

The grandmother's face is all earnestness. "You must think clearly, Livvy. I'm not saying your mother lied. She just had a way of shaping things, but always from truth. Can you remember exactly what she said?"

"I think it best if you stop needling me."

"*Needling* you." She looks at me confusedly, then sits back. "Perhaps I do, dear. I keep wanting to live through those last years of her life. Is that such a bad thing? Isn't that what you want— to live through those years your mother had with me?"

I stir the drawn butter, my mouth flinching with guilt. The grandmother doesn't notice, she's wringing her hands and looking sombrely about the kitchen. "What matters is what one thinks. If Cecile believed I said those wretched things to her, then that is what's true for her, isn't it? You know what's sad, dear—perhaps I did try to fashion her after myself: curling her hair and dressing her in pretty clothes. But isn't that what mothers do? Didn't she do the same with you? I swear, Livvy, the first time I saw you scrabbling out of the thicket on all fours, I thought you were a monkey falling out of a tree."

The image draws a reluctant smile and I turn down the heat on the stove. "Will you have some fish and potatoes? It's ready."

"Aren't you having some?" she asks, noticing I've laid a place only for her.

"I'm not hungry. I want to walk." I set her dinner before her and sit for a moment, finishing off a cup of tea.

"If this old table could talk," says Grandmother Creed. "I'm sure there's many a teacup that was rattled over its face throughout the years." She pauses. "Are you ill?" she asks, staring at me.

"No, I'm quite fine."

"You look pale. I imagine you're a bit homesick. Forgive me," she says after a small silence, "but some things cannot be hidden for long. Are you with child? Don't look so shocked, Livvy. It's quite possible."

"No. It is not," I say adamantly, and get up.

"For pity's sake, sit down. After what your father said about Henri—"

"Damn what Father said."

The grandmother chuckles. "So like your mother. Well, I don't defend Durwin, but Henri's shenanigans have set us all on edge."

"What shenanigans?"

"What, dear?" The grandmother pushes aside her plate. "Perhaps I'll eat later. Why don't we both dress and go to the club? I'm sure they'll give me a table without having to line up; I did much for their patronage before the war. We used to have our meetings there, the ladies' charity group." She reaches for her canes, refusing to look at me as I stare at her. Impatiently, she lays aside the canes and faces me.

"I swear, I'm in trouble every time I open my mouth. And the way you look at me sometimes is so hostile. It's not me who's punishing you, but your father."

"Tell me about Henri."

"There's nothing that sets him aside from other young men, they're all the same. Born maestros when it comes to playing the girls. They all try to woo them with their little sad songs and wheedling rods—"

"Their what?"

"Their rods, their wheedling rods, or however you say it these days. Oh, don't look so shocked, Livvy. Things don't change too much from one generation to another, and I'm sure young men never change in what they want with young girls."

"Just tell me," I cry out with frustration.

She purses her mouth, then reluctantly begins to speak. "The Reverend Cooley could be removed from his parish if you divulge this conversation, do you understand me, Livvy? You must promise me you will never speak of it.

"Very well, then," she replies to my nod. "Reverend Cooley spoke to me one day, after service. There was a young girl from his parish who'd gotten herself with child. He confided in me *simply* because he knew my connection to Henri's family and thought I could be of some help. She named Henri as the father. There. Now I've told you. She swore to the reverend that Henri had told her he loved her and had asked her to marry him. But he ran off when she told him about the child. She was distraught and so were her parents. I wrote letters to Missus Louis and Esmée, but they stood by Henri and denounced the girl. The girl's mother let her keep the child." Grandmother Creed shrugs. "I spoke with her several months ago. God help her, she's a sweet little thing, shy and sweet. And the boy is the spit of Henri.

"I'm sorry, dear," she whispers as I get up, take my cup to the sink and rinse it. She pulls herself onto her canes and stands quietly, watching me, then makes her way slowly to her room.

I wipe down the sink and the table. I sweep the kitchen floor and shift the upholstered chairs in the living room from the direct sunlight so the fabric won't fade. I wipe the wooden surfaces of the cabinet and tables, moving the damp cloth with the direction of the grain. It dries and I wipe it again with polish. I see his eyes in the dark of the oak, I hear his deep lazy voice, I feel his fingers soft as anything, stroking my belly.

Pulling on a winter coat, I go outside and trail through the few inches of snow to the back of the house and lean against the fence. The cats aren't there. A hoarse meow sounds from behind me. Ashes. She's crouched by the basement door waiting to be let in. She looks cold. I sit in the snow beside her, my back against the house, and she lets me touch her for the first time. I stroke her ears, staring into the snow clouds thickening the sky. It was only a few times we laid together, but I wanted more, expected more. I shouldn't have left, but I had to—and I was going back. Soon, quite soon I was going back.

What does it matter? He had taken her and denied her before he laid with me, and spoke nothing of it. *God help her, she's a sweet little thing, shy and sweet, and the boy the spit of Henri.* Ashes touches my cheek with a sheathed claw. Some of the other cats approach, sitting at a distance from me. They're expecting food. That night

I open my bedroom window and Ashes leaps onto the sill, then onto my bed, curling beside my pillow.

It is morning, it is one of many mornings in their sameness and I get out of bed into the cool air and the familiar band sounds coming from a nearby school that has been overhauled into a training centre for servicemen. I dress and make tea and eggs for Grandmother Creed, who is already up. She's almost always up before me, sitting by the window, scanning the newspaper.

"War's a poor business, Livvy," she says over the rustling of her paper. "I can't find the good in it, no matter whose side I study it from. I don't understand it—not that understanding would make it an easier monster to live with."

After breakfast, her face fraught with concern, she asks, "Is it safe to be going out, dear?" She tries to stand, but her legs are bothering her this morning, and she sits back with frustration. "I'd like to walk with you, if these silly bones would gain strength."

"I won't go far."

"You'll be careful. Everything's gone pear-shaped out there, the city's not equipped for all those soldiers roaming about."

I assure her I'll be back soon. She doesn't like that I've started taking walks downtown, and warns me constantly about the threats posed by this city with a war just outside its gates, a war that has doubled its population with servicemen and transient labourers. The news about Henri has set off that sense of aloneness inside me again, as did my failing grades in school that drove me to walking the hillsides alone, feeling confused and uncoupled with myself. But unlike the hills back home, I find no companionship with aloneness here. The outside air is too taut with the roar of planes cutting through the skies and the distant boom of cannons and sirens and ships' horns moaning from the harbour.

I feel the same sense of disconnection from the people swarming the Halifax streets as I felt amongst the people of Sables d'Or. I see myself in shop windows and think of Mother walking these very streets. It encourages me to walk further each time, past brothels and canteens, through narrow and narrower roads. I come to Water Street, where Father left me standing alone my first morning here, all those weeks ago. The salty winds of the harbour strike cold against my face. I hold onto a light pole so as not to be swept away by a loud knot of servicemen quarrelling amongst themselves as they bump against me, making their way along the sidewalk. I watch an older woman sharply elbow her way through a group of laughing air force men in blue, piling out of a pub.

I look for the spot where Father left me, and find it. I remember my panic, my holding tight to a frightened bladder threatening to stream piss down my legs. That he would leave me alone—a slip of a girl from an isolated strip of beach—on this war-frenzied street where even veteran citizens tread with care. Anger stirs inside of me. It stirs deep, for it has been growing for days now, in that tender spot in my belly that Henri had stroked. But it finds nothing there to feed upon but the emptied expectations of a silly girl. Perhaps they mightn't have been emptied if not for that crow-blackened heart of Father's driving me from home. There now, that's something for it to feed upon. My eyes fall onto the grey ships staggered like whales across the harbour. I see Father's face etched against each massive hull. And then Henri's. That he had loved before me, that it is within him to abandon.

Making my way back through the streets and up the hill, feeling grumpy and cold with wet feet, I am relieved to step into the warmth of Grandmother Creed's porch. I take off my coat and boots and pull on a pair of slippers and go into the living room, patting a cloth into place on the side table. Grandmother Creed is moving around the kitchen, the smell of fried fish searing the air, a thin veil of greasy smoke watering her eyes.

"I've burnt the darn things," she exclaims with a pout. With her curls sagging from the steam of boiling potatoes and her silken dress wilting beneath her apron, she looks like a lost princess from some fairy tale. "Tut tut, how can one do anything with these darn legs—too slow getting about, and I was never one for cooking. Go, sit, dear, I'll scrape the pan, it should be palatable in small doses. No, in there." She beckons me into the dining room where she's set the table with her china dishes and silverware. In the centre of the table is a large bronze candle holder.

"Please, light the candle, Livvy. Granny never sat for supper without lighting the candle. I hope you like flounder? A fisherman from down the shore came around. He said he caught it this morning."

I flick a match to the candle and trace the curves of the ornate holder. It is polished to a sheen in some places, dulled inside those hard-to-get-at places inside the scrolls.

"It's my old granny's, passed down to her from her granny," says Grandmother Creed, placing a steaming platter of fried fish and potatoes on the table and noting me stroking the candle holder. "Imagine all our grannies caressing that very holder as you're caressing it now. Every time I polish it, I think of them polishing it with their wrinkly old hands."

I look at her own hands, shiny and pink and wrinkled beneath her jewelled rings.

"Did Mother polish it?" I ask, trying to imagine her thick fingers getting into those tiny grooves.

"Oh, yes. That's one chore she didn't resist, polishing that candle holder. She liked thinking about her old grannies, too. It's yours now," she adds, nudging the candle closer to me.

Impulsively I lean closer, feeling the warmth of the candle-light on my face. Pouring each of us a small glass of port from a crystal decanter, Grandmother lifts hers towards me. "To chase away the willies."

The thick dark liquid slides smoothly down my throat, settling warm into my belly. "Now then, tell me what you saw downtown," says Grandmother Creed. "Is there a show you'd like to see? I'm sure I could manage if we called a taxi. If it wasn't for those darn lineups. I swear, the city is held hostage to this war, it's become an overpopulated war camp."

"We've never looked at the pictures of your charity work, and of my mother when she was young. I'd like to see them. And pictures of my great-granny, if you have them."

Grandmother Creed beams a smile brighter than the flaming candle. "Jolly good, that is just what we'll do." She raises her port for another toast and then we both lift our forks, eating raven-ously from our plates, the warmth from the room settling snug as a wrap around my shoulders.

The wind whips snow at the house every day for a week, staying my wandering feet from my daily walks downtown. I pilfer bread and leftovers from the table and carry them to the basement amidst loads of wash, and after feeding Ashes, toss the rest outside for the wild ones.

"Livvy," the grandmother calls one morning, and I run back upstairs to a gust of wind as she opens the door to the mailman.

His cheeks glowing reddish above snow-matted whiskers, he steps inside the porch, coughing and sputtering about the bad weather and the heavy sack of mail he carries, hoisted onto his shoulder by a strap. "Gone to hell," he says garrulously, "the overcrowding has shot things to hell. There's ten times as much mail as we used to have, and they still expect it to be delivered on time." I listen for a moment to his and my grandmother's daily rant about the city gone wild, about how nice and quiet it was before the war started and how it's burdened now with the tens of thousands of servicemen demanding its housing and streets and restaurants and movie houses. In return, the city is gouging the servicemen's pockets by jacking the prices of everything to be had or sold, and if the war didn't soon end, it would be this city and its soldiers holding each other at gunpoint.

"Then to have the rest of the country writing bad things in their papers about us—not being hospitable enough to their sons!" exclaims Grandmother Creed. "They don't know what we're putting up with here—we can't even go to a movie or a restaurant for dinner. And the newspaper is full of stories about fights breaking out between the citizens and the soldiers. We'll have a brawl one of these days, you watch and see. Livvy, go to my room, dear, and fetch the post on my night table. Thank God we're getting the upper hand on the war," she says, turning back to the mailman. "It might end yet, but this city may never be the same."

I enter her room, standing before a plump bed, amply pillowed. It's rare that I get to be in her room, since she insists on cleaning it herself. I peek into her walk-in closet and stare with astonishment at the row of dresses and coats and the shelves of hats, with countless pairs of shoes and boots and slippers neatly paired beneath.

I step back, and a tall vanity mirror reflects a scented display of perfumes and makeup jars, ribbons and combs. A square silver locket hangs from a little gold hook. I lean closer; it looks vaguely familiar. I touch it, then take it into my hands. It's identical to the one Missus Louis gave me all those years ago—it was from Grandmother Creed, she told me. I pinch it open to two young faces, one blonde and smiling, the other dark and scowling—the same two faces as are in mine. *It's your grandmother when she was young,* Missus Louis had whispered, *and the dark-haired girl is her cousin.*

I stare into those dark eyes. They hold a truth that sends my thoughts reeling. It is Missus Louis. How could I not have recognized those earth-dark eyes?

"Did you find it?" the grandmother calls.

Dropping the locket back into place, I go to the bedside table. There's an opened envelope addressed to Missus Louis, and with a cheque for fifty dollars partly slipped inside of it. Grandmother Creed calls again and I push the cheque inside the envelope and take it to her. She seems surprised to see it unsealed, and turns from me, hastily licking the envelope, and then passes it to the mailman. "Look, Livvy, the postie has something for you."

"Miss Livvy Higgs," says the mailman, passing me an envelope still cold from his winter sack. I hold it, staring at my name written in a lovely, flowing script. It is from Missus Louis.

I feel the grandmother's eyes watching me as I go to my room. I keep staring at the envelope, at Missus Louis's name. That she would lie about the girl in the locket hits me hard. But no, it is not a lie. It is a secret. What kind of secret, then, can be carried for so long? She can't possibly be Grandmother Creed's cousin, she must've said that simply to deflect my attention.

My fingers tremble as I slit the flap of the letter and quickly slip it out of the envelope, opening it before me.

Dear Livvy,

How are you? My old eyes aren't so good, I can scarcely see what I write. My soul, we miss you here. It's a tough winter, Louis is not himself, but he's resting lots with Henri doing most of the chores. Your grandmother said little in her letter, other than you are doing well and are a joy to her and I am not to worry. Pray you'll write soon. It's only been a few months since you left, but already Suzie has found herself a nice husband—a hard-working man, with two half-grown boys. Oh, and he's a Frenchman. Louis likes that.

Etna has gone back to Corner Brook. She has a family member there who's taking her in—it was your father's doing, luv. Henri is long in the face—we wonder if he misses a certain girl—? Perhaps a letter might do him some good? He plans to return to the war, but his leg gives him trouble. With Louis feeling so poorly, I count it as a blessing that he is here.

A letter comes from your grandmother as I sit here, writing you. How is that for harmony, macushlah. She writes that you've taken grandly to the city, exploring its streets and shops every day. I miss you, dear macushlah, but I am content with knowing you are where you need to be. Please write me, I care nothing for your errors with spelling and words, I should read them as I have read others who share the same writing patterns as yourself, I so crave a word from you.

Blessings, macushlah, I await your news.
Your Missus Louis

"I hope everything is well," says Grandmother Creed as I enter the living room. She studies my face like one fearful of being driven from the well before thirst is quenched.

"She's fine," I say, and take myself down into the basement, sorting the wash, a heaviness in my stomach. She didn't ask me to come home. But Henri, his face is long—perhaps he does miss a certain girl. I push away the thought and dump detergent into the wash.

⁂

It is three, perhaps four weeks since Missus Louis's letter. From my room, where I'm lying on my bed, reading a magazine article about new technology advancing the navy's positioning in the war of the Atlantic, I hear the phone ring and Grandmother Creed's voice. She sounds anxious. I perk up my ears, but the call is quickly over. I begin reading again, and am interrupted by another phone call and Grandmother Creed's voice growing more anxious.

Laying aside the magazine, I go to the living room where she sits on the edge of her rocker, wringing her hands, her face pinched with worry.

"Everything's fine," she says to my concerned look. "I— It was our Missus Louis. She's wanting to know how you are. I should wonder if you didn't miss her," she says, beckoning me to sit. "Such a good woman. She would've taken in your father too for a pittance, if he had landed on her doorstep. What's wrong, dear?"

"Take me in? She didn't take me in. I worked. I—I slept at home."

"Of course you worked, Livvy dear, she wrote as much. Please, come sit beside me, there's something I must tell you."

I remain standing, Grandmother Creed's words churning heavy in my belly. "Is that why you send her money—to care for me?"

"I've never mentioned money, where did you gather that idea?"

"I saw the cheque in the envelope."

Grandmother Creed sniffs her disapproval. "You ought not to be snooping as you do. I've a right to privacy about certain things."

"How much did you pay her? And why are you writing her cheques when I'm here, now?"

"I've a complicated relationship with the woman, Livvy. Some things are better left alone."

"Why? If they concern me, I should know."

"Don't distract me further. Something has happened. But first, you must promise never to mention anything to Missus Louis about money." She breaks off as the phone rings loudly beside her. "Hello," she says hurriedly. "I've not time to talk right now—" She falls silent, her face breaking into careful smiles.

"My dear, I'm just sitting with her now. Perhaps you'd like to talk to her? Livvy"—she covers the mouthpiece with her hand— "it's our dear Missus Louis." She widens her eyes to caution me. "She's phoning from the post office. Wait," she calls, for I've taken to my heels and am marching to my room. "Livvy! Something has happened."

She says a hasty goodbye to Missus Louis and then calls out to me. "It's your father, Livvy. Please, listen. He's all right, but his ship was torpedoed," she says to my startled look as I turn to face her. "He was taken from his ship almost immediately and brought ashore. There's to be an operation—don't look so frightened, he's fine, he's all right. The hospital rang a minute ago."

"The hospital? Why didn't you tell me?"

"I can't talk with you staring down at me like that. There's more, Livvy. Just let me speak, it's all happening so fast. It was Henri who called—"

"Henri!"

"Apparently he's back in Halifax and working on the docks. He was there when your father was taken from the ship and he accompanied him to the hospital. Wait, Livvy dear, let me finish," she pleads as I rush to the porch, pulling my coat from the closet. "You mustn't be angry with me. I told him I'd give you the message. I thought it prudent to give you time to prepare yourself before speaking with him. Where are you going? Wait for me, we'll call a taxi, I'm coming with you."

"There are no taxis, the roads aren't plowed. Please," I beg as she hobbles into the porch behind me. "I'll call you as soon as I've word."

"You're angry with me. I don't do things well sometimes, I tend to overthink things, I should've called you to the phone."

"I'm glad for it. Please," I say, staying her hand from reaching for her coat, "I have to go."

She stands silent, watching as I wrap a scarf around my neck and button up my coat.

"It's cold, bundle up well," she says, tucking my scarf beneath my chin. She reaches up to fix my collar, her wispy, coiffed hair brushing my cheek, smelling faintly of perfumed soap.

"You aren't angry with me?" she asks.

I take her hands to remove them, but hold them instead, impulsively turning my face into her hair for one brief moment before whispering goodbye. Outside, I push through gusting snow down the sidewalk, my mind instantly going to Father. My legs feel stiff and I'm surprised at how anxious I feel; I hadn't thought I'd mind if something happened to him. I think of Henri and my belly warms, then cools, *sweet little thing, shy and sweet, and the boy the spit of Henri.* Grandmother, the smell of her stays with me, and I recoil from thoughts of Missus Louis. That she was being paid to befriend me!

Shielding my face against the cold, driving snow that wets and blurs my eyes, I try to make out the shadowy buildings ahead of me—one of them, I know, is the hospital. Cutting across what used to be a green, public place but is now knee deep in snow, I arrive, coughing and practically gagging from exertion, at the hospital doors. Inside, I'm directed into an elevator and onto the third floor. The doors slide open and I approach the nursing station, trembling with fear. A young clerk, her face tired as though sitting through long hours working on her files, looks up at me.

"I'm looking for Durwin Higgs. I'm his daughter."

"That'll be room thirty-six, my love: three doors down to your right." The voice belongs to an older nurse with a long, calm face who rests on her knees, fishing things out of a bottom cupboard. She gets up and comes towards me, smoothing her hair beneath her cap and smiling kindly. "I would've known you for his girl, you've the same eyes."

"How is he? What—what's wrong with him? His ship was torpedoed, that's all I know."

She comes out from behind the nurses' station and leads me aside as a group of people pile noisily out of the elevator. "He was struck hard in his abdomen," she says gravely. "It ruptured his spleen. They'll be readying him for surgery any minute, so if you want to see him, you must be quick. There's his room." She keeps a staying hand on my arm, her face becoming apprehensive. "You need to be prepared: he's sicker than he appears. He's lost a lot of blood. There might be other damage, but they won't know till they operate."

"But ... he's going to be all right—?"

The concern in her eyes belies her smile. "They won't know till they operate," she says again. "For now, he is with us. You'd best hold up," she says, as my eyes widen with fright. "Go on now, and see your father. He's fully conscious, and quite able to talk. It's the unknown that's got us concerned. We've given him something to relax him, so he might be a bit sleepy."

I stand outside his door for a moment, gathering myself, gathering her words that flutter without pattern outside my head, trying to find entrance, *You need to be prepared … for now he is with us … for now he is with us.* Clasping my hands in prayer, I enter his room. The head of his bed is raised and he lies back sleeping, his face the tombstone white of the already dead. Even in sleep his jowls are tense, fusing into the broad of his neck that appears naked without his tightly buttoned collars. I keep staring at his face, so familiar, yet nothing so familiar that I cease to see it. He is the dance of numbers within the well-worn cover of a book I have never deciphered.

He groans. I stand back, watching his eyes moving rapidly beneath their lids. His breathing grows erratic and mine grows fainter still to be standing so close to his dreams. His eyes open, they are unfocused. Seeing me, he brings his head forward, but is forced to lay it back, wincing in pain. "The time, what time is it?" he asks, his voice faint, yet his words full of their usual authority.

"Half past two. How—how do you feel?"

His breathing becomes loud in the too-quiet room. He looks at the IV dripping into his arm, then back at me with a growing sense of discomfort. He opens his mouth to speak, but is jolted by a pain that brings terror to his eyes. He paws the sheet as though looking for something to grip onto.

"Should I call the nurse?" I ask, jolted too by his pain, but more by his look of fright. I've never seen fear on my father's face, this man who walked so decisively into war. Mother's voice sounds through the room, *I'd be scared of dying too if I were you,* and I am seized by that awful memory of his near falling from the rock ledge into the sea that morning he took me to see the bones of the ship in the cove where his father had drowned. His face had blanched with fear, as it does now as he looks wildly around the room, threatened by a far different enemy this time, one that sails beneath no man's flag.

"No. No nurse," he says, his voice harsh with drugs and sleep. "There are things you need to know. My will specifies that the house and store are to be sold. The money will be given to you."

Sell? A panic wells up. "Why? I won't stay there."

He turns to me with a hardness in his eyes that not even the fear of death can soften. "There'll be no Frenchman crawling into my bed. Or mauling the goods in my store. I've put paid to that."

"Pillaged goods," I say steadily. "And you ran Grandmother Creed's ship ashore, trying to pillage more goods. She told me."

His mouth twists derisively. "Her insurance was worth more than her ship. She made a deal with Captain to burn it midcrossing." He closes his eyes and I feel dismissed. His hand gingerly touches the sheet covering his swollen abdomen and I see his face flinch with pain. I should go, but I can't.

"My mother," I whisper. "Did she know about this deal?"

He is agitated now. A priest appears in the doorway, speaking softly, his silver cross flashing on his robed chest. Abruptly, Father holds up his hand, stopping his entrance. The priest bows and vanishes as quietly as he appeared and Father tries to close his eyes again, but is unable to escape the heat of the question that burns in mine.

"I'm not proud of some things," he says, wiping at his brow. A nurse's voice can be heard outside his door, and then the sound of a stretcher. They've come for him. Father's agitation grows and I lean closer towards him.

"What did you do?" I ask urgently. "Grandmother Creed said you fought with Mother."

His mouth flinches with scorn. "She put your mother up. Captain wanted a guarantee she would pay," he says, and is about to say more, but it's me now who's turning from him, trying to decipher his words.

"She was glad to be with me," he says, looking at me as though for understanding. "Her mother disliked her."

"At least she *had* dislike," I whisper. "With you she had nothing."

He looks at me as though I'm daft. "She had everything. But she still went against me."

"You gave her nothing. How could she betray nothing? It is you who betrayed her."

He tosses his head with exasperation. "She didn't leave, did she."

"She died! She died! You took her heart."

He looks fiercely into my eyes. "I had nothing to do with her sickness." Pain forces his head back onto his pillow, yet his eyes cling to mine like a sinner protesting his innocence before the gates of hell. But he'll receive no pardon from me, for it is out of fear that he seeks absolution, not a change of heart towards me or Mother.

"God will hear your confession," I say hotly.

"Mister Higgs, it's time, sir," says the nurse coming into the room, two aides wheeling in a stretcher behind her. The nurse is speaking to me about a cafeteria, but I'm hurrying out, my mother's words chasing after me, *Cares for himself, cares nothing for what I want, I don't do nothing good enough, don't clean the house good enough, don't dress fancy enough, I'm a disappointment.* No wonder. No wonder she felt those things. She could never be good enough for someone who didn't want her, who wanted only those things she could bring him. No wonder she yelled at him. No wonder she wouldn't wear pretty dresses and fix her hair nice and clean the house the way he liked—she felt his nothingness. That's why she was all the time ranting—anything to keep herself from fading into that awful nothingness.

I stop walking. Henri stands before me. He's wearing one of Missus Louis's bulky knitted sweaters, its cream-coloured neck coiling beneath his chin and a matching wool hat capping his shiny black hair. He smells like sheep and his dark eyes are all over me.

"Livvy," he says, but he doesn't come to me. I begin to tremble. I want to run to him and hold him and breathe him deep inside of me to fill this sense of emptiness that is Mother. But I back away from him as I did Father, *Sweet little thing, shy and sweet, the boy the spit of Henri.*

"Hey, I didn't put him there," says Henri, gesturing towards Father's room. "And I wouldn't start grieving yet; there's a chance he'll survive. I've been talking with the doctors."

I stare at him, the familiarity of his voice, his face, the smell of Missus Louis's wool. I close my eyes, drawing my hands down over my face. Amidst such madness as pummels this moment I distrust myself to say anything or to absorb anything Henri might have to say. He takes my arm and I let him take me down the elevator to a quiet corner inside the cafeteria. I note his stiff-kneed limp as he brings us coffee and collects a milk jug from a nearby table.

"Nothing like warm milk to settle the stomach," he says, pouring a good dollop into each of our cups. "Least that's what Mam always says. She should know, she had enough of us young-sters wimping around her legs with sore throats or sore elbows through the years. Most times we were just wanting to get away from doing chores, but she never thought for a minute one of her darlins might be telling the lie to get a little snooze."

He keeps talking in that slow, lazy voice I know so well, giving me time to gather myself, and I slip inside his words as I used to slip inside the river, letting him carry me over the jagged edges of Father's words still cutting their way through me. He rambles on, finding different eddies for me to rest in—Suzie snuck out of the house and married the widowed man from down near Gut Bridge, sending Esmée and Missus Louis into the fits. Blissfully the widower has two strapping sons, he says. And it looks like they're all going to move into Missus Louis's, another blessing for *Grand-père* who is rapidly failing this past month, and needing extra sets of hands to help with the work.

Blessing for Henri, too, he says, for he's been able to rejoin the navy.

I come out of my stupor. "What about your leg?"

He grins, patting his leg. "Me and old limpy here, we get around as well as we want to. There's ships from every port on the planet sitting out there in the harbour. My job's to help search them all for bombs—spies out there, planting bombs for a mid-ocean bonfire. Tons of steel got sunk in the last war by time bombs," he adds at my perplexed look. "They load them on with the cargo. We're making sure it don't happen here."

"That's your job, searching ships for bombs?"

He pulls a long face. "Yeah, not too romantic, eh? But there's a fun part. I get to meet all them different flags strutting about. Some are pretty pissed with them torpedoes coming at them. You might say they're taking it sitting down, refusing to sail. Perhaps tossing a wrench or a couple of rocks into the engine. Lots of ways of keeping a ship from sailing. Me and my buddies, we try and fix their problems, whether it be nerves or a rusty propeller.

Got to keep the convoys moving. Fifty, sixty ships at a time, sailing out of that harbour: the weakest gets nestled in the middle, the strongest sails the outside. Like organizing playtime. Better: I'm not aiming a gun at anyone."

"You're just fixing others to do it for you."

"Least I don't have to watch the fireworks. You're looking at me kinda strange, Livvy. Never seen a coward before? Hell, baby, take a walk to the docks and see the brave young seamen boarding their boats, all proud and strong and with seven shades of shit in their pants. Scared of what's waiting for them on the seas, and just as scared of turning back and facing their pappies watching them from onshore."

"You're sounding proud, Henri, as if it takes courage to be a coward."

"Hell, I'm nobody's hero, least of all my own. I'm thinking I must be missing something, Liv. Most of them bastards boarding those ships got some moral purpose for doing so. I expect it's no different with those bastards hunkering beneath the water, firing back up at them. Me, I don't got that moral thing. We're all the same feckin' bunch to me: English, French, Irish, German, all the same smarmy crew. Just wrapped in different colours some fat arsehole hiding behind a flag-draped desk picked for us. Perhaps I do sound proud. You know where I learned all that, Livvy? I learned it from you," he says, and my heart catches itself on a beat as he leans towards me. "Remember what you said about Mam's sheets? About them being the only flag worth fighting for? Well, I thought about that a lot since you left, about it being the only real thing."

His voice has softened, but there's a hardening in my chest that won't let me feel it, that keeps my voice dispassionate as I ask, "Why don't you stay home then, if you're not wanting to be some kind of hero?"

"Gawd-damn, and have *Grand-père* railing Mam every day about her Limey traitor having chicken knees?"

"You could have played up your limp at home as well as here."

"I could have done that. Yep." He sits back, nodding. "I suppose I could've done that. Why didn't you say goodbye to the girls before you left, Livvy? They were hurt, you running off without saying goodbye."

And you, were you hurt? I want to ask. "I didn't just run off. Father—he threatened to do things."

"Must've been one hell of a fight you put up. Heard you squealing all the way across the marsh."

"Is that what you're thinking, that I just hopped aboard Father's train, singing tiddly-do?"

"I expect if he'd gagged and tied you to the steering wheel, you would've been back on the next boat out. Course, by then I figured the pretty shop windows had a say."

"*Grand-père* would say you're as bad at figuring things as you are at stacking a tier of wood."

"*Grand-père* wouldn't expect nothing from an English girl. Thing is, I didn't figure any of it. Your Grammy Creed wrote *Grand-mère* all kinds of nice things about the two of you sitting cozy, looking through the catalogues and catching up on lost stories and fashions. There weren't any letters coming from you, so I expect there was truth in them."

"And do you always leave things nice and tidy behind you? What of the child you ran from?"

His smile fades. "I've never claimed to always do things accordingly, but there's nothing wrinkling my pillow at the moment. Wait, where you going—hold up, now. Livvy, hey." He's on his feet following me as I march out of the cafeteria and down a corridor and inside a small sitting room.

I face him at the doorway, barring his way. "I want to be alone." He holds back the door so I can't close it and I look closely at his face. There are no twitches of guilt around his mouth, and his eyes are clear of anger. "Is there nothing that grieves you?" I ask.

"There are many things that grieve me, Livvy. The war grieves me. What that sick daddy of yours is doing to you grieves me. What *you're* doing to you grieves me. Having other people judging my business grieves me. Have your little pout, I'll be waiting out here."

"I don't need you keeping watch."

"That you don't, baby doll. You got yourself in a boat with too many anchors, you'll be going nowhere fast enough. Oh, and before you lock yourself in, *Grand-mère* will be here late this evening. Pays to be a sailor with pilots for friends," he says to my disbelieving look.

He walks away and I close the door. Missus Louis is coming. Perhaps there's money owing, I think nastily. Instantly I am shamed by my childish thinking. I sit on a sofa, staring at a pastoral scene hanging on the wall. I think of Father's house bleached of life from Mother's death and Etna's cleanings. I think of Missus Louis who now has Suzie with her man and the two strapping boys living with her. I look to the doorway where Henri waits outside, *Sweet little thing, shy and sweet, the boy the spit of Henri.* I think of Grandmother Creed. How could she have done that to my mother, her daughter? Perhaps she didn't. Perhaps Father lies. For certain he lied to Mother.

I sit for a long time staring at that pastoral picture, trying to think, trying not to think. A knock on the door disturbs me and Henri walks in. He stands there, scratching his head through his thick wool cap, his sweater sleeves pushed up to his elbows.

"I've news. Your daddy made it through the operation. There was no further damage," he says with resentment. "Must've bribed a few angels to take care of him. Can't see him for an hour, they're sewing him back up and he'll be sleeping like a baby for a spell."

My mind feels blank. I draw my hands tiredly down over my face. Father survived. I feel nothing. In my anger, he was dead the moment I left his bedside. It was my mother I had thought about, always my mother. Now, like one pardoned from his sins, Father has returned. And I feel nothing.

Henri hauls a folding chair from beside the wall and positions it before me. He sits, leaning forward with his elbows on his knees. "Let's have a chat. Where'd you get this idea about me being some poor little orphan's daddy?"

I shake my head, not wanting to talk right now.

"You start flinging about mud, you're gonna have to clean it up, Liv. Now, I'm not sitting easy hearing them sneaky little tales about me."

"You didn't deny it," I say stonily.

"I can't recall being outright charged. Besides that, it felt like the judging was already done. Now, for the record, I'm guilty as hell of turning tail last year, and running from the proud little mama-to-be when she sprung her happy news on me. But the *rightful daddy* soon stepped forward and now they're all happy in Happyland. What's that look for? You disappointed I'm not the daddy? Or that I once slept with his fine-looking mama?"

"They say the baby's the spit of you. Perhaps somebody else married her out of duty—or pity."

"I'll tell you how I know I'm not the daddy, Livvy. Marcella worked the streets every night for two years. I never touched that woman once without using double rubbers—hell, don't look at me like that, I'm no fallen angel. Just one horny, God-made man with a fear of going blind with dick-rot.

"Oh, now we're all sanctimonious, are we," he continues as I turn from him, aghast. "The whole city is rotting with the dose. The dose, Livvy, do you know what that is? It's a venereal disease that gets spread from one fornicating soul to another and this whole city's been fornicating since the war started and yup, I'm one of them. But I'm scared of pain, see," he adds, jabbing at his chest with his thumb. "And of going blind—that's what the dose can do to you, Livvy. It can rot your privates and blind your eyes. So I double up good on them rubbers, and that's how I know I'm no daddy to nobody. So when Marcella named me, I took the next boat out. I figured a wolf pack was more appealing than spending the rest of my life with Marcella—no matter that she's a fine woman.

"But I didn't have to worry long now, did I. Like I told you, the proud daddy came forth and as luck would have it, he loves Marcella to death and they're all just fine. Now tell me, Livvy, what part of the story did your dear old granny leave out?"

There's a sound behind us, and the ghastly faces of an elderly couple stare at us from the doorway. "Just sorting things through, folks," says Henri without flinching. He rises with a smile and invites them to sit on the couch across from us. "What's worrying you folks today? Got someone sick?"

They've a son, they reply, with a burst appendix, and I sink beneath their little stream of chatter as Henri assures the worrying elders their son will be fine because an appendix is of no worldly good, and he knows that because he's spoken to many healthy old men who had their appendix taken out when they were young-sters and they've never noticed it a bit.

The couple drift off into a conversation of their own, and

Henri turns his attention back to me. "What're you thinking now, Livvy? Did I leave anything out?"

"My grandmother," I half whisper. "Did anybody tell her about the father coming forward?"

Henri shakes his head impatiently. "I got more important things to dwell on than nonsense uttered by idle tongues—like whether or not my appendix was going to blow up like their Harold's over there. Imagine that, he had forty years of living in peace with something and the darn thing just blows up. Where you going? Livvy, hey Liv." He's chasing me down the corridor now. "Livvy, where you going?"

"Taking my idle tongue somewhere else, Henri, so's it don't disrupt your important thinking."

"There you go, acting like a flighty hen."

"I'm not a flighty hen. I'm just fleeing the almighty cock crowing alongside of me. Shouldn't you be back there, taking care of your adopted folk?" I ask as he leaps into the elevator alongside me.

"Calm your jealousy, Livvy, they're worried about their son."

"I've more important things to dwell on than a man who has a woman and then leaves her."

"Not a fair thing to say, Liv. How would Marcella make her money if I took up all her nights? Unless you're thinking I should've married her because I slept with her? Which means I would've been married before I turned fourteen because that's the first time—Livvy, hey, Livvy—stop!" he roars, and blocks the elevator doors swinging open. Jabbing the control buttons, he sets us going upward again. "Now, here's my take on fornicating—" he begins, but I press my hands against my ears so's not to hear that word again.

"That's just fine, I'll call it whatever word you want," he says.

"Some call it making love, some call it having fun, some even call it evil. So let's just call it 'having fun,' or 'a lot of fun' because I got a lot of fun in me, Liv. The good Lord filled me to the brim with it, which is a dirty joke because I can never get rid of it all.

"But I don't mind it too much either because it's good for you, empties the mind and fills the heart—like a good bottle of whisky. Except it don't leave no headaches in the morning. Well, that's not quite true either. Marcella sure laid one on me. Why are you looking at me like that? Half the world's doing what I'm doing. Most just wrap it up pretty and call it love. Now, there's the shame, dirtying something nice with lies. Hell, there's bigger things than fornicating to feel shame over. We're out there killing people we've never met or seen—how's that for something shameful?"

"You know what, Henri? You're too damn arrogant to feel shame." I push past him as the elevator lurches to a stop several floors past Father's floor. The doors swing open and I hurry past a couple of aides and an old man strapped onto a gurney and then half run down the deserted corridor. "Go away, go find yourself a brothel," I mutter as Henri catches up with me. "Spread around that good fun God overloaded you with."

I duck through a side door into a stairwell and clump down two flights of stairs to the sixth floor, ignoring Henri who's following behind, mercifully quiet for now. Looking back on his past bits of fun, no doubt, I'm thinking, for I'm nowhere convinced of the *rightful pappy coming forward*. Wouldn't the hard-luck Marcella point elsewhere if Henri suddenly vanished before her growing belly?

I push through a doorway onto the sixth floor and am directed towards the critical care unit on yet another floor. When I finally reach it, Henri behind me all the way, I watch with relief as the doors close in front of him. Only family allowed, the nurse is telling Henri, and I turn from the placating smile he's now using on the nurse, trying to gain entrance.

There is a row of curtained-off beds and Father's is at the end, a young intern tells me. I walk slowly past the makeshift rooms, catching glimpses of patients holding the hands of their visiting loved ones. I hear their whispers as they speak of the past hours, no doubt, that brought them here, and recount treasures of past memories and hopes of tomorrow. I come to Father's curtain, where he lies inside waiting for no one, his past hours, his memories, strung out like ill-written postcards that lead me not into his tomorrow, for my hand is already poised for a final goodbye. But first, there is one more question I must ask.

As before, he lies stiff and pale beneath his sheets, an IV in his arm. His jaw is slackened. A memory shoots through me of sitting astride his shoulders and grasping at his neck to keep from falling, but his neck was too hard, his skin too taut to pucker beneath my fingers. I wonder now, in the silence of this room, if he might have regrets; if the beating of his heart against that lone doorway through to eternity might not be squeezing its rock hardness, rendering it a little softer, an enticement perhaps for those same fingers now fisted beside him.

I sit and commence waiting. I wait for what feels like a long, long time for him to begin to wake up. I wait as he opens his eyes, then sleeps again, then awakens. For an hour or more he grapples with awakening, each time his eyes taking in more and more of his surroundings, his mind trying to assess whether he's in heaven or hell.

I stir when I feel him sensing me. His eyes touch mine and he closes them as if already knowing the question I am about to ask.

"You've managed fine," I say. "You'll be leading the next convoy out of the harbour soon enough." My words are clipped, cold. Yet a smile touches his lips and he speaks in a raspy whisper that's strengthened with pride.

"Aye. I'll not lead it onto the rocks."

I listen to those words long after he's spoken them. I watch them hovering like phantoms above his mouth. They take the shape of the drowned captain, the man-god who rescued him from mouldy bread and a piss-drenched bed, who stole him from a slovenly mother and enrolled him into the halls of scholars, who faced down the sea and warships with iron fists and taught him to climb riggings and ride the white horses through the ocean's fury. And who then allowed himself to be brought down by an old rogue Frenchman, cast off by the English and French alike.

I lean towards my father with growing wonder. "You're ashamed of him," I say. "You're shamed by the captain's drowning."

He opens his eyes; they are drugged and clouded with confusion. "No wonder you hate failure," I say, my voice low. "Seems like we all failed you. Your Captain. Mother. Me."

He stares at my mouth, trying to understand. A nurse peers through the curtain.

"Don't tire him," she says. "He needs his strength." She slips the curtain into place and I take hold of Father's hand to jolt him back from sleep.

"Did my mother know?" I ask, slowly and clearly. "Did my mother know why you married her?" He doesn't open his eyes; he doesn't have to. I see the cords tense in his neck. I feel his hand tugging away from mine. I feel his guilt. "Grandmother's right," I whisper. "You are without soul."

His eyes open, their confusion partly clearing. "Was ... she ... that told," he manages to croak.

I back away from his bedside. I shiver from this room that darkens with the malice winging from his crow-black heart. For it isn't from fear, or a sense of being beholden to me or my mother that he speaks, but to strike another blow against Grandmother Creed in this battle he continues to fight against her.

I walk away from the unit on trembling legs, escaping the hospital without Henri seeing me. I walk through the snowbanked sidewalks of a city blackened by windows that are curtained against a war raging outside its shores. The early evening wind snakes through crevices in my tightly knotted scarf and shivers around my neck as I approach Grandmother Creed's door. Scuffing away a mound of snow, I enter the porch and she's immediately calling out to me.

"My dear, you've been gone so long," she exclaims with relief, opening the inner door and hobbling into the porch. "I was about to ring a taxi and join you. I swear, those nurses are so rude—but I did manage to find out about your father. My goodness," she exclaims, grasping more tightly to her canes as Ashes scoots around her legs. "Where did *you* come from? Was he in your room, dear? Can we keep him in the basement?"

I scratch the cat's ears as she sniffs at my wet boots, and then I open the basement door, nudging her down the steps.

"Is everything all right, Livvy? You're so quiet, dear, you're frightening me. Your father—he's all right, isn't he?" She stands watching me closely, her thin frame wrapped in a rosy-pink dressing gown, its wide sleeves gracefully covering the bony wrists and hands that now clutch the two black canes propping her. Her face is cleansed of rouge and lipstick and she looks pale, yet her eyes are sharp on mine.

"He's fine. Go inside, the floor's wet." Kicking my boots to one side and hanging up my coat, I follow her into the living room and sit on the settee as she makes tea.

"I'm relieved for you that it ended well. You look exhausted," she says from the kitchen. "Such a horrid night. You must be worn out, my dear. There, I'm adding a splash of whisky—an Irish tea, if you will. If there's one thing I take from the Irish, it's their manner of making a good broth for what ails you.

"There now, we'll wait for the tea to steep. Ohh, my legs are weakening by the day," she says, laboriously making her way back across the living room. "Why don't you take off your clothes, dear, and get into your dressing gown. We'll be two old grannies nipping our tea-whiskies, and you can tell me everything that's happened."

"Those pictures of you and your charities—and of Mother. Can we look at them now?"

"What? What, dear? But the light's not good."

"I want to see them. May I?"

"Certainly. I'll finish making our tea—"

"I'll make the tea. You get the pictures."

She looks disconcerted as I start for the kitchen. "All right, then. I'll get them out of the trunk. Put a teaspoon of sugar in my tea, and you can have two if you want, damn the restrictions."

I add sugar to the amber liquid in the pot, then pour the tea and bring hers to the side table near her rocker. Taking mine to the settee, I watch as she comes from her room, breathing heavily, her hair a bit mussed.

"I swear, I thought those pictures were in the trunk. But it comes to me now, they're still at the charity headquarters. They were using them for advertising. To think I was talking to Gertrude just last week. I'll ring her in the morning and have her bring them back. Now then, to a hard old day," she toasts, settling into her rocker and raising her cup to me. "You must tell me everything that's happened. Did you see Henri?"

"He doesn't have a child," I say quite chattily. "The girl—she cleared his name. It surprises me Missus Louis didn't tell you that."

The grandmother's eyes widen. "Well, I'm surprised too. Why are you looking so glum, dear? I would think it a good thing his name is finally cleared."

"I'm not sure I believe him. Plus, you said you saw the boy—and that he's the spit of Henri?"

She leans towards my questioning look. "I swear, he *is* the spit of Henri. You're wise not to rule it out, Livvy."

"I just don't understand why Missus Louis didn't clear it with you."

"The poor woman's endured so much over the years. This probably isn't the first time she's had to turn a blind eye to Henri's roguery. I've heard of other things," she adds, her voice dropping. "But I try not to listen to gossip. I couldn't bear bringing more hardship onto that dear soul, especially after what she's done for me and my girls. I say a prayer for her every night, Livvy. But she's blessed too, isn't she, with all of Esmée's children growing up around her? And now with Suzie moving into her house with her husband and those two big boys—I shouldn't worry too much about Missus Louis. She'll spend easier days now."

"I've never thanked you for the locket."

"Locket, dear?"

"The one you sent Missus Louis to give me."

"This foggy old brain," she says apologetically. "You'll forgive me, Livvy dear."

"It held two pictures: one of you as a young girl, and a

dark-haired girl. Missus Louis couldn't recall the dark one's name. I think she said it was your cousin?"

"Oh, the locket, the silver locket. How could I *possibly* forget! I tell you, there's no dignity for the old, we scarcely remember our names. Why would you think of such a thing now? It was so long ago."

I shrug. "I liked holding it. It was comforting, kind of like the candle holders," I add with a smile.

The grandmother holds her hand to her heart. "That you should say that," she whispers. "I slept with that locket under my pillow from the day dear old Gran passed on. I used to hold it in my hands each time I said my prayers. It was my greatest treasure, Livvy. I so wanted you to have it. The thought of you wearing it so close to your heart, it brought me comfort too."

"Who *is* that dark-haired girl? She looks familiar."

The grandmother smiles sadly. "That's my old granny, dear. Your great-great-grandmother—when we were the same age. I told you, you look like her, that's why she's familiar. It's the only picture I have of her, that's why it was so sacred to me. I begged Missus Louis to caution you against losing it. What did she tell you when she gave it to you?"

"She told me to keep it in a safe place."

"Such a good soul, our Missus Louis. She said nothing more?"

"I don't remember."

Grandmother Creed gives a solemn nod, as though I've just offered her something noble. Then her face brightens. "I've an idea, Livvy. Why don't we hire an artist to paint a portrait of our old granny? Perhaps we can have a painting done of your mother, too. And why not you—and me? Wouldn't that be grand, dear, if we decorated the hallway with our portraits? All of us women who lived in this fine old house? They'll be wonderful items to pass on to your children someday."

She looks away, her face saddening. "I wish I had a picture of my mother to put there. I've often wondered what she looked like; there are no pictures of her. Well, I can imagine her, I suppose. I only have to look at you and know what she probably looked like. My goodness," she exclaims, dabbing at her eyes that are all misty, "why are you letting me prattle when you've so much on your mind. Now, tell me about Henri. And your father."

I watch, sickened by her smiles, her sadness, her cajoling tones, the fluttering of her little wasted hands as she weaves herself into being with each and every lie. *Like the fox, she's like the fox,* said Mother, and I rise, my limbs heavy, and walk to the door. What other lies has she told me? What other lies are hidden amongst her half-truths that were slowly distorting my ears to my mother's warning cries, even starting to distort my thoughts of Mother? And of Missus Louis, and of Henri. What lies, what other lies has she told? I see now her poisons, all concealed within truisms that play themselves through the mind, contaminating thought more lethally than a direct strike from an outside foe. Poor Mother. Poor, poor Mother. How dizzy her young mind must have felt from all those lies transforming into truths and truths transforming into lies, the only consistency being a little voice within her ear whispering *Something's not right, something's not right.* She must have been strong. She must have had courage to listen to such tiny whispers and pack her bag and do their bidding. Only to have the same whispers disturbing her sleep with Father. Small wonder she ended up walking the shoreline, ranting. It kept her from hearing the whispers. She probably thought herself a lunatic, imagining them. She probably feared having to pack another bag—two, this time, for she'd a youngster now in tow—and move where? Back to the same lair of lies she'd managed to spring herself from?

"Where are you going, dear?"

I go into the porch, stepping around puddles of water from the melted snow on the floor, and put on my boots. Grandmother Creed is lifting herself onto her canes, following me to the door, standing there watching as I take my coat from the closet and push my arms through the sleeves.

"But where are you going, Livvy? Surely not back to the hospital?"

I look at her frail form hiding behind her rosy-pink robe, her perfectly coiffed hair, her mouth quivering with unspoken words. Her eyes, their startling blue the one thing of colour on her pallid face, are deeply lined from their long years of scrutiny, from their searching up close and far away. And yet they're empty, they will always be empty, her desires never to be fulfilled, for her lies, like Etna's germs, are a symptom that blinds her to the far greater illness preceding it.

"Father told me things," I say.

"What kind of things?"

"They weren't nice things," I say quietly.

She takes a step closer, staring at my mouth, drinking in my words; I hear them plink inside the empty chambers of her heart. "Will you tell me what he said!" she cries.

"He said you put Mother up as a guarantee against a payout to Captain Higgs."

She blinks with confusion. "What are you *saying*? What has he done now? He stole my daughter with lies and now he does the same with you?"

I pull open the door to leave, and turn back to her. "Do you think I can't hear *your* lies?"

Her mouth quivers violently. She presses her hand against it, her face becoming all pious. Giving the slow, knowing nod of a sainted one dealing with a mouthy heathen, she whispers, "It's all right, dear. I understand you must heed your father. Please, close the door, dear, and let's have us a talk."

"Why did you tell her?"

"Tell her what?"

"Tell me or I'll leave. Why did you tell my mother about the guarantee?"

Her mouth quivers, her eyes flit about the porch. "Because she needed to know, dear. She needed to know why Durwin ran off with her."

She reaches out a bony hand to touch me. And it is here, in this irreparable moment, that rage snaps its coiled self through my veins and I lift up my hand as Father had raised his that time with Mother. But the grandmother doesn't stand rooted in the truth of her convictions as Mother had. She draws back as I raise my hand threateningly above her, and her weight comes to rest on the one cane not properly positioned on the wet floor. The cane slips and the grandmother makes a piteous crying sound as she's thrown against the basement door that I'd left slightly ajar after nudging Ashes down the steps. The door smashes open behind her and she hovers on the brink of falling. And in that frenzied second of still-ness, within that hundredth of a second it would take to wrestle back hate, I could grab her with my raised hand. I could grab her. But I don't. I don't. And the stilled moment springs itself forward and she falls. I shriek and throw myself after her, but too late, too late, and I too am falling, *thud thud thud* down the basement steps.

My face strikes something sharp and I cry out, opening my eyes to darkness and a pounding heart and a knowing that snatches at my breath: anger—it distorts things, muffles your nose as you try to breathe. It is an easier thing to spot than this other thing, this *hatred,* that just now caroused through me with such ownership. How long has it been growing silently within me, plying itself gently around my bones, nestling within my belly, sleeping, waiting for its moment to strike? And now it has. And I lie here atop the grandmother's twisted body, her little silken slipper lying next to my hand and a dark pool of blood forming beneath her on the bottom step. I hear Henri and am surprised. He yells my name and he curses, coming down the basement stairs. I close my eyes, turning from him, from my grandmother, and feel again a stinging on my face. It stings again, and I open my eyes onto an oval, creamy sheen appearing before me like a pallid moon through a night sky. It grows in lustre, becoming clearer, much clearer, less dark, and it is Gen, it is Gen's face staring down at mine, her hand poised to strike me again, across the face.

EIGHT

"Wake up! Wake up, Livvy," Gen cries. "Are you awake? Were you having a nightmare? Sweet Jesus, you were making noises, unearthly sounds, like a freaking demon had you by the throat. Are you okay?"

I nod and she flops beside me with relief. "Christ, you scared me. You're pale, you don't look well. I know, I know," she says as I glance past her to the clock on the wall. "It's six o'clock, time for mortals to be just stirring from sleep, not getting ready for bed. Look." She raises her foot. "The cuffs are off. Stu's gone to my place and I'm staying here with you. Let me help you to bed. I'm freaking exhausted, and you must be, too."

"I—I'm feeling a bit rested," I say, the fluttering of my heart leaving me breathless.

"Well, you just had a good nap, almost two hours. I kept sending Stu up to check on you. What do you think, Livvy? Later, if you're not looking better, I'll have to call the ambulance. I'll go with you," she insists over my protests. "Listen, I owe you so much for helping me. More than helping me, you saved me and I'll do anything you want. I'll kiss your rosy little toes." Her eyes are bright and she's smiling and I want to hold her hand to keep her near me. I'm frightened, my dream has frightened me, and I don't want to go back, don't want to see the grandmother lying there.

"I've been thinking, Livvy—don't let me keep you awake, though, will you? You want me to stop talking?"

"I'll just close my eyes."

Gen smiles. "While I was downstairs, getting those things filed off, I kept thinking about what you said, about me being sad. I thought no one could see that. If you see it, then Ronny does too. Hell, that's what I felt from my mother all those years, her sadness—whatever it is that makes her sad."

She shrugs. "Maybe she don't know either. Maybe I should ask her, maybe we're sad for the same reasons." She smiles, tucking my blanket around my chin. "You're sad, too. I think that's the first thing I saw in you, your sadness. Maybe that's why I was drawn to you, I see my sadness in yours. Do you know why you're sad?"

I avert my eyes to hide their shame. *We're all drunk on something, luv, some a bit more than others.* Missus Louis's words. I close my eyes—there's so much I'd like to tell this girl—but the fatigue weighs me down with a weariness I feel straight through to my bones. "Go back to sleep," Gen whispers. "I'll just sit here, if there's anything you want. What?" she asks, as I tug on her sleeve.

"Clean my house."

She laughs again. "First sign of aging: prettying up the house before one's self. Righto!" She glances around, noting the dusty curtains, the cat fur starting to crowd the corners, the dust starting to coat the bookshelves and tables, the dull floor. "Righto! Nothing too strenuous here. Tomorrow I'll clean your house."

"Now," I whisper.

"Now? It's six in the morning, and I haven't been to bed yet."

"You asked," I say.

"What, we can't wait till later? You expecting company?" She touches cool fingers to the bump on my head from where I fell. "You sure you didn't addle yourself?" She does away with her grin as I brush aside her hand with impatience.

"Hey, I'm sorry," she offers, "I was just joking." She sits quietly for a moment, staring at my averted face, and then stands, pushing up her shirt sleeves. "Fair enough. I owe you. Crap, I've pulled all-nighters before, studying Durkheim's theories of suicide and baby-bearing. This should be a treat. By the way, those kittens in the basement, you're joking when you say they're mine, right?" I shake my head. "Ronny's?" she asks. "Shit. I hate cats. I mean, I really hate freaking cats. He's not getting them, then. One, he can keep one. Little frigger," she mutters, going into the kitchen. "I should've known he was up to something, he's been so sweet, lately—"

Her words are lost to a blast of tap water gushing into the sink and a clatter of dishes. I cling to her sounds as she scrapes plates and drops cutlery into the sink and drags around chairs and the garbage cans. I close my eyes and see her washing down the kitchen table where I sat with Grandmother Creed, listening to her made-up life. With her foot she nudges a bucket of water into the living room. She's wearing a pair of yellow gloves up to her elbows and holding the mop in one hand, with the broom, dustpan and rags in the other.

"First we'll do the sweeping, then the dusting and then the mopping," she says. "You can close them eyes, I don't like being watched when I'm working. Fine, keep them open, spy if you want. Pray tell, if I'm as stubborn as you when I'm old, I'll pop pills and end it." Gen keeps chiding me as she works, and it's a comfort to hear her voice. She's tired, her eyes are shadowed, and she keeps stopping her sweeping to blow on her burned wrists. Yet she chatters away about Ronny and the kittens, and about her mother and what she'd said earlier about her mother blubbering and feeling shameful after she gets drunk. "Perhaps I am too hard on her. Maybe she's not even feeling shame, perhaps I'm putting that onto her, perhaps she's ignorant, and aren't we all? Frig, we don't even know who we are, how's that for ignorance, uh?"

A small pain starts up in my chest. Gen hums now, like Etna, as she cleans. The pain deepens a little, but just a little, there is no nausea, and yet my pulse seems to flutter more erratically. I try to lift my hand; I cannot. My breathing isn't so bad and I don't feel uncomfortable either. If this is dying, I feel strangely fine.

"Who's this?" asks Gen. She's holding a picture frame, wiping the dust from its glass. "He's bloody handsome, was this your man?"

I look at her, reaching hungrily for the picture. "Wow, he's *gorrrgeous*," says Gen. Those eyes, full of fun, and that grin. "You going to tell me about him someday?" she asks, passing me the picture.

I take it, holding it against my heart.

"Look at her, still in love," Gen murmurs. "Promise you'll tell me about him."

I nod. I'll tell you, I want to say. I'll tell you how he helped save me, how he never left, at least not in the way I thought he would, that night the grandmother fell down the stairs like a kicked dog. He almost saved her. Before she and I hit the basement floor, he'd been coming up the side steps. The door was already open, I'd left it open when turning to confront my grandmother. He heard her cry out. He heard my shriek immediately following and was instantly inside the door. So close! So close he was to that moment, that small, small moment, that he could have almost snatched it back, snatched us both back, me and Grandmother Creed, from our wretched fall.

"Don't move, don't move, either of you!" he shouts, feeling my shoulders, feeling my arms and legs for broken bones. He lifts me aside and I see her stick legs, naked outside her pink robe, her one slipper half off her foot, the other beside my hand. I watch in silence as he feels for a pulse in her throat, looking to me through the dim basement light.

"She's alive, she's bleeding, I think she's cut herself somewhere." He reaches for me, but I draw away.

"Save her," I whisper, eyes frozen on the grandmother's crumpled form. He scrambles up over the stairs, roaring from the side steps for someone to call an ambulance. Somebody must have heard, for he's yelling about the grandmother falling down the stairs, and within the minute he's back down with a coat from the closet and gently laying it over my grandmother's twisted limbs.

"What happened, tell me what happened!" he demands. "Livvy!" He's shaking me. "Tell me what the fuck happened!" And I shrink from him in shame, I've failed, I've failed again, and I start sobbing.

"Did she slip?" he demands.

"I could have caught her—I—my hand, it wouldn't move."

"Goddammit, Livvy, how'd you end up down here if you hadn't tried to catch her. Tell me what happened. Hurry up, baby, before they get here."

"She—she told me lies. I wanted to hit her. I raised my hand and she drew back. She hit the basement door. Her cane, it slipped."

"And she fell against the basement door. It fell open and she fell, and you tried to grab her, and you fell, too."

"My hand, it wouldn't move."

"That's because you were stunned. It's not your fault. She slipped and you slipped trying to catch her. When they start asking questions, that's what you'll say. Start mixing it up with I shouldas, I couldas and people start hearing other things. Keep it clean and simple, you listening to me, baby? You say no more than what I told you. No matter what that old bird there says when she wakes up, you keep it clean and simple. She slipped, you tried to catch her. I was here. I saw exactly what you just said. We don't want *Grand-mère* worrying, she'll soon be here, she's enough to worry her."

An ambulance wails to a stop outside. The door opens, voices call out, and feet stomp down the steps to Henri's shouts. Henri holds me to one side as a stretcher is rattled down the steps. He tells them about the fall, about Grandmother Creed's cane slipping and my trying to catch her and taking a fall myself, but am unhurt. They lift her, her head flopping back like a dead chicken's.

Hustling me up the stairs, Henri helps me find my coat and boots and half carries me to the ambulance. The driver tells us to get inside, and we crawl into the back, squeezing against the cold metal sides as the ambulance men come soon after with Grandmother Creed. I turn from her tiny, wrinkled face, her closed eyes as they slide her in beside me and Henri. I burrow my face into the damp of Henri's sweater, listening in fear to the men as they talk loudly to each other and to the driver. Within minutes we're at the hospital, the men manoeuvring the stretcher out of the ambulance, Henri's arm protectively around my shoulders as he guides me through the emergency doors behind them. The nurses, the filing clerks, the interns, they all ask question after question, all the same: what happened, is she on medications, what is her name, what is yours. They hustle us to a small room off the crowded waiting room. There's no one here, only a few chairs and a small wooden table.

We sit, Henri rubbing my shoulder for comfort, the harsh ceiling lights heightening the pallor of my hands lying lifeless on my lap. I look at Henri's warm dark face sequestered between his creamy worsted cap and the coiled neck of his sweater. With the smell of Missus Louis's sheep still living in the wool and a trace of saliva dampening his lower lip, he is the one element of life in this austere room and my cold hands reach towards him.

He takes them, rubs them between his and holds them to his mouth, blowing warm rushes of air over them. I wait for him to start asking me questions too, but he doesn't, he just keeps leaning forward, massaging my hands, not looking at me.

"She said bad things, Henri," I say tonelessly.

"Tell me about the bad things, baby."

"Father said bad things, too."

"Tell me what they said."

"Father said he'd cut your credit at his store if I didn't leave Sables d'Or. He said he'd blacken your name like a winter's spud. He said you'd be eating salt fish and cowhide before the winter was halfway through."

Henri shakes his head. He pats my hands and then leans back, rubbing his face like he's rubbing away dirt. "He lied, Livvy. *Grand-père* would starve before taking credit from your old man. Your Grandmother Creed's been lending Mammy money for years for spring startup. We pay back every copper come fall and the books are tallied. He lied to you, your old man's a goddamn liar, we've never taken credit from him."

I bend over with a cramp and he wraps an arm around my shoulder. "Can't let something like this touch you, Livvy, it's bigger than you. That's why there'll always be wars. Men like your father

and old *Grand-père,* they gotta find someplace for what ails them.
Damn sight easier sighting subs on the bottom of the sea than the
rot in the hearts of fools." He shoves himself up onto his feet and
knuckles his palm, his words rambling on like a river again as he
paces, looking for places to hide himself this time from the rage,
the guilt and the fear smouldering in my eyes.

He sits, giving me a gentle shake. "You hear me, Livvy? You
can't let it get to you. You didn't stand a chance against him. I
would've done what you did. It shows your heart, it shows your
big heart, you tried to save us by leaving."

"He *did* bad things too, him and Grandmother Creed."

Henri stops talking. He listens as I tell him of what Father did,
the deal he made with the grandmother. He remains quiet long
after I've finished talking.

"Did you hear, Henri?"

"Yes. I heard."

"What they did to my mother?"

"And you too."

"They lied. They took her heart."

"And yours too, baby."

"My poor mother. My poor, poor mother."

"She had you. She had Mammy and *Grand-mère* too, and all
of us."

"She told me lies about you. And the child. She—she let me
think things about Missus Louis. She was twisting my thinking,
Henri. I was starting to think bad things about Missus Louis, like
I done you. I would've started thinking them about Mother too.
That's how crafty she was. Like the fox. That's what Mother said,
she's like the fox. I never listened."

"Hard listening to someone who's dead, Livvy. You got to
find out things for yourself. If we could learn from others, there'd

be no war. And, hell, baby, if there was hanging for bad thoughts, we'd all be swinging."

"I've done bad things too now."

"No." His eyes spark with anger. "You froze up, that's all you done, you froze up like any of us would have in the same situation. It was probably for a second. You was probably frozen for a second and it felt like minutes. I know about things like this—you don't go to war and not learn about things like this. If you hadn't fallen yourself, you would've caught her. You didn't do nothing wrong. I was there and I saw it and I don't want to hear no more about that."

He sits back, folding his arms tight before him.

"How come you don't let things bother you?" I ask. "How come you never minded *Grand-père* yelling at you all the time?"

He snorts. "Hell, I minded. I was always mouthing back when I was a youngster, spent days mouthing back at old *Grand-père*. One day I figured he wasn't bullying me for any good reason, he was just bullying because he'd been bullied. That's the difference between me and *Grand-père*. I had time to sit back and mull things over. Didn't have to spend every minute of the day prowling and scheming for a bite of mutton or bread like he done."

"But things got good. They didn't have to fight and scavenge in the end," I argue.

"By then they already had their devils."

I think about his words for a moment, then ask in a whisper, "How do we know when we're not being evil?"

He shifts impatiently. "That's when I listens to my heart, Livvy. I takes what it says and moves on and tells myself there's no sense dwelling. What's good today might be a sin tomorrow. You just got to feel in your gut that what you're doing is the right thing, and what happens after that is a different kettle of fish." He clasps his hands behind his head, his arms against his ears as though closing out my words. I try to see into his eyes but he swings onto his feet as though avoiding them; he's afraid, he's afraid of what he'll see there. I understand. I understand why he doesn't want my story. He needs to believe in his own, in my innocence, in order to defend me.

Our attention is suddenly taken by a white-coated doctor looking anxiously inside the room. His eyes are small like a sheep's behind thick, black-framed glasses as he looks from Henri to me. I read Henri's worry in the pressure of his hand as he takes mine and we both stand to attention like frightened schoolchildren as the doctor begins to speak. She has a cut on her lower back that took stitching. More serious is her concussion, a *severe* concussion, he emphasizes, and they won't know the effects till after she's woken up.

"How long before she wakes?" I ask.

"An hour, ten hours, perhaps days. There's no telling, we just wait."

"And after she wakes up, will she—will she be all right?"

He begins to speak, then pauses, rubbing the bridge of his glasses. "She's an old woman and very frail. We just don't know. There's the worry of blood clotting. The best we can do is wait. Someone will let you know when you can see her," he adds kindly. He turns to the sound of voices in the hall. It is the police. I must have gasped out loud, for Henri jerks my hand. I sit, my knees shaking so hard they knock against each other, my heart pounding with panic.

"The doctor's news isn't so great," Henri says to them, and sits beside me, hugging me. "She'll be fine, Livvy, she's going to make it," he says soothingly.

"You're Livvy Higgs?" asks one of the policemen. They come towards me, their backs straight, their chests big, and there's an ominous glistening in their eyes. Or perhaps I put it there, for their voices are kind when they speak, asking me what happened.

"She—she slipped," I begin. "I tried to catch her. She—she was already falling—" My voice croaks, my mouth so dry I can scarcely move my tongue. I keep looking at the older policeman with the grey tufts of sideburns curling down around his jawline. The younger one keeps looking at his watch and I'm heartened that there are other things taking his mind. Henri points out the scrape on my cheek, the bump on my head. "She fell too, trying to catch her," he says. "I got to the door just as it happened. I tried to catch them, but I was too late, just a second too late. I got detained on my ship—goddamn. Just five more seconds and I probably could've prevented the whole thing."

"What ship you on?" asks the older policeman, and Henri stands, patting his wounded leg, telling briefly of his being torpedoed and how he's now searching foreign merchant ships for bombs. He is sparing me their attention and I look up into his eyes, which are so filled with concern as he looks back at me that a shudder of passion shoots through my heart.

The policemen are looking at him favourably as well. "You take care of those ships, soldier," they say, clapping his shoulder with pride, "and we'll take care of the rest."

"We wish the best for your grandmother, ma'am," the older policeman says to me, and they take their leave.

Informing the nurses at the station where to find us, Henri leads me down the hallway to a more comfortable waiting room. I sit stiffly on the sofa, but Henri pushes me back against the pillows.

"Lie down," he instructs, and taking my coat, he drapes it over me as he had earlier with Grandmother Creed. I lean back, seeing her lying unconscious somewhere down the hall. And Father, recovering from surgery somewhere above me. I close my eyes against the ceiling light shining garishly down. It's how every-thing feels right now, like a garish light burning inside my eyes, and I want only to sleep, to escape into darkness. And I must have, for when I open my eyes, Henri is gone.

I lie there for a while trying to absorb the quiet, trying not to think about my grandmother in a coma down the corridor, or my Father recovering from surgery above me. Footsteps sound out in the hallway. I hear Henri's voice. I close my eyes again and face the back of the sofa, not wanting to talk just yet.

"You awake?" he asks, entering noisily. He drags a heavy piece of furniture to where I'm lying on the sofa. I smell her first: the grassy sweet of dandelion greens, the earthiness of growing things. I sit upright, gasping to see her lowering herself into an armchair Henri has provided: her white hair tucked behind her ears, her eyes dark and soft and staring concernedly down at me.

"*Macushlah*," she whispers as I fling my arms around her neck. She holds me tight, speaking softly. "Henri's told me, he's told me everything. Your poor mother having to learn such a thing. And your grandmother, that she'd *do* such a thing. Aye, it's a day for prayers, luv. And now, for her to have taken such a fall! Enough to make one believe in a punishing God."

I feel the sting of tears and catch a cautioning look from Henri as he hovers near the door. In the slow shake of his head I read that he's not told her everything, only those things that he himself believes. "I'll go check on the old soul," he says. "Be back in a few minutes."

He closes the door behind him and I look back at Missus Louis. The softness has left her eyes, replaced by an earnestness that creates more unease within me. "I shouldn't have let you come," she says wearily. "I was wrong to let you come."

"But you had nothing to do with my coming. It was Father who made me leave."

"I encouraged you to go. I was always encouraging you. I should have just up and told you everything, but there it is now, no sense puffing on dead embers."

Her words don't catch me at first, for I'm thinking about how to tell her the things that Henri won't listen to—how my hand felt frozen, how I could have caught the grandmother had I not been struck with rage. But the weariness in Missus Louis's eyes takes my thoughts. Her brow crumples as though sorting through too many things and I make myself smile, my heart falling into silent despair. She has become old. Too old to bear another failed heart.

"She—she slipped on the wet floor," I whisper. "But I'm glad I came, for I know the truth of it now, and I could never have rested without knowing. What did you mean, you should have told me? About the deal Grandmother Creed made? Did you know about the deal with my father?"

"My soul, no. I could scarcely believe my ears when Henri told me about that," she exclaims, crossing herself. She glances towards the door beyond which Grandmother Creed lies and opens her mouth to speak, then closes it as if resigned to the futility of words in helping her express this thing that shadows her.

"I know you're the girl in the locket," I say. "You—you used to be friends?"

She sighs, wiping at her eyes. "It's not a good story, luv. It's been my plague for most of my life and it don't seem right I've to burden you with it."

"Please, I want to hear."

"Of course you do. Nothing will ever make sense if you don't. Do you remember Neave, the little girl born in the orphanage?"

"You kept her from fading."

Missus Louis nods. "There's no easy way to say this, luv. Neave is your Grandmother Creed."

I stare at her, trying to grasp the meaning of her words.

"It's hard to take in, but that's the truth of it. Your grandmother is Irish. She's as Irish as I am."

"But—but that's not possible."

Missus Louis nods. "Hers isn't a nice story, Livvy. There's reasons why she wanted to rid herself of it. But the day is long gone when she should have set things right. Or I should have. I was about to. I wrote Neave—perhaps I should say Julia? That's the name she took. Would it make it easier for you, luv, were I to call her Julia?"

"No. No, I've never known anyone to call her that either, not even my father. Why did she change her name, why did she lie?"

"Cecile knew nothing of her mother's past, about her time in the orphanage. Before she died I wrote many times to Neave, urging her to come forth with the truth. Perhaps it might have changed things between her and Cecile. But mostly it might have helped Cecile to learn the truth about herself."

"But—but *Father*—"

"Aye, it would've struck like a maw at his teeth. It would've eaten like maggots at his brain that he'd been had by the Irish. But it wasn't for him that I held my tongue, it was for your mother. Durwin would've stoned her with words had he found out, that he would've. But she was finding her feet, your mother was. The time was coming when I would've told her. I'd already threatened Neave."

"But she's so *English*! She's more English than anybody—and why?"

Missus Louis wearily shakes her head. "It's hard to tell where a story starts, who hove the first rock. All the way back to Creation, I suppose, like the scriptures say." She smiles, but with effort. "There it is now, blaming God for our weaknesses. I take my share of Neave's sinning. But it does go back, all the way to Neave's great-grandfather. Joseph. That would've been your great-great-grandfather. He wasn't a good man, *macushlah*. He was convicted of murder in Ireland and wheeled in a cart to a convict ship anchored off the Cove of Cork. The saints be praised, if there'd been any good in him when he boarded that ship, it would've rotted before he left it—a hundred men all chained together for a year, sitting in that filthy ship in the harbour, waiting to set sail to a penal colony. They were fed just enough maggoty fish to keep them from starving, and rats scratching at their faces while they slept. Treated like dogs, luv. When they finally sailed they were supposed to be taken to a prison in Botany Bay, but a fever broke aboard ship. The captain dumped his load instead on the shores of Bay Bulls, near St. John's—a hundred convicts with scarcely no food nor clothing. That was back in 1789. They lived for three days fighting over a bit of butter and beef, and were half starved and half froze by the time they made it to St. John's. Imagine, luv, 1789. And it's still playing itself out. Are you sure you want me to go on?"

"Tell me," I prod her with a grim fascination.

"Very well, then. Most of the prisoners got rounded up and sent back to England, but Joseph—he managed to escape. But he was found again and hanged a couple of years later—"

"Hanged?"

"That's the truth of it. I'm sorry to startle you, *macushlah,* and I wish it ended there."

"But *why?*"

"They say he was addled by the time he got off that boat. Instead of making a run down the shore when he escaped, he joined in with a hard crew of Frenchmen in St. John's. He hated the English and was plotting to mutiny, to murder those with property. He was caught and hanged for it. It was evil what he was plotting, and there was no one who cared enough to wrap his bones in cloth before they buried him. But he left a part of himself behind—his nasty part, God forgive me. A young daughter he had with Lizzy. Lizzy was an Irish woman who was put ashore from the same prison ship as himself. The daughter's name was Gertrude, they called her Gert. That would be Neave's grandmother, and there was no harder heart in all the Dominion than that one."

"She said her old granny raised her," I cut in with surprise. "She said all these nice things about her old granny loving her."

"Her old granny rotted in prison for helping incite riots amongst the English Protestants and the Irish Catholics. Ahh, it's a hideous tale. After she was jailed her two boys and a girl were placed in the orphanage where my mam worked. The youngest was Milly—that would be Neave's mother. My mam took to Milly. She was a meek little thing. She never bore up well with the talk and it was hard talk, *macushlah*. No one forgot about the murderous crimes her grandfather was plotting, and then with her mother, Gert, helping to incite riots—it stirred the old stuff back up again and it settled like dregs on the backs of her youngsters.

"When Milly was of age, she took off on a merchant ship to New England. Mind you, like her grandfather, she left a little something behind. An infant—Neave. Nobody knew Milly was pregnant till she gave birth. However in the name of God you can hide something like that."

"She said her mother died! She said she died giving birth to her. Is there *nothing* that wasn't a lie?"

Missus Louis looks at me with pity.

"Did she ever travel the country with her charities? What *did* she do then?" I ask as Missus Louis slowly shakes her head. "Somebody must've raised her, somebody had to care for her. The house—it belonged to her granny and her mother? Didn't her mother grow up there?"

I catch the pleading in my voice. I want something of Grandmother Creed and her old granny to be true, the floors creaking beneath their step, the candlelight warming their faces, their withered hands.

"She bought the house after she married, before Cecile was born. What is it, *macushlah*?" she asks as I lower my head with a pained look.

"My mother would never have believed those lies."

"You can't think yourself naive, Livvy. She fooled more than you with her tales."

"She's evil," I croak.

"Pity her, luv, pity her loneliness. She was afraid of losing you. She didn't trust the truth, for it was a black mark against her name. And that's no lie, since it was the family shame that drove her mother away."

"Well, she's shamed herself with her lies now, hasn't she. She's worse than my father. At least he believed his."

"Perhaps she believed hers."

"No, no, they're too made up. You don't know—I hate her and I don't want to hear nothing more."

"Then know what it is you hate, and why," says Missus Louis harshly. "My granny, who yoked herself to a plow and worked like a horse for a spud a day, was slandered as wicked and idle by ignorant tongues. She never learned why. My mam was a fallen woman because her husband left her when she was pregnant and the priest ruled her unfit to enter his church. She never understood why either. She took herself to an orphanage and worked to have a place in which to raise me, and there wasn't a day she and my granny didn't give thanks for small mercies. If you're going to yoke yourself to a plow, *macushlah,* let it be one that feeds you and not fields of malice."

I lower my eyes and sit stiffly on the edge of the sofa. Missus Louis looks around the small room as though it's closing in on her, and then sits back, dabbing at the sweat prickling her brow, and takes up the story. "Her mother, Milly, committed the first sin against your grandmother. But I committed the second. You remember I told you how I treated her like a doll, she was so pretty? And then she was taken in by this wealthy English family, the Crenshaws, as a playmate for their daughter, Frances? Do you remember all that?"

"You said she was happy there."

"Yes. She was. And after a while she started talking in an English accent too, like Frances and her parents, and taking up their mannerisms. I thought it was cute," Missus Louis exclaims. "I actually encouraged her because she sounded so cute." She shakes her head. "I didn't see it, luv. I didn't see it happening. But Missus Crenshaw did. She was uncomfortable with Neave's talking like that. And her manner of putting on airs. Then," Missus Louis shrugs, "to be expected, I suppose, Neave began to get demanding, expecting a certain dress or hair ribbon whenever Frances received one. When she turned thirteen, she wanted to sit in the dining room with the Crenshaws for her birthday cake. Instead she had to eat with the servants. She threw a fit and the next day she was sent back to the orphanage. We both were. It mattered little to me. I had met Louis on one of my Sundays home, and was already thinking of leaving with him when he sailed back to Sables d'Or. But Neave, she was stunned."

Missus Louis falls silent, her eyes fixed on some point ahead as though she's come to that part of the story she still can't figure. "Dear heart," she murmurs. "She sat for days, wouldn't speak, wouldn't let anyone touch her. I begged her to come with me and Louis, but she wouldn't leave. She believed Missus Crenshaw would come for her, that Frances would miss her and it was all a horrible mistake. So, she waited.

"I wouldn't have left her if not for my mam. Mam promised to care for her. I kept writing to her all while she stayed in the orphanage. She stayed till she was a young woman, teaching the younger children and earning her keep that way. I went back when my mam died. Then I saw what Neave had done. There was nothing Irish left in her, she had it all washed out and was introducing herself to everyone as an English teacher working with the poor little orphans."

A shudder passes through Missus Louis. "You see how it happened, *macushlah*? Somewhere, the truth of herself got lost. It was how she coped. Some might envy that she didn't lie down, bawling over her fate. She took it head-on and then met an Englishman who was smitten by her and took her to Halifax to be married. That would be your grandfather, the dentist. They lived here all their lives. Hard to imagine, but he knew no more about her past than you did. Till I tell it to you now. That Cecile should end up in Sables d'Or ..." She shrugs. "Well, that's not such a strange one. It was—and still is—a major shipping area, everybody goes there.

"So, there it is now, there's your grandmother's story. Find the good in it, for it's part of yours too now, and you can't cut it out like a canker."

I shake my head disbelievingly. "What good? It was all a lie. All those lies for a pretty dress and a fancy house."

"Must be something of her old self left inside, or else why did she keep in touch with me?" asks Missus Louis. "She saw what I had with my daughter Esmée and my grandchildren, everybody caring so much. I could see she wanted it. She felt so lonely, and she suffered so much from losing Cecile. I thought she'd find her way through you, at least I'd hoped she would. You said you hated her—could you have hated her if you didn't feel something, *macushlah*? Is there nothing?"

"She wasn't lonely," I say with scorn. "She was jealous that you had something she didn't, that's how vain she is. I'm no more to her than a locket. She's no different from Father, wanting me and Mother as a way of getting more insurance money." Instantly I regret the words, regret the despondency in my tone and the disdain on my face, for they heap more anguish on Missus Louis's long-suffering heart. Sagging back in her chair, she crumples a tissue to her eyes.

"No, don't worry," I cry, falling to my knees before her. "I mightn't have been born if not for you, and I'm glad I'm Irish. Mother would've been glad, too, she would've been proud." I lay my face against her bosom, pressing hard, wanting to push back those tremors passing through her, wanting to push inside her big, comforting self and into those days of running about her door-place, helping with carding and spinning and knitting wool, and scrubbing sheets with Suzie, and laughing at Henri and Mister Louis fighting between themselves, fighting with the youngsters flattening the hay with their play, and all things pulsing through the one heart, the one river of blood muscling us through our chores. But I've been nudged into a stream of my own now, and like the egret I must claw through its water, searching for another source of nourishment.

Henri enters, his wool cap pushed above his ears as he mostly wears it and his sweater pushed up to his elbows. The grand-mother is still unconscious but the doctor has given permission for a family member to visit.

"Don't worry, I'll be fine," I say to Missus Louis, and impul-sively squeeze her hand before following Henri down the hall. He remains quiet, but I feel his strength in the way he touches my shoulder, my arm, guiding me through the corridors and in through the emergency room for the second time that day. As I did with Father, I falter before the pale pink sheets curtaining off her bed. But I muster my courage and step towards her, feeling faint. She lies beneath the sheet, looking like little more than a child's doll withered with play, her face white as bone, her eyes sunken in her skull. And her hair, as with Mother's, appears to have darkened, and I know she will not awaken.

I sit weakly on a chair, the horror of the basement steps coming back to me. I keep looking at her eyes, wanting them to open and save me from the awful guilt of having let her fall, but my revulsion at her lies and her made-up self keeps me from speaking. So I sit. I sit for a long time watching her pale, stilled face and listening to the whisper of breath seeping through her thin, colourless mouth, and I feel nothing. Trembling, I rise from her bedside and hurry outside. Henri is waiting. I run to him, wrapping my arms around his neck, feeling the rough of his sweater on my cheek as he grips me to him.

"I don't feel nothing for her, Henri, I don't feel nothing."

"Feel this, then, baby," he says, engulfing me in his arms.

"You'll leave with Missus Louis."

"I'll not leave you, Liv."

I cling to him, letting his words stroke me as he murmurs, "Nothing to be afraid of, I won't let anything happen to you, you've got nothing more to worry about, I've got you now."

Fetching Missus Louis and assuring her there is nothing more to be done this evening, he cabs us through the snowy night to Grandmother Creed's house. Tucking Missus Louis into my grandmother's bed, Henri takes himself into mine. He holds me in the way I remember, his big bear body wrapped around mine, our hearts beating hard, a passion growing between us that empties me of thought, that tolerates no restraints, and every pent-up emotion inside of me finds its way into sweet release.

I reach for him again and again in the days that follow. During those moments with the smell of his skin and his breathing suffusing mine, I am too full to feel anything but the immediacy of being with him. He awakens more than my numbed senses, he awakens my courage to take turns with Missus Louis sitting at my grandmother's bedside. I sit there for hours, saying nothing, just letting it be, my mind empty of thought and my heart of feeling. My father is being released from the hospital, one of the nurses tells me. Missus Louis has tried visiting him, but he wouldn't see her. Nor would he see Henri. Yet he is aware of what has happened with Grandmother Creed, and wishes to speak to me.

I sniff with disdain. "He has nothing more I want to hear," I say, and go to my grandmother's bedside to relieve Missus Louis.

"Are you sure, luv?" she asks, after I tell her of my father's request.

"He is not my father," I reply, and a feeling akin to lightness comes over me, as though I have just shed a winter's cloak. It is a feeling short-lived. Several days later, about eight or nine days now since the fall, there is a call from Sables d'Or. Mister Louis has taken a bad turn. Missus Louis accepts the news with knowing. She looks down onto Grandmother Creed's shrivelled form lying silent beneath her bedding and reaches for her hand, but it is me she speaks to, her voice scarcely an utterance.

"When the sea swallows a man, does that make it evil, *macushlah*—when it's just following its nature? It's only evil to them who think it to be. I'd be careful with how I judge her, luv. Only she knows the truth in her heart, and even that's known more by God."

I sit by the grandmother's bedside long after Missus Louis is gone, staring at her tiny face withered like a leaf in winter's wake. I stare at those sunken eyes, imagining how pretty they once were, and how Missus Louis worked to keep them pretty, to keep them from fading to grey. The wretched memory of searching through the dune grass for Mother comes to me and I am not without heart and I lean closer to Grandmother Creed, asking in a whisper, "Did you search for your mother? Is that why you made up your old granny, because you couldn't find your mother?"

My words vanish into Grandmother Creed's silence. I speak them again, and then again, striving to break through her silence and the nothingness that fills me. Thoughts of Mother come to me, images of her that build with an urgency as though trying to break free from some hold I have on them. I let them come. I begin speaking them out loud to my grandmother, telling her, finally, those things she's been wanting to hear. My voice croaks over words I have never spoken, words heavy with sound and yet sparse in meaning for I tell nothing of my deepest moments with Mother, none of her secret anguish. I tell only those things as seen by clouds: Mother walking along the yellow sand beach, Mother standing atop a rock, her hair a reddish plume in the wind, Mother stretching out her arms like the wings of a bird.

Sparse though my words may be, they ring deep in my heart,

triggering images so sharp I close my eyes, seeing myself scooting over the sand like a crab, gathering cold, shivery lances to drop beside Mother as she watches the sea crumpling at her feet. I see me burrowing beside her in the dunes as she stares through her smoke clouds at thoughts known only to her. I see me running to catch up with her those times when she walks angrily ahead. I see me bribing her with catalogues as she puffs smoke out my bedroom window, and me choking on food trying to keep her from fighting with Father, and I am no longer telling Mother's story. It is a tale of a frightened child clinging to her mother's dress as her mother becomes more and more caught within herself and her ongoing fights with Grandmother Creed and Father.

Something strikes me and I start towards the grandmother. *There's no soul lonelier than the one without a mother,* she had said. "Did you know? Did you know my loneliness?" I ask into her silence. I push away from her bed. She knew. She knew my loneliness, she knew it better than me. It was how she had seduced me, through my loneliness. I hold my hands to my mouth and push further away from that parched face that shrivels more and more with each passing day, her soul slipping as silently from her old woman's body as it did from the young girl Neave's.

I lie awake, cuddled against the near-sleeping Henri, staring at the night sky sprinkling starlight through my window. "My mother didn't talk to me like a mother," I say quietly. "Do you think that's all right, Henri?"

"As long as she talked to you, baby, and it was comforting."

"She would've seen how caught in herself she was. Missus Louis said she was finding her feet, she would've seen it."

"There's them who never do. That don't mean nothing either, they probably got the biggest hearts."

"I felt her loving me."

"Pity your mother and grandmother both, baby. Neither of them had a mam. Makes it even more special, your mother making you feel love like that."

"If she wakes up, do I tell Grandmother Creed about all her lies?"

"That's a hard one, Liv. Be like hitting her with a sledge-hammer, don't you think? Can't imagine spending my life staking out enemies, then finding at the end there weren't none, only my own fool heart. *Grand-mère* would tell you to pity her. Let's sleep now."

The next morning I sit beside the grandmother. After a while I sink to my knees and try to pray. I take her cold, emptied hands and try to whisper into them words of forgiveness, but my voice is silent. I try to pray for my father, for his heart greased with a greed that stole from him any small joy, and I try to pray for his father who committed that first great sin against him. But my voice is silent. And so I pray to God to burn the anger from my soul, and I take comfort from the reverence with which those words resound through my heart.

Grandmother Creed passes and Henri stands beside me as we lay her beneath the sod. And he stands beside me again when the police return several days after the burial. There are questions, many more questions. I am the heir to my grandmother's house and her substantial wealth. Had I known I was her heir, they repeatedly ask, before her fall? And Henri, who stood as a source of their pride in the hospital, becomes a questionable character, too, in light of his relationship with me and my newly acquired fortune.

"They're just doing their jobs," says Henri. "They'll get bored soon enough, there's a gawd-damn war on. And that's pure crap," he continues, gesturing to a newspaper article appearing just that morning about my grandmother's death and the visits, lately, of the police questioning her granddaughter who is heir to her sizeable estate.

"They make it look as though I killed her for her money," I exclaim in horror. "I've never thought of her money, I've just never ever thought like that."

"That's their job, baby, to cut off other people's heads so's they can stand taller themselves. Five ships got sunk last evening. They'll not waste more ink on you."

"The neighbours, they're looking at me every time I go out."

"Dress real pretty, then. Make them want to keep looking. You want to marry me, Livvy? Don't help you're living in sin."

"You want to marry me to save my reputation?"

"I can think up more reasons. Just need some supper right now." He laughs and ushers me into the kitchen. "Gawd-damn, nothing makes a man foolisher than a woman serving him tea."

I make his tea. I know his heart is deep beneath his joking ways, but I don't feel right in standing before God just yet, asking for blessings. As for living in sin, perhaps I'm just tailoring truths to serve me, but I read somewhere that when you're young, honour is everything. And that when you're old you see the silliness of such thinking. This, then, I adopt into my thinking and for the rest of that miserably wet winter and the damp summer to come I ignore the critical looks of my neighbours and watch in comfort as Henri leaves my door each morning and goes off to work, sweeping ships in the harbour for bombs and other forms of sabotage.

But nothing can lighten the weight of the secrets I carry in my heart: my mother's, my father's and my grandmother's. And now my own. They circle my heart like a moat, keeping me separate from all things. I try to understand the secrets, sometimes wanting Henri to help me, but he's impatient.

"Leave all that stuff where it belongs, Livvy, in the past," he keeps saying. "I told you, baby doll, you got too many anchors weighing you down. Cut the ropes, set yourself adrift. I would think you'd be more concerned with making a respectable woman of yourself," he adds more than once. "But a man, well, this man, only asks a woman once to marry him."

"Do *you* think what we're doing is shameful?" I whisper one night in the aftermath of our lovemaking, his heart still pounding hard and fast against mine.

He bellows a laugh. "Hell thunderin' jeezus *no.*" Lifting me to him, his eyes search out mine as though they hold some mystery he's yet to figure. I squirm with discomfort, unable to hold such intimacy, and nuzzle into his neck. "Whoa, get back here," he commands, cupping my chin and lifting my face to his. "Open your eyes, open them eyes." But instead I lower my head again against the thick, pulsating column of his throat. "Gawd-damn, Liv, I don't know half the time what you're thinking," he groans.

"I was thinking about shame. I was asking if you ever felt shame."

"Perhaps when I was firing guns at some poor bastard crawling through the water beneath my ship. That's what shame is, killing each other in wars without ever figuring what the wars are about. I'll tell you something else that's shameful: not living the life the good Lord give us. And that's what worries me, Livvy, the way you're always to yourself, thinking about everything gone wrong in the past."

"I'm trying to figure things, too. You just said, it's a shame to not figure things."

"It's a shame when you starts feeling shame for not catching old granny."

Even when I could have caught her? I want to ask. I don't, though. His voice is soft and he's cradling me comfortably against him, but I hear the impatience in his tone, and it frightens me that he'll grow tired of my trying to figure things and walk away.

He doesn't. He stays through another hellish year of war, and then the day comes when peace is called and I anxiously pace the floors, waiting for him to come home. As great as my relief is that this war has ended, I can't help but worry how it'll affect me. Will Henri want to go home now? I know I will never go home again. My father's presence in Sables d'Or is a darkness that would forever cloud my days, and the ghost of my mother would forever haunt those yellow sandy beaches of Sables d'Or. No. This is my home now. Halifax. I will learn to be its friend.

Henri gets home late. He twirls me around the house in his excitement about the war ending, and practically carries me downtown to dance. The city has erupted into a frenzy of joyous whoops. Thousands of civilians and sailors pour through the streets, shouting and cheering over the horns blasting from the ships in the harbour and the trams and cars honking all around us. Windows are thrown open overhead, flags are unfurled and rolls and rolls of toilet paper stream down the sides of the build-ings into the crowds below. But beneath the joyous madness is an undertow of resentment and scorn that have built up, in sailors and civilians alike, from the four long years of living in cramped, sparse conditions, with both sides gouging the pockets and comforts of the other. Capping the resentment is the city closing its liquor stores and restaurants and movie houses the day peace is called—so that everybody can join the celebration, they say. But it's because they're nervous about riled sailors getting drunk and rowdy, Henri tells me as we squeeze inside a dance hall that's flooded with sailors waltzing with their girls to loud, piped-in music. Henri slips his arms around me and it doesn't matter that I can't dance. All one has to do is hold onto one's partner and try to keep from being trodden on. Cupping my chin, Henri lifts my face and smiles. "You might try smiling, baby doll," he says.

"I'm trying to dance, Henri, but you just won't keep still."

He laughs and the brown of his eyes pours into mine and I start feeling flushed and tongue-tied. He keeps smiling and I try to look away, but he imprisons my face between his hands and I start getting anxious, my mouth quivering like a neglected youngster's who's suddenly singled out from her horde of siblings and offered a mother's kindness. "Stop squirming and look at me," he says in a low voice, and I'm relieved by someone hauling on his shoulder, passing him a foaming bottle of beer. He guzzles from it, foam washing down his chin, then holds it to my mouth.

"A taste, just a taste," he urges. I touch my tongue to the harsh, yeasty fluid, and when I draw back with a sour face he grins and swings me upward with a violent roar of approval. I laugh as he sets me back down. A civilian pushes his way through the dancers, shouting something about riots, and Henri sobers.

"Let's get the hell home, Liv," he says, and taking my hand, he pushes through the crowd. Others are leaving as well, a flotilla of sailors and civilians, all suddenly serious and intent, swarming out behind us. It's getting late, but thousands of people are still thronging the streets. The sound of breaking glass shatters the air. Taking the corner, I gasp to see mobs of sailors flinging rocks and bricks at storefront windows and howling like wolves as they tear inside the shops, tossing out racks of coats and dresses and shoes like piles of garbage. Everywhere there are mobs of military people and city folk drinking and smashing windows and looting stores and restaurants and setting fires. Henri stops at the barred entrance of a liquor store with a group of sailors and civilians crowding in front of it. Someone shouts to Henri, a woman.

"Wait right there, Liv, I sees what they're up to," he says, nudging me inside the alcove of a nearby storefront.

"I don't care what they're up to, let's go home!" I yell in fright, following after him, but I draw back as three women in navy uniforms, their arms linked, stagger drunkenly towards Henri, calling his name. One of them breaks away, throwing herself into Henri's arms with a whoop, and he laughs, lifting her as he lifted me only minutes ago at the dance. The other two women raise their drinks in cheer as the one he's hoisting smacks his face with kisses. He puts her down and she clings to him as he fists a roar of approval towards a couple of men who're coming out from beside the liquor store dragging a heavy plank. Thumping one of the men on the back, he lifts the plank with a dozen others, and, holding it waist high, rams it at the door, splintering it from its hinges. Henri disappears inside while the men fall into a brigade and I watch in dismay as crates of beer and liquor start being passed out of the store and along the line, vanishing into the hooting, hollering mob.

Incensed with Henri's helping in such a thing, and resentful of being left alone amongst such carnage, I leave the alcove and hurry down the street. Within a minute I'm standing, frightened, amidst the rioting exploding around me, the streets being littered with store display cases, goods, garbage, broken glass, furniture. There are buildings burning and the stench of smoke burns my eyes as civilians flee in all directions, some snatching armfuls of clothes and shoes and coats from the street and ducking quickly out of sight down alleyways. I turn back to find Henri, but I'm thwarted by a tram rattling past. A group of sailors tackle it, hauling it from its tracks, and start rocking it, hooting and jeering at the frightened passengers now streaming through its doors. One of the sailors climbs onto its roof and starts bashing it with an iron lever. An explosion rocks it from its rear end and I stand frozen, staring in stunned fright at the burning tram.

A car comes towards me from the direction of the dance hall. It stops and the driver yells out to me, his face pinched with panic. Inside, the cab is crammed with women from the dance. A back door opens and I hold out my hand and am pulled inside a cramped nest of furs and rustling satin and starched hair and gloved hands and more assorted scents than a meadow in summer's bloom. Looking through the back window, I search for Henri. He'll be looking for me, panicked. Instantly, I am shamed by my running off.

"Stop, stop!" I yell, "I want to get out!," but I'm shouted down by the anxious voices of the other women urging the driver onwards.

The house rings with silence as I enter. Taking off my shoes and coat, I stand looking about. I wrap myself in a shawl and pace the rooms with a fervour that keeps me from putting my mind to anything but thoughts of Henri searching for me.

He ought not to have left me, I tell myself. He ought not to have involved himself with the riotous behaviours of those men.

I go to Grandmother Creed's rocker by the window, and for the first time, I sit in it. I pull back the curtains as she must've done a hundred times a day, and look out onto the darkened street. I wonder what morning will hold for this city's devastated downtown. But even in the silence of the living room my mind falls blank and my heart races as though I'm struggling up a steep hill. I look about this grand house with its flowery wallpaper and heavy drapes and lacy lamps and wooden cabinets and settee with the rose-carved edgings. Silence. It rings with a silence no word can enter. I leap to my feet, berating my foolishness over and over for running off and leaving Henri. Suppose he doesn't come back. Suppose he goes off with those women who were smacking kisses all over him. Perhaps he shouldn't come back, perhaps he should stay downtown with those silly girls.

A dog barks savagely outside and a man's voice barks back. I run to the window: it's Henri. He sees me and his body slumps with relief. Mine, too, slumps with relief, and then fear of his pending response to my running off.

I flee to my room, dismayed at the violence of my shifting emotions. I listen as he quietly enters the house. I listen as he takes off his boots and pads softly down the hallway, pausing outside the door. Opening it, he enters. I am lying with my face to the wall, my eyes half closed, feigning sleep as he lies on the bed beside me, the weight of his body pinning me beneath the covers. He grasps my hands from behind, holding them like two warm coals between his cold ones.

"I shouldn't have left you," he says quietly.

"Why did you help those men?"

"A drunken man is less trouble than a rampaging one. They should never have closed the damn stores, none of this would've happened."

"You shouldn't have left me."

"You always going to be running off, Liv?" His voice is soft, but tense. "Look at me," he says, tugging me onto my back. "Why won't you look at me?" I keep my face averted. "Gawd-damn it, Liv, I don't know nothing about you. I don't know if you're shy or just plain not interested. Or perhaps you're just a scared little girl, still hiding behind them big skirts your mama used to wear."

"Perhaps I don't like my man hoisting other women about and kissing them," I say pointedly.

"You're jealous? Well, gawd-damn, baby, but that's a love song to me." He wraps his arms around me, his big hands smooth and thick like the bark of a dogwood as he slides them down my bare back, chasing away chills and creating others. "Come on, Livvy, talk to me," he coaxes. "What's wrong, are you cold? Are you cold, baby, you're shivering, are you cold?"

I try to speak, but my tongue won't move, my lips won't part. I open my eyes and Henri is no more, it is Gen who is speaking.

"Are you cold, Livvy, are you okay? You were moaning," she says, seeing me awaken. "You were having more bad dreams. I'm sorry, I shouldn't have woken you. It's that bump, I'm just worried. Look, I've most of the cleaning done. Go back to sleep, then. I shouldn't have woken you."

NINE

I try to speak to Gen. I want to thank her for cleaning my house, but I'm not wanting to leave Henri. I want to make things right, but I don't know how and my heart cries out from its old woman's chest to my saddened younger self, hollowed out by a mother who took her love to soothe herself, giving her little in return upon which to build trust and honour with another. But Henri is waiting, his eyes tender with love, and it's easy to follow him into his lovemaking. I marry him in a judge's chambers and he bridges that small corner of my heart that isn't burdened with secrets. And given how the wounds of the flesh are easier to fix than the wounds of the heart, and how it's easier to be angry than to understand, I lock the secrets away. But he knows they're there, and perhaps it's his manly thing to try and fix all things right, or perhaps he's jealous of this place he can't enter, and so he gets testy sometimes.

"You should find a job, Livvy, get yourself out of the house," he says during supper one evening. "You're always brooding."

I look at him in surprise. Since the war ended he hasn't been home much, spending long stretches at sea with his new job on a merchant ship. "Why do you say that?" I ask. "I don't need to work. There's no work anyway, with the war over."

"There's lots out there for them who wants it. No need to be sitting home. Nobody's going to hurt you walking a few blocks down the road."

His words stoke me hard. "I'm not scared of going out," I reply. "And I'm not a coward, either. I took on coming here without you leading me."

"I'm not calling you a coward, Livvy."

"Yes, you just did."

"Hell, baby, I'm just grunting like an old pig here."

"Then grunt at your own self." I take myself from the table. He comes after me, offering apologies, and I can never be angry with him for long.

And perhaps it was his words that spur me through the want ads the following week. But it's my legs that take me to the hospital, answering their call for helpers. And blessed is that day and those to come, for it takes me outside of myself to help bathe, feed and rock those infants born into sickness, either their own or their mother's. And those unfortunates born into a world with no mother's arms waiting to hold them, those I rock the hardest to help keep them from fading into that grey that Missus Louis spoke of, and from falling into the silence of their missing mothers. They rock me, too. As I sit there, my cheek resting on their crowns that quiver with life, their little fingers clutching one of mine, they keep me fixed into this moment and from fading inside that chamber of my heart with its locked secrets.

But what's this, what's this now. This past while, it's been the girl who's demanding to be rocked, it's been my poor young self, locked inside a penitent heart and forgotten in the wearying pass of time. She waited all these years, till Henri laid his old *grand-père* to rest, and then his *grand-mère,* my beloved Missus Louis. I don't go with Henri to their burials in Sables d'Or. I sit at home and light a candle for each of them, lighting their way in the only way I know. I don't go when my father passes, either. Nor do I light a candle for him. He is too deeply tucked away with my secrets to be resurrected, even if it is to bury him again.

The day comes when I bury Henri in the graveyard behind the house.

I never need to light a candle for Henri, his light can never be extinguished, he permeates the air I breathe. It pained us both that I couldn't bear children, but as Henri repeatedly said, no use in pining for what can't be had. And now it's only me and the beckoning hand of God. And the girl who has awakened in me these past two days, and has helped lead me back through my garden of life, patrolling with me the soiled grounds where I battled, helping me gather those wounded bits and reunite them into my living heart.

My heart seizes again and I open my eyes, seeing her, like a shadow drawing closer, her skeletal bones all padded out now and swaddled in white, her hair tumbling forward, her eyes moist and dark and smiling. I hold out my hands, they are cold and I smile as she catches them in the warmth of hers and I feel her flowing like a river through my veins and my heart triumphs.

The girl's hair darkens and it is Gen, now, smiling down at me, my white cotton nightdress flung over her shoulder as she bathes my hands with a warm, soapy cloth. "Look who's waking up, now that the work's all done," she scolds. "Be still, then, I finishes bathing you. I found this lovely cotton nightdress in your drawer. Why are you smiling? You won't be for long, the plow just passed. Livvy, I'm calling an ambulance, I don't think you're well. We'll take the nightdress in case they keep you in for tests or something."

"No," I say, my voice much stronger than I would've imagined it. I grasp her hand and stare pleadingly into her eyes. She wraps her hand around my wrist, her fingers pressing against my quivering pulse.

"Jesus," she gasps, and her eyes widen with fright, but I'm still smiling at her.

"It's been that way all night," I whisper. "It's all right. I'm ready."

She's shaking her head, the colour draining from her face. "No. No, *I'm* not ready."

"It's not your life," I say softly.

"I can't let you die. I couldn't live with that decision."

"You'd have me live with yours?"

She stares at me, her eyes filling with defiance, and I know she'll call. She has to. Like Henri, she has to believe in her story in order to live with it, to defend it, if only to herself.

I roll my head aside with a weariness and it comes to me that Father, too, believed his story, else he wouldn't have fought so hard to protect it. And Grandmother Creed. Perhaps she became too lost, perhaps her made-up story kept her from falling into nothingness. What shame, what shame to suffer such loneliness when love was but a truth away. A thought comes to me, it comes hard and strong, that evil is swallowed by repentance, that only the sin of it carries on, and sin is little more than a smoky thought, clearing itself with the breath of prayer. I turn back to Gen, smiling again, how good, how good it is.

Gen's sitting there, her eyes on mine, not wanting to defy me, wanting my permission to lift the phone. She has been my unwitting confessor this past while as I lanced those swollen secrets, weaving their story into mine. Another thought strikes me: I've willed everything to Ronny. And Gen would have been my only companion during my last night. Would suspicion reign over her as it had with me?

Dear oh dear, how everything circles. I sigh again, giving her a slight nod. Frantically, she grasps the phone, shakily dialing. What odds, what odds, then. Let there be another sweet day if God so desires it. Perhaps another grace awaits me. Or perhaps it awaits Gen, one different from what I've already willed her.

"Now, right now, hurry!" she's shouting into the receiver. "Hurry, please, hurry." She puts down the phone and grabs my hands. "Don't die, don't freaking die. I need you for a while, I'm a fucking mess. Can we pray? Let's pray," she begs, and scoffs at her own words. "Prayers. At this point they're little more than begging, aren't they? That's what my mother, Treen, says every time she thinks she's dying—she must call the priest for her last rites. The beggar's prayer, she calls them. I think we're all beggars before God," she babbles, "I think life is one long prayer. Imagine that, Treen taught me something. Perhaps I should listen to her more. Don't die, Livvy, please, don't die." She puts her hands to her mouth to stop herself from talking and I gaze into her beautiful brown eyes, feeding them with the love flowing so freely now, from this too-full heart. Willaby leaps upon the settee and nuzzles his face against mine, soft as a summer's day. He stretches and bends his neck as though he feels my stroking him, and I giggle for this spirit that never mewls for yesterday, seeking only the comfort of the moment. Gen leans towards me, her hair tumbling forward as my mother's used to do, and I imagine it reddish, glowing and unfolding around me like a new dawn. "Shh," I say as Gen starts to cry, "I'll not leave yet, truly," and I pull her against me, feeling the warmth of her entering me, feeling her strength steadying my pulse—ahhh, sweet, sweet grace.

ACKNOWLEDGMENTS

I wish to express my extreme gratitude to my brother, Glenn, his
Diana and their Steven, whose love and courage humble me.

Thank you to …

My editors, Diane Turbide, publishing director, and David
Weale, and my agent, Beverly Slopen.

My dear friends Angela and Jim Sykes, and the girls: Lynn
Cochrane, Kimberly Matheson, Nancy Irvin, Pamela Stonehouse
and Mary Lynk.

My longtime friend Karen Pottle, her mom, Elsie Pottle,
and brother, Tony Pottle, and their common-wall neighbour,
Florence Tippett, who fed me their stories of growing up on that
old French shore in Newfoundland; and all my new friends in
St. George's Bay and on the Port au Port Peninsula who welcomed
me into their homes and shared with me their stories and heritage.
Especially, I would like to thank Debbie Coughlin, Peggy Bennett,
Lucy Simon, Naomi Felix, Ali Chaisson, Barbra King, Bill Pike,

Gerry Ryan, Bernie and Matilda Kerfont, and Elizabeth and Alban Cornect. My apologies to those whose names I've mixed up and/or mislaid; you burn bright in my memory.

I wish to thank Kirk Butt (*Early Settlers of Bay St. George*), Steven Kimber (*Sailors, Slackers and Blind Pigs*), Thomas Raddell (*Halifax: Warden of the North*) and William D. Naftel (*Halifax at War*).

Thank you to the spirited Royal Merchant Marine veteran Angus McDonald, Commander William Gard of the Royal Canadian Navy and Lieutenant-Commander Murray Knowles.

And thank you to Dr. Kay Singleton, that bon-vivant sailor Bob Royle, the Writers' Federation of Nova Scotia and the Department of Tourism, Culture and Heritage for being every writer's friend, John Robichaud for gleaning the title and Ismet Urgursal the Turk for his breath of warmth.

Mostly, I want to thank my dear departed friend, May Halloway, who took time to take tea with a boy, and whose story inspired this novel.